Using his foot, Oliver nudged the door open. Anger flared within him. The office had been tossed.

Oliver returned his gun to the back of his jeans. He followed Darling into the small, disheveled room. She stood in the doorway, eyes roaming over the mess. Then, like a switch had been flipped, she hurried to the other side of the desk and started to move through drawers on the floor.

"It's gone, Oliver!"

"What's gone?" But before she could answer, it dawned on him. "The security tape."

Darling nodded, clearly upset. An overpowering urge to comfort her pushed him forward. He put his hands on her shoulders, making her look up into his eyes. The moment from the night before played back into his mind.

She was close enough to kiss.

"Oliver, there's something I need to tell you."

"Yes?" His voice dropped low. Her green-eyed stare could stir up a drove of feelings in mere seconds.

"I think I know who did this," she whispered. "And you aren't going to like it."

PRIVATE BODYGUARD

—

TYLER ANNE SNELL

HARLEQUIN® INTRIGUE®

This book is for one of my best friends, Rachel Miller.
Thank you for listening to everything I had to say about Darling's story,
as well as every other story I've ever created! Your enthusiasm,
wisdom and friendship have made my life exponentially better. Here's to
many, many, many more years of staying up late and talking about books!

Also, the quickest of shout-outs to Hunter Hall.
Our friendship is also killer!

ISBN-13: 978-0-373-69895-0

Private Bodyguard

Copyright © 2016 by Tyler Anne Snell

The publisher acknowledges the copyright holder
of the additional work:

What Happens on the Ranch
Copyright © 2016 by Delores Fossen

Recycling programs
for this product may
not exist in your area.

Printed in U.S.A.

www.Harlequin.com

CONTENTS

Tyler Anne Snell genuinely loves all genres of the written word. However, she's realized that she loves books filled with sexual tension and mysteries a little more than the rest. Her stories have a good dose of both. Tyler lives in Florida with her same-named husband and their mini "lions." When she isn't reading or writing, she's playing video games and working on her blog, *Almost There*. To follow her shenanigans, visit tylerannesnell.com.

Books by Tyler Anne Snell

Harlequin Intrigue

Orion Security

Private Bodyguard

Manhunt

Visit the Author Profile page at Harlequin.com for more titles.

PRIVATE BODYGUARD

TYLER ANNE SNELL

CAST OF CHARACTERS

Darling Smith—Trying to keep her business afloat, this private investigator gets a case to take down the most beloved resident of the small town of Mulligan, Maine. However, when the case takes a deadly turn, can she look past her deep resentment for the rich and privileged to see the truth behind a Jane Doe's murder? All while trying to protect her heart from the only man who ever broke it?

Oliver Quinn—Regret has followed the Orion Security Group bodyguard around for years. First with the woman he left behind and then with the woman he couldn't protect. Since then, the bodyguard has made a promise to always provide safety to those who deserve it, even if they can't afford it. When his newest client throws him directly into the path of his past, can he also protect the woman he never thought he would see again?

Jane Doe—A young woman with no identification found murdered in a seedy hotel room sets in motion a series of events that leaves everyone involved questioning who and why.

Nigel Marks—Back in his hometown of Mulligan for business, this millionaire gets thrust into a murder investigation where he's the prime suspect.

Elizabeth Marks—Nigel's wife and Darling's newest client, this high-society woman has just as much motive to kill Jane Doe as her husband does.

Derrick Arrington—Ex to Darling, this deputy puts aside their romantic past to try to help catch a murderer who seems to elude them at every turn.

Nikki Waters—Founder of Orion Security Group and one of Oliver's closest friends, this boss tries to keep the bodyguard in line when the situation becomes complicated.

Chapter One

"It was just a little misunderstanding."

Darling Smith was standing behind the bars of one of two holding cells in Mulligan, Maine, and not at all amused.

Deputy Derrick Arrington, however, was all humor. Maybe that was due to the fact that the two had dated on and off the year before with less than favorable results. They were normally amicable if not downright pleasant, but Darling figured it wasn't every day he was able to arrest his ex. Her thoughts slid back in time for a moment.

Oh yeah, she would have loved to put a certain man from her past in the slammer and throw away the key.

"That should be tattooed across your forehead, Darling. 'It was a little misunderstanding, Officer. I'm too cute to be up to no good.'" He grinned.

"Deputy Arrington, did you just say that I'm cute?" she replied with a big dose of sugar.

He pointed at her and laughed. "See? That right there is what I'm talking about."

"Oh, come on, Derrick." Darling dropped the cuteness from her tone. She was tired. "We both know that George Hanely overreacted." Just saying the gate guard's name made her mad. He'd acted as if he was a Secret Service agent and Darling was an enemy of the state.

"He did his job. George saw a *suspicious person snooping around private property*." He eyed Darling a moment, waiting for her to confess. He'd keep waiting, too. "What's more, that *suspicious person* was found going up to his employer's garage."

"Not confirmed, just accused," she said.

The deputy shook his head. "I'd take this a little more seriously, Darling. You were caught breaking and entering into Nigel Marks's house. He's a beloved figure in this town. This will be the first time he's been back to stay for a while in years. The last time he came, do you know what he did?"

Darling let out a long breath. She had already researched the millionaire, but that didn't mean she was buying what he was selling. "He donated a new wing to the children's library."

"That's right. He was here for a little over a week, and he brought joy to an entire town's kids. Now he's coming to stay for almost a month. His visits, even if they are work related, usually benefit our community." He paused, making sure he let his words sink in before he tacked on, "We want him to enjoy that stay, not worry about some spunky private eye."

"I preferred 'cute,'" she grumbled.

"Well, I preferred starting my Tuesday morning with a cup of coffee and not picking up a criminal just as the sun rose."

"Accused criminal."

He rolled his eyes and checked his watch. Derrick was tall, had jet-black hair and the bluest eyes she'd ever seen. He was handsome, sure, but he also wasn't anywhere near her type. Though, admittedly, her type had revolved around one man and one man alone throughout the years. She stopped herself before she could picture him, angry for entertaining thoughts of a past best forgotten.

"Okay, I'm going to head back up," he said. "I just wanted to come check on you and see if you wanted that one phone call."

"But Deputy, why would I call you when you're already here?"

"Oh, Darling, how I've missed your sarcasm." They both knew that was a bold-faced lie.

It had been two days since Elizabeth Marks had walked into Acuity Investigations and asked for the twenty-five-year-old's help. Darling could recall with almost perfect precision the way the graceful woman had breezed in. She had shaken Darling's hand with a firm grip but had seemed hesitant to introduce herself. However, Darling hadn't needed to know the woman's name to understand she was important, if only financially so. It had been Elizabeth's shoes—silver-toed, red-soled, python-heeled Louboutin shoes—that had spoken volumes to Darling. Mrs. Marks came from money, and that always made a case more interesting.

"My husband is having an affair," Elizabeth had said after adjusting the Gucci sunglasses that sat atop her crown of bleach-blond hair. "I just need concrete proof now."

Darling had been taken aback. Normally when a spouse sought out a private investigator, it was to confirm a suspicion. The way Elizabeth's back had straightened and her shoulders had squared had suggested there were no doubts in her accusation.

"If you already know he's cheating, why do you need the proof?" Darling had asked.

A surge of energy had seemed to pulse through Elizabeth. Her face had become lively for a moment.

"We married when I was young, my husband, Nigel, and I. His career was just taking off, and we were so in love. He drew up a prenuptial agreement that I should never have signed, but I was foolish and naive and believed he was the man I wanted to spend the rest of my life with." She had stopped herself then, as if trying to pick the right words. "If I divorce him right now, because of the prenup, I'll receive almost nothing. Even the money I personally earned. But if I get proof that he's cheating, it will void the prenup and I can take at least half of what he owns, which will be enough for me."

So that had been the bottom line.

Darling sat on the uncomfortable cell's cot as the memory of their first meeting came to an end and a new wave of determination washed over her. She wasn't the biggest fan of the wealthy—having a past like hers left an unforgettably sour taste in her mouth for them—but she had believed in the woman's pain and anger enough to want to help. Just because Darling had fought her own personal battle against the rich, and lost, didn't mean Elizabeth deserved the same fate.

"You sure you can do this?"

Oliver Quinn looked up from the desk to see his boss leaning in the doorway. Nikki Waters's tone was light, though her demeanor carried unintentional importance. Since she not only founded the Orion Security Group but also ran it, he decided that importance was deserved. He certainly respected it.

"Excuse me?" he asked, half of his mind still going through the travel details in the open folder between his hands. He was twenty minutes away from heading to the airport to start a three-week contract and, since Oliver was the lead agent of Team Delta, he was triple-checking their route. He wanted to avoid as much traffic as possible—a goal made easier by the somewhat remote location.

"Maine," she replied, staying in the doorway. It was almost seven in the morning and she was dressed in her workout clothes, her dark red hair slicked back in a short pony tail. Most likely she was headed to the twenty-four-hour gym across the street. There were several of them spread throughout downtown Dallas. "In April, no less."

Oliver raised an eyebrow at her.

"Oh, come on," she continued with a smile. "Every time I checked in on you during that stint in Montana two years ago, you talked about how crazy you were going from being in the cold."

If he had been a rookie like Thomas, the newest addition to Delta, or even someone who had been around a year like Grant, he would have thought she was serious in questioning whether he could do the job or not. However, if there was one thing he rarely doubted, it was Nikki's faith in his abilities. If she hadn't believed in them, she wouldn't have sought him out when Orion had only been a name.

"What can I say? I'm from California. We tend to love the sun and heat. I don't think Maine will be too bad, though. I'm just glad we aren't going there a month earlier. I can handle April."

She laughed. It was clipped. He knew something was bothering her and waited until she spoke again.

"Listen, I wanted to thank you for not giving me grief about this client," she said. "I know Mark and Jonathan think taking him on is unnecessary." She was referring to the lead agents of the other two teams and Oliver's closest friends. They had worked together before Orion, sharing a past that had been fused together by tragedy.

"They don't like thinking about the big picture," he said, trying to lighten the mood. He knew she had been struggling with her decision to accept millionaire Nigel Marks as a client.

"It's just…" She hesitated. "We've spent the last few years claiming to protect those who need it but can't afford it. That's the Orion Group's bottom line. We provide security and guarantee safety to those who don't have bottomless pockets. And now we're taking on an almost monthlong project with a millionaire?" She sighed. "I feel like I'm selling out."

"But if we don't occasionally pick up an elite client, then we can't continue to be Robin Hoods. Right?"

Nikki snorted. "Robin Hoods, huh?"

"Well, we don't steal from the rich, but you get the idea."

She seemed to like that way of thinking and nodded. "You're right. I need to be firm in this decision. You're heading there soon?"

Oliver pulled out his plane ticket. "Since he insisted on us meeting him there, I want to head up there a little earlier to make sure everything is okay," he said. "The rest of Team Delta will follow but might be a bit late since their flight last night was cancelled."

"Team Delta. It still sounds as corny as it did when Mark suggested the name."

"Says the woman who named her security group

Orion," he replied. Though as he said it, he glanced past her to a picture framed on the wall. The real reason behind the name.

The picture weighed less than an ounce, but it left an unbelievably heavy weight on his heart.

Nikki didn't have to follow his gaze. She knew what he was feeling. Her pain had turned to anger over the years. His had only drowned in guilt.

"Well, be careful," she said after the moment passed. "And, Oliver? Keep this client happy. We need him, as much as I hate to say it."

Oliver needed to ensure everything was on the up and up since Nigel had been clear he didn't want to start the contract until Wednesday morning. He still didn't understand why the man had hired a security group to protect him while he traveled if he didn't want to use them as he traveled *to* Maine. He'd been cautious enough to hire Orion after he'd earned a few nasty anonymous letters at work. He clearly had felt threatened. Oliver didn't think about it too much, though. He'd learned the hard way that most of the upper class was stubborn, and arguing with them did little to change their minds.

Oliver tried not to dwell on the past as he arrived at the airport and then boarded his plane.

Nigel Marks had been transported by way of his private jet; Oliver's long legs were pressed against the back of a snoring man's chair in coach. When he finally landed, stretched and turned on his cell phone, he wasn't in the mood for the voice mail from Nikki.

"Oliver, I received a call from the security guard who watches Nigel's house. I think his name is George? Anyways, he found a woman lurking around early this morning and had the cops come pick her up. They are holding her on trespassing and potentially breaking and entering. George didn't give me all of the details. He seemed too excited. I already talked to Nigel. He's actually at work in the next town over and will be delayed until later this afternoon. He liked the idea of you going to talk to her to see if she's a threat. Call me after you do." She didn't say goodbye. She was in business mode. Nikki the boss, not Nikki the friend.

He hung up, aggravated.

"Great," he grumbled, making his way to baggage claim. "Not even in town and already having problems."

The town of Mulligan—a name that Oliver found humor in—was thirty minutes away from the airport via one dust-covered SUV. Oliver hated rentals. Due to the company's track record, no agent was offered the rental insurance that was an option with each vehicle. In his line of work, there was a high chance they would receive damage in some form. Oliver knew from experience the rental companies were a pain to deal with when that happened, and as team lead, he was the one who dealt with it. The man he'd rented the car from had taken his sweet time passive-aggressively warning Oliver about how it would be unwise to bring it back in anything less than pristine condition. Every pothole he bumped through made him cringe.

Thinking of the uptight man only dampened his darkening mood. He mentally ran through a list of questions he would ask Nigel Marks's intruder as the vehicle's GPS directed him to Mulligan's police department. It wasn't until he was nearing Main Street that his phone blared to life.

"Quinn," he answered, pressing the speaker button.

"It's Nikki." There was no mistaking the annoyance

in her voice. "I wanted to warn you that our intruder is a private investigator."

"A private eye?"

"Yep. I finally got the chief on the phone, and he said she's a local. And she's feisty. Try to figure out why she was snooping around, but don't make her too mad. If she's a local, it might make the next three weeks unpleasant."

"Okay. Don't tick her off. Tread lightly. Yada yada."

"The sheriff also made a point to warn me not to let her name fool you."

Oliver raised an eyebrow to no one in particular. "Her name? What is it? Candy? Bunny?"

Nikki laughed. "No, even better. Darling."

Oliver almost swerved off of the road.

Before he could stop himself, the image of a woman popped into his head. Dirty-blond hair, round green eyes, a button nose and a set of soft, curvy lips.

"Come again?" he asked. He was already certain he'd heard Nikki wrong.

"Her name is Darling. Darling Smith."

A silence followed before Oliver found his voice again. "I hate to say this, but I can almost guarantee she's already pissed at me."

FOOTSTEPS SOUNDED FROM the stairs, bringing Darling out of her haze of absolute annoyance. Derrick had been coming down a few times each hour to talk her ear off. She wished Nigel Marks's lackey would hurry up and question her. Anything was better than staying any longer in the mildew-scented cell. As the steps got closer, she ducked her head and rubbed her eyes. She didn't think she could take another round of Deputy Derrick.

"If you're going to keep bothering me, the least you could do is bring me a coffee," she called when the footsteps stopped outside of the bars.

"Well, I haven't been in town long, but I'm sure I could find some somewhere."

Darling's heart skipped a beat. Slowly she raised her head to look at the new speaker. She could only stare.

Out of all of the town jails in the world, Oliver Quinn had picked hers to make a grand appearance in.

It had been almost eight years since she had seen him, yet she recognized him instantly. Brushing six feet, the twenty-eight-year-old had broad shoulders and a stocky but muscular build, giving him the look of a well-toned soccer player. His blond hair was cut short but not too short, still covering the top of his forehead with a golden swoop. His amber-colored eyes and ridiculously soft-looking lips only added to the attractive angles of his tanned face. Not to mention a jawline that simply begged to be touched. For a moment Darling wondered why she ever had ill feelings toward the man who looked like an angel. But then, all at once, she remembered not only who he was but also what he had done.

No matter how handsome he was, Oliver Quinn had crushed her heart. A fact Darling wouldn't forgive or forget anytime soon.

"Miss Smith, this is the security agent Nigel Marks sent," Deputy Derrick said, coming up behind Oliver. "His name is—" He stopped, noticing Darling's deer-in-headlights stare. "You okay?"

Oliver, with a small smile attached to his lips, was about to interject, but Darling found her voice. Though she had to tamp down several less-than-pleasant responses.

"Deputy Arrington, this is Oliver Quinn," she said, standing. "We used to make out in my father's Ferrari." Derrick raised his eyebrow before looking at Oliver.

"What can I say? Fast cars and pretty girls equal a winning combo in my book," Oliver shot back with an easy laugh. It was not the response she had expected, but Derrick thought it was funny enough. When Darling didn't show signs of joining in on their shared mirth, the deputy sobered.

"Do you want me to stay down here during the questions?" Derrick asked her directly. They might not have had the best romantic relationship, but they did consider each other friends.

"I can handle this one," she answered. It earned another little laugh from Oliver.

"When you're satisfied she isn't a threat, let me know," Derrick said, turning to leave.

"She isn't a threat. You can let her out now." Oliver moved aside and motioned to the lock. Derrick and Darling exchanged a confused glance.

"You don't want to question her?" Derrick asked.

"I do, but unfortunately, I have to get back to work." He looked at her. "I was thinking we could pick this up tonight?"

Alarm bells as loud as the Monday-morning trash pickup rang in her head.

"Like on a date?" she blurted, heat rushing to her cheeks.

Oliver gave off another short laugh. "More like catching up with a few pointed questions concerning my client," he said. Then, when she was about to decline fiercely, he added, "I need to make sure I was correct in saying you aren't a risk. If you are, my client will press charges."

Both men looked at her, waiting for an answer.

If Oliver was the only thing that kept her from receiving the potential wrath of Nigel Marks, she'd have to take up his offer. She sighed, thinking about her bad luck so far on this case.

"Fine, but you're buying."

Oliver produced a business card as Derrick opened the cell door. He handed it to Darling, never dropping his grin.

"Would it be okay to stop by your office around seven?" he asked.

"Do I have a choice?" she replied with one of her sweet, yet not sweet at all, smiles.

"Of course you do, but it might be better if we could have that dinner."

"Then I guess that's what will happen."

The three of them went back upstairs. Oliver the Bodyguard didn't even hesitate to get into his car and leave, while Darling got into her car that had been brought to the station. She sat in the driver's seat, trying to process all of what had happened in the past ten minutes. Fate? Coincidence? A cruel joke? She couldn't decide which category her situation fell into.

She might have kept wondering had her phone not buzzed with a text she had been hoping to receive. Looking at the caller ID, she couldn't help but feel better.

Darling pulled up to the Mulligan Motel a few minutes later with excitement coursing through her. Her caller was Dan Morelli, a transplant from New Jersey and the owner of the less-than-ideal motel. There was a Holiday Inn fifteen minutes south of Mulligan, but those who participated in not-so-legal extracurricular activities often stayed at the Mulligan Motel.

Or people who wanted to meet someone in secret.

"Hey, Dan," Darling greeted him, walking into the lobby with her camera swinging around her neck. Dan had been a valuable contact throughout the past few years, keeping an eye out for certain persons Darling had cases on. Though since she had tried to stay away from the dirty-laundry spectrum of stereotypical private-eye jobs, she hadn't seen him in a good few months. She'd paid him in cookies, movie rentals and the promise of an exciting bust in the past. There wasn't much else to do in Mulligan for a man who hated the cold. Plus, he'd confessed once that Darling reminded him of his little sister, which apparently worked in her favor.

Dan didn't look up from his paper when she stepped inside.

"Room 212," he responded, intent on his crossword. "And you figured that out all on your own."

"Of course I did. You know nothing—everyone knows that, Dan."

He laughed but didn't say anything more. Darling went behind the desk and grabbed the key with the chain marked 212. Some people might have felt guilty for what she was doing, but Darling could justify it easily enough. Nigel Marks had spent a few hours in the Mulligan Motel's room 212 last night. And what's more, he hadn't been alone. The millionaire had left while the sky was still dark, but his mistress hadn't checked out yet. It was time Darling paid a visit.

She walked up the stairs and down the length of the second floor until she came to a stop at the last door. A TV could be heard on the other side, but no voices. Darling, using a method her former boss had applied in the field before, adopted a high-pitched voice and knocked.

"Room service," she sang. There was a Do Not Disturb sign hanging from the doorknob. If she kept nagging, the woman would answer, annoyed yet visible. Then Darling would do what she did best and question or trick her into confessing. Who needed pictures when the mistress would admit publically to the affair? Sure, it was a little brash of her and maybe not what she would have done under normal circumstances, but she felt oddly off-kilter after seeing Oliver. Even though they'd barely had a conversation.

She knocked a few more times and waited.

And waited.

"Room service. I'm coming in," she sang again in a lower voice. She slid the key into the lock and turned, an excuse for her intrusion ready on her tongue.

But no one yelped in surprise or yelled in anger. Aside from the TV, the room was still and spotless. Maybe Dan had gotten it wrong, Darling thought. There was no luggage or bags of any kind, the trashcans were empty and all the lights were off. She walked past the two double beds and peeked into the bathroom, hoping for some kind of clue that would prove Nigel Marks's mistress had been there.

However, the proof she found was more than she had bargained for.

Lying in the bathtub was a woman wrapped up in the shower curtain. Blood was everywhere.

Chapter Two

"And you're sure she won't be a problem?" Nikki asked after Oliver more or less summed up his visit to the police station. He had admitted to knowing Darling, just not *how* he knew her.

"I'm sure. She was just curious, that's all," he said for the third time. Nikki might not have been fond of taking on Nigel Marks as a client, but now that he was under contract, she was going to make sure nothing bad happened. "Listen, I don't blame her. This place is impressive. I'd have done the same thing. If it makes you feel better, I'm catching up with her when Thomas and Grant relieve me tonight. I'll bring it up again and if she lies to me, I'll catch it."

"Well, just try not to tick off the long-winded gate guard, George, while you're there. I'd really like to avoid talking to him again."

Oliver agreed and they ended the call. He looked through the window to the gatehouse down below. George Hanely had been like a kid on Christmas as he recounted the story of how he had saved the Markses' home from the more-than-suspicious private investigator. Oliver had been at Nigel Marks's home for less than ten minutes, and in that time he had watched George re-enact what had happened.

He had led Oliver from his post in the small one-room, half-bathroom house that sat at the front of the drive around to the garage. It, like the house, was large. It could easily fit several cars. Darling had been spotted next to the side door. Her story of just being close to the gate that surrounded the property was hard to believe. The iron gate was a good forty to fifty yards away. If she had been trying to get back over the fence, then why come so close to the garage?

Oliver could guess the answer. She was trying to get *into* the garage. But why?

Ever since he had seen Darling, he had been assuming that she was still the same girl he'd known before. The fact that she was in jail to start off with had proven the opposite. And a private investigator?

He smiled to himself. *That* he could believe. Darling had loved the challenge of a good mystery.

He remembered the first time he'd met her. She had been butt up in a Dumpster behind an office complex, rooting around in discarded papers and files. At the time he'd assumed it was a part of some weird bet. She hadn't looked homeless with her designer clothes and perfectly manicured nails. Then, when she found exactly what she didn't want to find, she had opened up in a burst of emotion to the nineteen-year-old him. Her world wasn't over, but it had changed. Through the next few months the once-spoiled, once-naive teenager transformed into a thoughtful, compassionate young woman. The people around her hadn't appreciated the changed Darling, and slowly she had become isolated. Oliver, however, had formed a bond with her, staying by her side until…

Self-loathing pulsed through him at the memory of the last night he'd seen her. *Time can heal all wounds, but seeing the girl whose heart you shattered only breaks out the salt and pours it into the gashe*s, he thought with a frown.

Seeing her after all those years had been a shock to his system. One he wasn't sure was entirely good or entirely bad. As he tried to clear his mind, he marveled at the fact that he still felt so strongly about what had happened almost a decade ago.

Oliver left the guest bedroom Nigel had assigned to him and started to go through each room of the house. He checked windows, catalogued all exits and got his bearings of the Markses' second home. Its large size didn't surprise him in the least.

After finishing his sweep, he made his way back over to the gatehouse. George, a slight man in his thirties with dark hair and a pasty complexion, could barely keep his excitement at bay at having someone to talk to. Oliver didn't blame the man one bit. Even though Nigel Marks hadn't been at his house in years, it was still George's job to watch the gate daily. If it had been Oliver's job, he would have hated it. However, George seemed to take pride in his tasks, and Oliver spied a movie player and several movies under the front desk, which must have made sitting in one room day in and day out a little more bearable.

"So, have you ever met Mr. Marks in person?" George asked when Oliver was satisfied with each part of the property. Aside from the gatehouse, garage and house, there was nothing but open land surrounding the acres the Markses owned.

"No," Oliver admitted. "My boss handles the client

interactions before the contract start date," he explained. "Do you see him often? I was under the impression he didn't come visit much."

George shrugged. "He calls to check in from time to time and ask about things," he said. Oliver noticed the gate guard puffed his chest out a bit. "I keep him informed on what's going on in Mulligan." There was no mistaking that George definitely took pride in working for Nigel. Oliver could respect that, even if he wondered what kind of social life the guard was left with after the hours he worked. Having a good boss was an absolute must for Oliver, especially after the nightmare of what had happened with his last. "That's how I knew that woman was up to no good."

They had just stepped outside the gatehouse and were facing the private drive. It wasn't as cold as the Montana case had been, but there was a chill in the air that moved with the breeze. Oliver tilted his head as another gust pushed against his clean-shaven face, and he thought about his next words carefully before speaking.

"You mean the private investigator? She seemed harmless enough," he said, not believing himself as he said it.

George snorted. "Private investigator. Yeah, that sounds a lot better than what she really does."

Oliver raised his eyebrow. "What does she really do?"

"Sneak around, break the law and ruin lives. Just like the rat of a man she got her office from," he explained with a surge of anger.

"From what I could tell Derrick seemed to like her," Oliver added.

"Deputy Derrick and her are close, if you know what I mean."

A quick burst of jealousy flashed through Oliver. The

idea that Darling was with someone romantically hadn't yet breached his thoughts. Not that it should matter either way.

"And as for the chief, he's one of many people here that have fallen for her charms. If you ask me, she uses her looks to get what she wants. It's repulsive. She should be using her time better, you know? Get married, have some kids."

Oliver's brief jealousy turned to a not-so-brief anger. It was true he couldn't claim to know this new, older version of Darling the same way he had known the younger one, but he seriously doubted she was this repulsive person George was claiming. He was about to set the man straight when his cell phone beeped.

"They're almost here," Oliver said instead. "I want you to call me if anyone other than my team and Nigel comes to this gate. No matter the time. Are we clear?"

George straightened his back and almost looked as if he was ready to salute. "Yes, sir," he barked.

Within minutes a black SUV came up the drive, followed by a sleek silver two-door Audi. Originally, Nigel was supposed to be escorted from his home in California to Mulligan, but a week ago he had changed this detail, much to Nikki's frustration. He had spent two days in the neighboring city, working to put out business-related fires due to his company's newest merger while he stayed at a four-star hotel less than a block from that branch of Charisma Investments. The other two members of Team Delta had been ordered to pick Nigel up that morning, officially starting their contract time frame.

Oliver nodded to Thomas Gage, Orion's newest recruit, as he rolled down the SUV's tinted driver's side window just before the gate. His build was on the lean side, with narrow shoulders and arms toned but not as built as the rest of Team Delta. He had light brown skin, dark hair and bright blue eyes that Nikki had commented on more than once. Thomas never sported facial hair, and that decision often got him mistaken for younger than twenty-five. This was his third job as a Delta agent. Oliver liked his humor and lingering innocence.

"Hey there, Boss," Thomas greeted Oliver with a smile. He motioned to the backseat, where Nigel Marks sat with a laptop on his lap and a phone to his ear. He looked up and gave a quick wave before turning his attention back to his work. "He had an emergency call that couldn't wait," Thomas explained.

Oliver motioned through the gatehouse window for George to open the gate. George didn't hesitate, and Thomas moved the SUV the rest of the way up the drive, parking in front of one of the garage doors. Grant Blakely arrived next, driving Nigel's high-end rental. He was already grinning as he paused next to Oliver.

"This assignment may not completely suck after all, especially if we get to play with his toys," he said as soon as the window was down. He petted the dashboard.

Oliver chuckled. He missed working with his old team of Jonathan and Mark, but he had grown fond of Grant. The thirty-four-year-old was the epitome of intimidating without even trying. Tall, wide and thick with muscles, the dark-skinned bodyguard never looked as if he couldn't win in a fight.

"Just wait until you see the house," Oliver said. "Any problems getting here?"

"No, sir. It's about a thirty-minute commute with no traffic. How about on your end? Did you deal with the private eye?"

"The threat wasn't as threatening as we thought, but just to make sure, I'm going to ask a few more questions after my shift." Grant nodded, and Oliver once again told George to open the gate.

"The man driving Nigel is Thomas, and the one in the Audi is Grant," Oliver explained to George. "You have all our numbers. Don't hesitate to use them if you need to. At all times there will be two of us with Nigel."

George took the three cards with their numbers and put them in his pocket. Although he said he understood, Oliver could tell his attention had moved toward the cars, where his true boss had just exited.

Nigel Marks was over six foot, of average size and dressed in a proper suit. His salt-and-pepper hair was cropped close to his head, with a pair of reading glasses resting on top. The file Oliver had been given said Nigel was fifty-three, though he looked years younger. The file also said he was an avid runner, competing in marathons and triathlons in his spare time. That would account for the toned body his suit did little to hide. As Oliver approached, Nigel ended his call and extended his hand.

"Sorry about that," Nigel said with a smile. "This merger has made everyone forget how to do their jobs. You must be Mr. Quinn."

Oliver shook. "Call me Oliver."

"It's nice to meet you, Oliver. Nikki spoke very highly of you and your team. Hopefully you won't get too bored on this job."

"It's a good sign when a job stays boring," Oliver replied.

Nigel seemed to consider this and laughed. "I suppose you're right. Well…" Nigel waved to his house as Grant and Thomas joined them. "As I told Nikki, feel free to treat this as your home while here. There are no off-limits areas, but I do ask my office be left alone unless I'm with you. I have a feeling that my free time will be spent in there." He paused as his phone rang. His pleasant mood seemed to slide away in an instant. Replacing it was the look of a tired man. "My work is never done."

DARLING FELT AS if she was frozen yet couldn't stop everything around her from moving. It wasn't until her vision started to tunnel that she realized she was about to pass out. With a quick dose of good sense, she backed out of the bathroom and crouched, flinging her head down between her legs. In the moment she couldn't remember why that stopped a person from fainting, but she knew she needed to try it nonetheless.

So there she was, crouched just outside of room 212's bathroom and its body in the tub, trying to calm her stampeding heartbeat and erratic breathing.

This case was nothing but bad, bad luck.

A car door shut in the parking lot some time later. Whether it was seconds or minutes, she wasn't sure. The room hadn't been the only aspect of her reality that had warped when she had seen the body. However, instead of sending her into a bigger fit of worries, the sound of the outside world started to make her focus.

She took two deep breaths and slowly righted herself. The camera around her neck slapped against her chest, reminding her of the reason she had been there in the first place.

Nigel Marks and his mistress had been in this room the night before. He had gone, but his mistress hadn't checked out. It wasn't a stretch of the imagination to guess it was her unfortunate fate that she was the one wrapped up in the tub. Darling knew she had to call the police, just as she knew that once she left the room, she'd never be allowed back in.

At the moment, it was a thought that didn't sit right with her. So, blaming the impulse on her desire to solve mysteries, even ones seemingly cut and dried, she took her camera from her neck and walked back to the bathroom doorway. With hands she let shake, she snapped a few pictures of the bathroom and its deceased guest before she turned back and took a few of the bedroom. Another car door slammed shut in the distance. She glanced once more toward the bathroom.

Darling felt a mixture of anger and sadness pull at her heart. Nigel Marks might be a powerful man in the business world, but by killing this woman, he had unwittingly stepped inside Darling's domain.

Darling hurried to the main office and was thankful that Dan was still alone. He didn't look up when she came in, he just raised his hands.

"I know nothing," he said, still in a bubble of humor. It was a bubble she was about to pop.

"Dan, you need to call the police. There's a dead body in room 212."

Dan laughed, thinking it was a joke until he finally met her eyes. Darling figured she must have looked as serious as the situation was. She watched his face and mood sober.

"Where?" was all he could manage.

"Wrapped up in a shower curtain in the tub."

His lips thinned, and his brows pulled together. "You better give me the key and leave, then," he said after a moment. He pulled the only landline phone the office had from the second shelf of his desk. Darling felt a quick wave of fondness for the man. He was always trying to cover for her.

"I don't want you to lie about how you found the body," Darling said. "I'll tell the deputy the door was already open." She handed the key back to him. "We don't have to tell anyone about the key. Though I don't think they'll care either way." It seemed obvious to her what had happened.

Dan nodded and pocketed the key.

"Then you call them," he said, already shrugging into his coat. "I want to go see it for myself."

Darling sat behind the front desk with a very loud, long sigh and did as she was told. Deputy Derrick wouldn't be happy she had managed to get into this mess, but at least this time she wasn't guilty. Not that she would have admitted she had been guilty that morning. Instead of dialing 9-1-1, she called the man directly. In a small town like Mulligan, where the members of police force could be counted on two hands, Derrick had the dual duty of being their trusty investigator as well as deputy. Instead of puttering around with someone else in the bull pen, Darling went straight to the source.

"Deputy Derrick," he answered on the second ring.

"Derrick, it's Darling. I hope you're not busy right now."

She heard him snort. "Is that your way of trying to ask me out? We both know how well that works," he said, all humor.

"Well, not quite."

"Where are you calling from?" he asked after a pause. She knew him well enough to recognize something close to suspicious concern creeping into his tone.

"The Mulligan Motel," she paused for a moment and

then dove in. "There's a body in room 212, wrapped up in the tub."

"A body?"

She nodded. Then, realizing he couldn't see her, she said, "And Derrick? The last person seen leaving the room was Nigel Marks."

There was silence on the other end.

"Stay there and tell Dan don't let anyone else in that room," he finally said. "And I mean it, Darling. No one else goes in there."

Darling agreed to his no-tampering-with-a-crime-scene rule. Suddenly her morning indiscretion didn't seem as bad. She even bet Oliver's need to question her would disappear when he found out.

Oliver.

She pulled his card out of her back pocket and looked at his number.

If Nigel did kill whoever it was in the tub, where did that leave Oliver?

Chapter Three

Oliver didn't answer when Darling called him.

Somewhere in the back of her mind, she felt she owed it to him to give him a heads-up that the man he had promised to guard was about to need a lot more protection than he could offer. Oliver had said she wasn't a threat, vouching for a woman he no longer knew. Plus, it was no fun to be blindsided. She knew that from experience.

"This is Oliver Quinn. Leave a message and I'll get back to you as soon as possible," his voice mail recording answered. Darling felt her face heat up after the beep to leave a message came and went. She realized then that giving him a heads-up might also give Nigel one before the cops were even able to see the body in the tub. She didn't want to be the one responsible for giving the number one suspect time to lawyer up or possibly run. Although he probably had already done one or the other. It wasn't as if the body could have gone unnoticed for too long.

"Um, hi, it's Darling," she floundered. "I need you to call me as soon as you get this. Something's happened. Thanks." She let out a long sigh as she ended the call. She liked to believe she was a very confident and sure woman, but mix any part of Oliver into her life and she suddenly felt off her game.

Darling went back up to the second floor to find Dan, trying to push thoughts of her ex clear out of her head. She had walked into the crime scene that, most likely, her current client's husband had created. That gave her a new set of problems and concerns without adding the complication of the man from her past.

"I talked to Deputy Derrick," Darling told Dan, who was standing in the doorway to room 212. "He said no one else needs to go in there until they get here."

Dan didn't answer right away. His eyes were stuck on a point somewhere in the main room. She wondered if he had peeked in the bathroom yet. When he met her gaze, she knew he had. He looked haunted.

"Do you think he really did it?" he asked. "Nigel. Do you think he really killed her?"

Darling shrugged. "I can't say for certain, but I can make the leap and say I think there's a pretty good chance he did. You said yourself that he stayed the night here."

Dan nodded, but there was no enthusiasm in it.

"Do you want me to wait in the lobby and send the cops up when they get here?" she asked when it was clear Dan wasn't going to talk. He nodded again and returned to staring into room 212. She patted him on the shoulder and made the walk back, thinking a dead body in your hotel couldn't be good for business.

Darling sat behind the desk again but didn't let her mind wander. Instead she thought about Elizabeth Marks, the only other woman who knew about her husband's affair. Or, at least, she had thought so. If Nigel went to jail for murdering his mistress, she'd be in the clear to take what was hers, and possibly his, and leave without any strings attached.

A coldness seeped into Darling's heart.

She pulled her phone out and went to her email. Searching through discount offers and social media updates, she found the itinerary Elizabeth had sent to her after she had signed on to the case. During the duration of Nigel's work trip, Elizabeth would be with her mother in the Bahamas. She claimed that if she were far away with no chance of accidentally spotting Nigel and his mistress, he might get careless. It would be easier to catch him, she had said with vigor. If the schedule Darling was looking at was correct, the two women would have left for the trip on Sunday, two days ago. That meant Elizabeth wasn't even in the country when the woman had checked in.

Plus, why would you hire a private investigator if you were just going to kill the problem?

All at once, Darling realized there was an easy way to figure out who the mistress was.

Jumping up, she hurried to look out the door to make sure no one was coming. Derrick had been at the police station when she had called, which meant she had very little time left before he arrived. She ran back behind the front desk and pulled a big leather-bound registry book out. Dan hated leaving it on the desktop because he claimed it got in the way of his crosswords. He only pulled it out when a new guest had already handed over the money. It was also the only way he kept tabs on the people who checked in and out. Darling could have slapped herself. She couldn't believe she hadn't thought of looking at the registry as soon as she had come in.

She flipped through a few pages until she found the

entries from the night before. Three people had checked in. All were after 6:00 p.m., and none of them were Nigel Marks. A car door shut in the parking lot, and for the second time that day, Darling took a picture of something she probably shouldn't have. This time it was with her phone, but that reminded her she needed to hide her camera or else Derrick would take it from her. He was always suspicious of her, which, she guessed, was deserved in this case. She grabbed the camera, put it in the bottom drawer of the desk and replaced the registry seconds before Deputy Derrick came into the office.

"Two times in one day, huh?" she greeted him. Derrick didn't think it was funny. She sobered. "Sorry, it's been a weird day."

Whatever he had been about to say, he must have changed his mind. His face softened.

"What room?" he asked.

"Room 212. Dan is waiting outside. I told him not to go back in, like you said."

Derrick nodded. Behind his knitted brows, he was probably running through police procedures.

"You okay?" he asked when she kept staring. "I mean, like emotionally," he tacked on. He had never been that great at talking about feelings, so the question surprised her.

"Yeah, I didn't really see much."

He nodded and turned for the door that led to the stairs outside. He paused long enough to add, "And Darling, don't leave. I have a *lot* of questions for you."

"I know."

"I NEED YOU to call me as soon as you get this. Something's happened. Thanks." Oliver hadn't recognized

the number, but he sure did recognize the voice and the oddness behind it as he listened to Darling's message. He didn't have long to think about it, though, before his phone rang again.

This time it was George.

"Oliver, the police are here," he started. "They want to know if they can come in."

"The police?"

"Yeah, they say they need to talk to Mr. Marks."

Oliver looked up as if he could see his client through the ceiling.

"Let them in," he answered, ending the call.

He left his spot in the kitchen next to the back entrance and walked down the long hallway to the front. Grant, off duty until seven that night, was sitting in the dining room, reading one of the many books he had brought with him. He looked up as Oliver opened the front door.

"Something is up," Oliver said over his shoulder. A police cruiser was parking next to his rental SUV. Two male cops got out. "I need you on duty right now," he added, seeing their facial expressions. This wasn't a courtesy visit.

"Good afternoon, officers," Oliver said when they were a few feet away.

"Afternoon," the first one responded. He was in his upper fifties and had almost no hair left on his head. He was built strong but didn't look intimidating with his short height. "I'm Officer Barker and this is my partner, Officer Clay." He motioned to the much younger black man next to him, whose lack of hair looked more intentional than his partner's. "You must be one of Mr. Marks's bodyguards."

"Yes, sir. How can I help you?"

Officer Barker looked considerably more uncomfortable than Officer Clay. They shared a glance before Barker straightened his back and answered.

"We need to talk to Mr. Marks," he said. "Now."

"Okay," Oliver said. He turned to nod at Grant, who had been hanging back in the dining room to listen. "Can I ask what about?" Oliver ventured as Grant walked out of the room, heading for the stairs.

Again Oliver caught the feeling of unease that passed between the officers.

"Something's happened," Officer Clay answered. Oliver instantly recalled Darling's voice mail. "We shouldn't say anything more until we've talked to Mr. Marks."

Oliver wanted to push for more answers but had to remind himself that he was the bodyguard, not Nigel's personal assistant. He let the officers stand in silence until the man of the hour made his grand appearance.

"Officers," Nigel said, a question already in his tone. "What can I do for you?"

"We'll give you some privacy," Oliver said, falling back into the house with Grant but maintaining a sight line. Nigel didn't seem to notice, and as soon as they were out of earshot, the officers began to talk in lowered voices.

"What's going on?" Thomas asked. He had come down the stairs with Nigel, face filled with curiosity. Not that Oliver could blame him.

"The cops are here," Grant answered. He turned to Oliver. "Do you know what's going on?"

Oliver watched as Nigel's entire body visibly tensed.

"No," he answered. "But I can guess it's probably not good."

Probably not good was an understatement. In less than

five minutes, Nigel Marks was in the back of the cop cruiser and as mad as a hornet. Before they had driven away, the businessman had asked Thomas to call his lawyer.

"About what?" Thomas had asked.

"I'm being accused of murder," Nigel had bit back.

All three bodyguards didn't have time to hide their surprise.

Oliver had had many interesting things happen in his line of work, but he could definitely say a client being accused of murder was a first. No matter the new unique circumstance, he couldn't forget he was team leader. He sent Grant and Thomas—who had followed Nigel's directions and was calling Nikki to get the man's lawyer's information, and also an earful of confusion from her— to the police station. There they would continue to work as his bodyguards until Nigel was officially convicted of the crime or cleared of it.

Oliver made sure George knew he needed to keep an extravigilant eye on the gate and jumped into his rental, already calling Darling. It wasn't a coincidence she had called. She knew something.

She always did.

Minutes later, Oliver pulled into the lot of the Mulligan Motel. The coroner's van along with two police cruisers were parked next to the entrance, while a few guests stood around, but he had eyes only for one woman.

Darling was sitting on a bench next to the lobby's front door, concentration aimed at her phone. She had been brief during their call but had admitted they had found a dead body. Though how it was linked to Nigel, he wasn't sure yet.

"Apparently my questions are going to have to be

asked a little earlier than planned," he said by way of a greeting. It made the woman jump, but she didn't appear angry when she met his eyes. His body tensed at her gaze.

"Believe me, you aren't the only one who has questions." She stood and stretched. He was acutely aware of her five-five height, having to incline his head down slightly to look at her. A memory of how easy it was to pick her up into his embrace flashed across his vision. "Where is Nigel, and why aren't you with him?"

Since Nigel was a client, what went on in the man's private life was confidential. Oliver was under contract, which meant, unless it was public information, he couldn't divulge the fact that the businessman had been taken to the jail. Even if the person asking was Darling.

"Grant and Thomas are with him," was all he gave her. "Now, what's going on here, and how is it connected with Nigel?"

Darling was visibly trying to hide her anger at not being given a full answer, but she reined in the emotion along with any words born from it. She pushed her shoulders back when she was no longer actively trying to hide her displeasure.

"A body was found in the room your boss was staying in last night," she answered. Oliver didn't correct her with the difference between boss and client. His interest level had jumped off the charts instead. He was about to push for more when the Mulligan Motel's front door swung open and the deputy walked out. His mouth was set in a grim line, one that thinned when he saw Oliver.

"I'm surprised you're here," the deputy said, coming over. "I thought you'd be at the station."

"So Nigel was arrested?" Darling cut in before Oliver could comment.

"He was picked up a few minutes ago," Derrick said, relieving Oliver of having to withhold the information. Even though Darling kept her face guarded, he didn't miss the satisfaction that the cop's words brought her. "Which is why I didn't think you'd be here," Derrick said to Oliver.

"The rest of the team is with him," he repeated. "I came here to find out what's going on." Oliver sent a pointed look to Darling. "And how you're involved."

Darling crossed her arms over her chest.

"I was actually about to ask the same thing," Derrick said. The two of them focused on the private investigator. She shifted under their collective gaze. A long exhalation escaped between her lips.

"I was working a case," she admitted. "It led me here and, to my surprise, right up to a dead body. But as soon as I found it, I called you," she said to Derrick.

The cop outdid her earlier sigh and pinched the bridge of his nose.

"What's your case?" Oliver had to ask.

Darling set her jaw. "I'm not at liberty to say."

"Dammit, Darling, a woman is dead. You need to tell me everything you know," Derrick said with tried patience. Oliver guessed murder wasn't a normal occurrence in Mulligan.

"So it is a woman, then?" she asked. Derrick nodded. It was her turn to skate around a direct answer. "I didn't look hard enough. How was she killed?"

"And how is Nigel connected, again?" Oliver tacked on.

The deputy wasn't happy about the questions. "It's my turn to say 'no comment.'" Darling opened her mouth to argue, but he held up his hand. "This is an ongoing murder investigation, Darling. I can't give you anything right now. Not even for old times' sake."

Oliver didn't like the way he said the last part or the way the deputy brought up their shared past. The past that Oliver's past few years didn't even touch. However, a small part of him did feel a sort of odd joy to know that whatever relationship they'd had was now seemingly over.

"Now, please go wait inside so I can take your statement," the deputy said to Darling before focusing on Oliver. "And I suggest you head to the station. We're going to need to talk about that client of yours."

He was gone after that, leaving Oliver and Darling speechless on the sidewalk.

"You said Nigel was the last to see the woman alive?" he asked, voice low and serious.

"He spent the night with her, Oliver."

"Are you sure?" Nigel had said he was in his hotel in the city until the morning. Neither Grant nor Thomas had said otherwise. "It could have been a mistake."

Darling's lips turned down. "It looks like Nigel Marks isn't the saint you thought him to be." There was no mistaking the undercurrent of anger that coursed through her words. He was a step away from a dangerous territory with her.

"This isn't how I pictured running into you after all of these years." Silence stretched between them as neither had a response ready for the topic of their past. Oliver then continued, "I'd still like to catch up, but it looks like tonight might not be good." He had already started a mental list of things he needed to do. "Can I treat you to breakfast tomorrow instead?"

Darling seemed to be thinking it over. Eventually she

nodded before she, too, disappeared back into the building. Oliver retreated to his SUV, pulling his phone out to call Nikki along the way.

The job was officially no longer boring.

Chapter Four

Darling chewed on her bottom lip, not stopping until she tasted lipstick. She was standing in the lobby of Acuity the next morning, staring into a folder, confused beyond belief.

The afternoon before had blurred by after she'd given a statement to Derrick and then been ushered home. He wasn't happy with her investigating, or the fact that she wouldn't say for whom, and had in so many words let her know that she wouldn't keep that secret for long. So instead she had tried to reach Mrs. Marks. The resort manager she had spoken with had taken a message and promised to give it to her when she returned.

It had eaten Darling up as she lay awake in bed, fuming that Oliver knew more about what was going on with Nigel than she did. Here he was, stepping into her town, and he had already managed to be on the inside loop with the infamous Mr. Marks. She could have called Oliver, sure, but her pride had shut that idea down quickly. Admitting she needed the fair-haired man in any capacity was something she refused to do ever again.

After only a few hours of rest, she had opened Acuity to find a folder filled with curious things lying on the hardwood floor, slipped under the door as an unmistakable greeting.

Now between her hands were four eight-by-ten pictures of Nigel Marks with a woman who wasn't his wife. Each picture—printed on glossy card stock and dated—was focused on the businessman and a red-haired woman in four varying shows of affection. The first two had them in an intimate embrace, while the third and fourth were of the two sharing meals. In one of those, Nigel was even holding the woman's hand, a smile splitting his lips. None of the four pictures had a clear shot of the female's face, but there was no denying it was the same woman in each and that the couple was happy. All pictures were dated from the previous December up until March, the month before.

Elizabeth Marks had been looking for proof that her husband had been seeing another woman in secret. From what Darling could tell, she was holding that proof.

But why?

She stood there, cycling through each picture again, when a knock at the door made her jump. The folder fell to the floor. She hurried to pick it up when she noticed there was something still inside it.

"Knock, knock. It's me," called Oliver from the other side of the locked front entrance. "You in there?"

Darling didn't immediately respond. Her eyes were glued to a newspaper clipping that had been stuck to the inside of the folder. It was a picture of her parents that she knew to be almost nine years old. However, it was the words written in red across it that grabbed all her attention.

Do the right thing this time.

"Hold on," Darling said after another knock sounded. She hoped Oliver didn't catch the waver in her voice. She put the pictures, including the clipping, back into the folder and tucked it under her arm to unlock the door.

"You okay?" Oliver asked immediately. Perhaps her poker face wasn't at its best today. He wore a zip-up black jacket over a black shirt that looked good contrasting with his lighter hair. Staying away from the all-black body-guard stereotype, he'd donned beige cargo pants with more pockets than she cared to count. She didn't recognize the brand of tennis shoes, but she bet that he could run fast in them if needed.

"Yeah, just tired," she lied, leading him into the lobby. "Let me just freshen up and I'll be ready to go." She stuffed the folder into her purse and excused herself to the bathroom. There she turned on the faucet and took a deep breath.

What had briefly felt like a gift that could close her case against Nigel now felt tainted and wrong. As far as she knew, no one in Mulligan was aware of her parents' past, especially the quiet part she had played in the background.

Do the right thing.

She didn't need to wonder what that meant.

Whoever had sent her the folder wanted her to turn it in to the cops. But why not just do it themselves? If the red-haired woman was the same one who had been left in the tub, that meant the pictures definitely linked the two before the hotel room. Why would they give them to her?

Darling ran her hands under the cold water but didn't splash her face. For the first time in a long while, she had taken pains to look nice. She wore a pale pink blouse that dipped down into a V—not enough to be seductive, just

feminine—a pair of comfortably tight light blue jeans
and dark brown boots that folded down at the ankle. Her
hair was twisted up into a purposefully messy bun so the
yellow daisy earrings she loved so much could be seen
with ease. A subtle coral tinted her plump yet small lips.
They were downturned at the moment.

She'd convinced herself that Oliver's presence in Mulligan was a good thing. What Oliver had done in the past
had broken a big part of who she was, but she liked to
think she had come out stronger because of it. As soon
as she had turned eighteen, she had left California, her
family and all of those bad memories behind. There was
no reason to dredge them up now. If she could keep her
head up while Oliver was in town, then she could get
through anything.

That thought alone pushed a wave of new purpose
through her bones until it made her stand taller. Putting
away the man behind the murder of the woman in the
tub was more important than her failed love life. Nigel
Marks's mistress deserved better.

Darling eyed her purse before nodding to herself in
the mirror.

She *did* need to do the right thing.

"You ready for some breakfast?" Oliver asked when
she emerged. He was talking to her but looking around
the office's lobby. Pride swelled in her chest.

Acuity Investigations was housed in an old strip mall
that predated half of the other businesses in Mulligan.
Acuity was at the tail end of the shops, next to a narrow
road that deposited drivers back on Main Street. The
reason Jeff Berns, Darling's former boss, had rented the
particular space was its proximity to traffic yet its back-
door access so clients could be as discreet as they wanted.

Darling remembered the first time she had walked into Acuity. The cream-colored walls, leather and oak furniture, pictures of boats nestled in calm water and slightly musty smell had been a sharp contrast to what she referred to as her former life. Instead of turning her nose up at Jeff and his place of employment like her parents would have, Darling had embraced it with vigor.

Acuity wasn't fancy or elegant, but it was important to her. As Oliver's eyes traveled along the hardwood floors to the heavy oak door that led to her office, in the back of her mind she hoped he felt that truth ring through his bones as she did.

"Actually, would you mind if we swung by the police station really quickly?" Darling asked when his eyes finally moved back to hers. "I need to give something to Deputy Derrick." When he didn't immediately respond, she tacked on, "If you don't have enough time, we could reschedule."

"No, it's fine," he answered. "Just as long as we actually eat afterward."

Darling slipped into her black faux-leather jacket and smiled inwardly at its comfort before ushering Oliver out and locking the door behind her. They walked in silence up to his SUV. She was oddly saddened when he didn't open the door for her. The Oliver from younger years had not only opened the car doors for her but also occasionally put on her seat belt, laughing and mock-admonishing her about the importance of car safety.

The memory tugged at long-forgotten heartstrings. Now as they settled into their seats, the disconnect between the present and the past stretched between them.

"Is this visit for business or pleasure?" Oliver asked as the SUV pulled out of the parking lot.

She gave him a sideways glance. "Business."

He nodded to the road. "Does it have to do with Nigel?"

"It does," she admitted.

"What is it?" he ventured.

"Something very important."

She didn't elaborate and he didn't push.

"I don't think he did it, Darling," Oliver said. "I don't think he killed that woman."

Darling couldn't help the reflex to tense up, her body readying automatically for a verbal spar. It was a response she had picked up out of necessity as a young female investigator. She rolled her shoulders back to ease the new tension and answered with a controlled voice.

"Did he admit to being at the hotel last night?" she asked.

She knew Oliver sensed the mood change. He shifted in his seat and lost his smile.

"I didn't get a chance to ask. As soon as he was released, he locked himself in his study with his lawyer and son. They were still there when I left."

Darling's control cracked. "They *released* him?"

Oliver nodded. "I don't think there was enough evidence to hold him."

"But he was there," Darling exclaimed. "He spent the night with her!"

"Just because he spent the night with her doesn't mean he killed her, Darling." Instant anger filled her veins at how he said her name, as if she was some confused child.

"So, what, it's just a coincidence, then? You can't comprehend that a man like him, an adulterer, could ever do something like kill his mistress?"

She watched as his jaw hardened. "We don't know for

sure he was having an affair," he said. "The visit could have been business-related for all we know."

Darling laughed. "Oh, you're right. They probably just sat around and talked business all night."

"It's possible," he tried, but Darling wasn't having it. Defending men like Nigel, bending to their wills, was unforgivable in her book. Heat rose from the pit of her stomach, but it wasn't embarrassment. It was the force of an old wound breaking open. She yanked the pictures from her purse right as they turned into the station's parking lot.

"He seems to like to talk to women in secret," she said, barely able to keep her voice level. Oliver took the pictures from her hand and cycled through them just as she remembered the clipping was on the bottom. Operating on the assumption that Oliver knew he was dealing with an angry Darling, she snatched the pictures back and threw open the door. "I'll be right back."

She marched into the weathered, blue-painted building without looking back. Her head was almost spinning with the range of emotions she had experienced in such a short amount of time. It amazed her how Oliver brought out the worst in her, no matter what attitude she wanted to convey. Instead of seeming put together, she had come off as truly childish in the end. Her cheeks heated; this time it was all shame.

The Mulligan Police Department was poorly insulated. Derrick had liked to joke that was one of the reasons the town's crime rate was so low. No one wanted to spend the night in the cells. She hadn't even liked spending the morning in one. Darling wondered how Nigel Marks's act would shake the community's relative peace and quiet. She made a mental note to grab a newspaper after her breakfast date was finished to see how the media had handled it.

"Hey, Trudy," Darling greeted the bundled-up secretary. She was the first and only barrier between the front doors and the bullpen.

"Darlin' Smith, I hope you're not in trouble again," she said. Her tone was laced with disapproval. Trudy had more grandchildren than most people had fingers. She was proud of this and often acted as Mulligan's mother hen, believing she had earned that right even more with every relation that had come from her and her children.

"Not today," she said with a small smile. "But I do need to see Derrick. Is he in?"

"No, ma'am. He should be in soon, though. Do you want to wait?"

"Um, no, but can I just leave something on his desk?" Darling flashed the woman the folder, though the pictures were in her other hand. Trudy nodded and let Darling around her to the rows of desks. Another cop sat focused on his computer and didn't seem to notice or care as she went to Derrick's space in the corner. Glancing at a picture of Derrick's niece and nephew positioned next to his keyboard, Darling felt as if she was making a good decision by turning the evidence in. Derrick wasn't her Mr. Right, but he was a good, just man.

However, in true Darling fashion, she quickly snapped pictures of each individual image and their corresponding dates before slipping them into the folder, minus the newspaper clipping. She stuffed that into her back pocket.

A source dropped these off at my office today. Darling.

She scribbled down the lie and was suddenly glad that Derrick and his questions weren't there yet. He'd call her, no doubt, but not until after he had investigated the evidence. If he caught her now, it would be the other way around, a thought that made her hightail it out of the station.

Dodging one ex only to get into the car with another.

THE RED LEAF was one of two local coffee shops in Mulligan. Like the town, it was quaint, yet endearing in its own right. They also made a mean coffee, Darling said after she had returned from the station. She hadn't apologized for her outburst, but he hadn't expected her to, either.

Bailing Darling Smith out of jail had never been on Oliver's list of scenarios for when, and if, they ever met again. Sure, he'd thought of the possibility of crossing paths when he went home to California to visit family. Maybe even a random encounter in an airport as he traveled for work. But never like this.

Occasionally, he'd wonder what he would say to her during a chance encounter. *How have you been? Isn't the weather nice? Have you cut your hair?* They weren't good greetings, but how else could he skate around the topic of their past? Now, as they sat across from each other in a worn leather booth, he doubted such a thing could be accomplished. Darling hadn't forgotten or forgiven what he'd done, and he couldn't blame her for that.

He hadn't forgiven himself yet, either.

"Expecting a call?" he asked as she took care to adjust the volume on her cell.

"Expecting? No. Hoping? Still no, but I can't ignore it." He raised his eyebrow so she explained, "Work-related."

"Ah, I know the feeling." He pulled his phone from his pocket and placed it on the table, as well. With the recent changes in the job, Nikki had made it clear she wanted all guards to have their phones on at all times, even when they were off the clock.

"So, I have to ask. You didn't seem at all surprised to see me yesterday… Why?" she asked, getting the conversational ball rolling. Darling had never been a fan of silence.

Unlike the seventeen-year-old he had left behind, this Darling was all grown and all woman. Oliver couldn't deny she was beautiful—she always had been—but now there was something more as he really looked at her. The way her dark green eyes bore into his, trying to figure him out, was so fierce it almost shook his resolve to leave the past just where it was.

"My boss told me the name and I couldn't imagine it being a coincidence," he said honestly. "Though I wasn't a hundred percent given the circumstances."

"Ah…circumstances. You mean the trespassing accusation."

Oliver made a gun with his hand. "Bingo."

"Well," she said, "given recent developments, I'd say that *accusation* is the least of everyone's worries. Wouldn't you agree?" she finished, crossing her arms over her chest. That movement meant Oliver needed to tread softly.

"We wouldn't have taken on this case if he was a bad man, Darling. I stand by what I said earlier. Just because he was there doesn't mean he did it, and I'd like to ask you to drop whatever case you might still have that involves him," he said. And, apparently, it was the wrong thing to say. Almost instantly the color in her cheeks rose, her brows lifted and her lips thinned. Knowing a storm was brewing, Oliver made a second conversational mistake, hoping to pacify her. "For old times' sake, Darling."

He might as well have kicked her beneath the table.

"I can't believe you're still simply rolling over for the big dogs," she bit out, angry. "Nigel Marks is a millionaire, so that makes whatever he does justifiable? Is that why you do what you do, Oliver? Do you get some kind of thrill from protecting the rich? Did you ever stop and wonder why that's even necessary? No, you probably don't, because all you care about is pleasing the elite, just waiting for them to yell 'jump.'"

She stood so abruptly that the booth's seat pushed back and scraped the tile. The waitress and few patrons looked over, but Darling seemed oblivious. Like them, Oliver looked at her, but in a state of awe.

"You know what?" she said. "I'm not going to sit here and be talked to like I'm still the girl you used to know." She grabbed her purse and started to leave, pausing for a second to finish her tirade. "And Oliver, if I still had a case, I certainly wouldn't drop it 'for old times' sake.'"

And just like that Darling Smith became the one who left.

Chapter Five

There was a reason Darling had picked the café as a place to talk with Oliver—it was only a block away from her office. He watched her through the café's front windows as she walked in an angry huff down the street, turning into the strip mall's parking lot and disappearing around back. Each step had been rigged with tension, each movement forced.

The waitress waited until Darling was out of view before coming to the table. She also didn't look so pleased with him.

He let out a long breath.

"Can I place a to-go order?" he asked, glancing back out the window.

For the first time in years, Oliver let the past wash over him, bringing in the flood of memories that pieced together the last conversation he had had with the younger Darling.

She had been wearing a white dress with daisies printed across it, a stark contrast to the tears that had streaked her cheeks.

"They're horrible, Oliver," she had yelled. "They'll never change! They of all people have no right to tell me what I do and don't deserve. So, please, let's just leave. Let's run away together and never look back!"

"We can't."

"Oliver, I love you," she had said, taking his hands in hers. They had been soft and warm. "And if you love me as much as you say, we *can* make it." There had been so much hope in her eyes, despite the tears she had shed because of her parents. Despite everything she had gone through in the past year. So much hope that Oliver could still see it clearly today.

"But, Darling," he had whispered. "I don't want to."

Just like that, the hope had died, and the memory of breaking Darling Smith's heart had burned itself into his mind, becoming another moment he could never forget.

It still amazed him that such a brief conversation had made such a big impact.

"Order's ready," called the waitress, holding up a paper bag and a cardboard cup holder. Oliver pulled himself out of the hardest conversation he'd ever had and paid for the food.

Instead of climbing into his rental, he followed the same path Darling had taken until he was, yet again, at Acuity's front door. He didn't knock this time. She wouldn't have let him in if he had.

The private investigator was standing behind the lone desk in the front room, a scowl still attached to her face, when he pushed into the lobby. Her hair billowed around her head, a crown of dark blond that seemed to crackle to life as the rest of her grew angry at the sight of him. Before she could get on a verbal roll again, he held up his café spoils in surrender.

"I'm sorry," he said, smile wiped from his face. He let his hands fall and took a step closer. "After all this time, I shouldn't have asked, and certainly shouldn't have expected, you to listen to me. It wasn't fair." Her lips parted to talk, though he wasn't sure which emotion was trying to push through. He continued before he could find out. "Although you weren't fair, either. It's clear you've made a few assumptions about me—some I'd like to correct—and, again, I can't quite blame you for that. But the fact remains that it's been eight years since we last saw each other. Our lives have changed—we've changed with them." He took one last step forward, testing her waters. "Give me the chance to set a few things straight, Darling."

"You don't have to answer to me," she replied. Her voice was low.

"You're right," he agreed. "I don't have to, but I need to."

Darling's expression—brows drawn together, lips thin, jaw set—slowly changed to a more pleasant mask. For the first time since he had walked in, she looked at his peace offering. She didn't smile, though he knew she could smell the delicious chocolate-covered confections, but she didn't continue to frown. If he wanted to find a safe ground with Present-Day Darling, he was going to have to come to terms with the fact that she might not warm up to him again. He would have to settle for whatever she gave him and ignore how the idea of never being in her good opinion hurt deeper than he'd like to admit.

"I'm surprised Carla still served you after the scene I caused," she finally said. "You must have done some quick sweet talking."

Oliver smiled. Dangerous Darling was gone. He'd get a chance to explain everything now. Well, at least the real reason behind his love and respect for the Orion

Group. That explanation meant more to him than she could fathom. The desire to tell her what had happened three years ago had been replaced by the need to explain the past the moment she had stormed out of the café.

"I told her I needed to score some points with you." He motioned to the bag in his hand. "Hopefully freshly baked chocolate donuts and a coffee with two creams and three sugars will do just that."

Joy flashed through him as the corner of Darling's lip quirked up.

"You're lucky that my breakfast preferences aren't one of the things that have changed over the years."

Darling walked forward, grabbed the bag and led him into her office. It was a much smaller room, but Oliver instantly liked it. Exposed brick walls, once painted white and now chipping, were decorated with certification plaques, black-and-white pictures of Mulligan scenery and a rusted sign that said Acuity across it.

"So you actually own Acuity, then?"

"I sure do. Expenses and all." Even as she said it sarcastically, he saw the pride in it. She was comfortable behind her desk. He was sure her ease was subconscious. Darling Smith had found her place in the world after all. He wondered how her parents felt about it but knew he'd never ask her that. If he was a gaping wound, they were bottomless caverns. "I interned here when I was eighteen. Jeff didn't tell me then, but he was ready to retire. So, he started to groom me as his replacement. When I was done with all my certifications and schooling, he split. Now it's just me." She bit into her donut and her eyes fluttered closed. "And more than occasionally the sweet, sweet Red Leaf pastry."

"Sounds like a good setup. I'm happy for you."

Darling flashed a small smile. "Thanks," she said. "Now, what about you? What assumptions do you need to clear up?"

"I feel like you have the wrong impression of me."

"I still stand by the fact that you don't need to explain yourself to me. You could be married with kids and living in the suburbs of Canada for all I know. Not that it would be bad if you did. I just want you to know that you don't owe me anything, Oliver."

This made him laugh. He lifted his left hand to show ringless fingers.

"No marriages, children or suburban Canadian living. Just an apartment in Dallas, where Orion's located." It might have been his imagination, but he thought she looked pleased at this information. He had already done his research on her. She wasn't and hadn't been married. Although he wasn't sure if she was attached currently. He decided against asking her that, too. "I know you aren't forcing me to explain, but I'd still like to do it."

"All right, then, I'm listening." She set her pastry down and laced her fingers together on the desktop. Oliver took a deep breath and began.

"I know you think I've sold out by working for a company that caters to the rich and privileged, but that's only partially true. Before I worked for Orion, I was hired as an agent at another security agency called Redstone Solutions out in California. I was excited—thrilled—with the offer because, one, I needed the money, and two, I was good at what I did. A lot of people think bodyguards just stand around and occasionally have to tackle someone, but the truth is there's a lot more to it. Strategies and problem solving, for instance. Redstone let me lead an exciting life of travel and leisure while also challenging me at every turn." Oliver felt pride and nostalgia surge through him. Though it didn't last long. It never did. He felt his smile sag and his face harden. Darling leaned in closer. "But then Morgan Avery was killed, and everything changed."

Darling's eyebrows rose in question, but she didn't interrupt.

"Redstone is a large company with more connections and funding than you can imagine. Its reach isn't limited to the US, either. I was based in the California branch as a part of a three-man team when Morgan Avery first came in and asked for our help. She was twenty-one and an astronomy student, utterly brilliant. She'd been competing for a spot in an elite university program in the UK that, if she made it in, would make her career. But when she was invited to the final round of the competition in England, she started getting these really nasty letters. Anonymous letters that threatened her life. So, she came to Redstone Solutions asking for a team to escort her while she traveled there. The only problem was, she didn't have enough money to come up with the minimum payment. My boss turned her away after she practically begged us to reconsider." Oliver's jaw tightened and his fists balled. "For a week straight, she tried to convince us, and for a week we had to turn her away. The day before she was scheduled to fly out, she was found dead in a ditch near the airport—beaten and almost unrecognizable. The police were able to find the killer—a competitor—and send him to prison for life, but it didn't matter. The damage was done." Oliver took a long pull from his coffee before continuing, finding a better place in his mind. "Morgan's death was an eye-opener for us."

"Us?"

"Nikki, the secretary, was the person who talked to Morgan the most. After Morgan's death, she became furious and left Redstone to start her own security agency. She asked me and my then-team to join her." He smiled. "We did, and that's Orion's origin story."

"Secretary to boss, huh?" Darling sipped her coffee. "I like the sound of her."

"Nikki was and is a beast in the business world. When she left, she already had a few connections willing to fund Orion. Since then, she's kept it going *and* growing with no issues."

"She sounds like my kind of woman," Darling replied with a smirk. Oliver laughed.

"She's something, all right." He sobered. "We've spent the last three years offering our services to those who can't afford it but need it, specifically when traveling. Without her connections and the occasional sponsor, we'd never be able to take on our clients for basically free."

He watched as Darling's ears seemed to perk right up.

"Basically free?"

Oliver smiled, but he was sad. "We'll never turn away another Morgan."

"Wow," Darling breathed. "And Nigel Marks is one of those sponsors you have to take on occasionally?" she guessed.

"Bingo. Team Delta was assigned and now, here I am."

"Team Delta?" She snorted. "What are you, five?"

Oliver held his hands up and grinned. "Hey, don't look at me! My bud took the Orion Belt theme and went with it. He got a kick out of Orion Belt's three stars also being referenced as Delta, Epsilon and Zeta."

Darling's eyes widened as she understood the meaning behind the name. Her voice softened. "Morgan was in astronomy. The name Orion was chosen to honor her memory," she said.

Oliver nodded. "It was her favorite constellation." A warmth that was equal parts fondness and sadness pooled in his chest as he remembered Morgan. "Darling, I know I have no right to come into your life and start trying to call the shots, but I have to state this again. I don't think Nigel killed that woman, and unless he's convicted or decides he doesn't need us, he's my number-one priority while in Mulligan." Oliver wanted to put his hand out to touch hers, to show her that she should trust him. To show that even though Nigel was his top priority, he still cared for her. Even though he shouldn't.

Darling, to his surprise, seemed to choose her next words carefully.

"I understand," she said in almost a whisper. "But, tell me, why are you so sure that he's innocent?"

"The surprise on his face when he found out about the body," he answered.

Darling huffed. "Surprise can be faked, Oliver. I do it every Christmas when Trudy gives me a can of peanut brittle wrapped in reindeer-decorated paper."

"True, he could have faked the surprise," he conceded. "But not the pain." Oliver replayed the moment when he'd watched as the cops had told the wealthy man about the body. He didn't need to hear the man's response to know it had caught him completely by surprise…and hurt him.

Darling hesitated, brows pulling together, but she didn't have time to respond. Her phone blared to life, a cute jingle that felt out of place within the conversation. She let out a long sigh as she read the ID.

"Excuse me a second," she said, standing.

"No problem."

Oliver was able to drink the rest of his neglected coffee, pairing it with one of Darling's chocolate-covered circles of delicious sin, before the private investigator came back. The look on her face made him stand.

"What's wrong?"

Darling bit her lip. "Do you want a list or a long-winded sentence?" It was a less-than-halfhearted attempt to lighten whatever mood had erupted around her. Oliver answered with an equal lack of mirth.

"List."

"One, the medical examiner believes our Jane Doe was killed yesterday morning," she ticked off. "Two, that puts Nigel in the clear since he was apparently eating breakfast with your team while you were bailing me out." Oliver wanted to feel relief at her words—that he had been right about Nigel's innocence—but Darling's grim expression had every part of him on guard. "Three, they haven't been able to identify the woman yet." There was a hesitation after the words left her mouth.

"Couldn't Nigel identify her? If he met with her he had to *know* her."

She held up four fingers. "Four, Nigel is denying that he was ever even at the hotel, let alone in Mulligan, last night. No one has stepped forward to prove otherwise, and it's Nigel's word against Dan's. There are no security cameras at the hotel, either. None that work properly, at least."

Oliver's instinct was to question Dan's claim of seeing Nigel in the first place, but he felt an irrational loyalty to him, because it was obvious that was how Darling felt about him.

"I don't think prints take that long to process," he said

instead. "Surely they'll figure out who she is within the week and go from there."

Darling's face darkened. She held up her hand. "Five," she said, voice shaking despite her calm exterior, "all of her fingers and teeth are missing. Someone removed them."

Chapter Six

Any chance of normal conversation disappeared at the grim news.

"Removed?" Oliver repeated.

Darling let her hand drop to her side and settled back behind her desk. Her half-eaten donut wasn't as appealing as it had been minutes before.

"Postmortem, but yes," she confirmed.

Oliver also sat back down, though he didn't relax.

"Who told you all this?"

"Derrick," she admitted.

"You two must be close if he'll disclose information about an ongoing murder investigation."

"We used to date, but now we don't," she said matter-of-factly. "I think he told me to warn me."

Oliver's eyebrow rose at that. "Warn you? Of what?"

"That my case against Nigel isn't safe anymore," she said. "Considering the murder."

"So he thinks Nigel is still connected even though he's denied being in town?"

"I'm not the only one who trusts Dan. Just because Nigel has an alibi for where he physically was at the time of the murder doesn't mean he isn't connected." Darling recalled the pictures of the millionaire and the red-haired woman. Derrick had confirmed their Jane Doe also had red hair. If they could prove it was the same woman, Nigel would have no choice but to offer her identity up.

"You think he's denying knowing her because he had someone else kill her," Oliver summarized. Darling didn't nod or shake her head. She was trying indifference. "Why would he go through all of that trouble?" he asked.

"Something tells me he can't afford an affair right now."

Darling froze. She was being too candid with Oliver, though she wondered if it even mattered anymore. Soon the town of Mulligan would hear the rumor that Nigel had been at the hotel and the woman who had been with him was dead. With or without denials, the idea that Nigel was an adulterer would cross each resident's mind at least once. The beloved Nigel Marks was about to have his image tested with or without her saying a word.

"Ah," Oliver said with a slight nod. "The prenup loophole. If he cheats, the wife can take at least half of everything Nigel owns."

"What?" She feigned ignorance but barely concealed her surprise. Oliver wasn't buying it.

"You aren't the only person with connections," he said. "If working for Redstone Solutions taught us anything, it was to be thorough in knowing the clients we take on. That includes the threats to them. Orion may be small and less well funded, but that doesn't mean our analysts are anything to laugh at." That piqued Darling's interest, but she didn't interrupt to follow up. "If Elizabeth Marks wasn't in the Bahamas right now, she would be the first person I would suspect. Although, like you said about Nigel, she could still be connected even though she wasn't physically there."

"But, even if what you say is true about this prenup

thing," she said, "why kill the mistress when you can expose her?"

"Why expose the mistress when you can kill her?"

"Ah, casting blame on the jilted wife. An overplayed card, don't you think?" Darling quirked her lip up into a grin.

He laughed. "I'm assuming the case you have against Nigel is about infidelity. Why else would you be snooping around his house and then the hotel he was at?"

"Nigel Marks is almost a legend in Mulligan. Who's to say I'm not his number-one fan?" Darling had her eyebrow raised high, a smirk across her lips to match. She knew Oliver wasn't dumb, but she wasn't going to admit to her deal with Elizabeth yet. There were a few questions she needed to ask the millionaire's wife first.

"Last time I checked, you weren't the biggest fan of the upper class," Oliver said. She couldn't deny that. "That's why I assume you asked the hotel owner to keep an eye out for Nigel, just in case."

Darling held up her hands. "Okay, you got me," she said. "I am Nigel's number-one fan. I have a poster of him over my bed and everything."

Oliver laughed, and the mood around them softened. They lapsed into small talk while picking up and finishing their food, avoiding the topics of murder and blame. They were delving into their individual pasts, while the one they shared wasn't brought up. Darling silently marveled at how the Oliver that sat across from her was so similar to the one all those years ago, and yet completely different. She couldn't quite put her finger on it, though she didn't want to, either. Trying to define Oliver Quinn would be a slippery slope—if she found she liked the new one, then what? It was better for everyone if she just played nice and treated the man as an old friend, nothing more and nothing less.

"Speaking of the job," Oliver said, "I need to go relieve Thomas. He worked well past his hours last night."

"Not to pry into your work, but where does the whole murder accusation leave you with Marks?" she asked, standing with him and ignoring the small part of her that wanted him to stay.

"Innocent until proven guilty." He shrugged. "The fact that he was with my team during the woman's death is an ironclad alibi, in my mind. The only way we'll stop working for him now is if Nigel terminates the contract or Nikki calls us off. Considering he already signed a contract, it'll cost him more to get out of it than to stay in it, and last time I talked to Nikki, she said we continue to do our job. She's a good person, Darling. There's a reason we all trust her to make the right call."

Darling nodded, not wanting to point out that everyone at some point was wrong. If this was Nikki's time, it meant Oliver and his team were protecting the man behind a woman's murder. But she let that thought slide. She wasn't Oliver's mother or wife or even his girlfriend. Darling couldn't dictate his choices just as he couldn't dictate hers.

"It *was* nice catching up with you, though," he added, meeting her eyes and holding her gaze. "Even the bumpy parts."

Darling couldn't help but smile back. "It certainly has been interesting."

Oliver picked up his coffee and slid his phone back into his pocket. Darling didn't know if she was supposed to hug him or shake his hand as a goodbye. It wasn't as if they had done either in greeting the day before when he had strolled into the town jail to get her out. As she struggled with trying to figure out what to say to the man who had broken her heart, Oliver saved her the trouble.

"I would say goodbye, but I have a feeling you'll pop back up in the middle of wherever you aren't supposed to be. So I'll just see you then." She returned his smile with a mischievous one of her own and watched as he walked out of her office.

He was absolutely right.

An hour passed without any new leads, evidence or answers. Darling was feeling unbelievably restless. She half expected Derrick to call or stop by with a no-nonsense attitude about her case, but Acuity's door remained closed and her phone remained quiet.

So Darling, unable to cope with the fact she wasn't making progress, made a list of all the evidence and facts she had. It reminded her that her camera was still beneath Dan's desk at the hotel.

"Better than sitting here and doing nothing," she said to the office.

Despite yesterday's discovery, the Mulligan Motel looked as normal as it ever did. No one was in the office, but Darling preferred that. She hurried to grab her camera, hoping to avoid explaining to Dan why she was back.

It took a few seconds to register that there was no camera to grab.

"What the?" she asked herself, squatting to make sure it hadn't been pushed out of view.

Darling's blood ran cold.

There was a piece of paper where her camera had been. Written across it in red ink was a message.

You already did the right thing, Darling. Now stop.

Chapter Seven

He wasn't tall, he wasn't big and he wasn't intimidating. His shoulders weren't wide, either, but he still held himself up straight and proud. With dark hair, muddy-green eyes and a surprisingly hard jaw, Jace Marks was sculpted with equal parts his father and the most average of people.

Oliver shook the twenty-six-year-old's hand and couldn't help but compare him with Nigel.

While his father dressed to impress, Jace wore a blue flannel button-up, jeans and tennis shoes. Instead of having a cropped haircut like Nigel's, Jace slicked back his short hair with a pair of sunglasses resting on top. Despite the past forty-eight hours, he looked rested enough.

However, one detail that matched his father to a tee was the trademark smile he wore easily. It spoke of wealth, privilege and many, many secrets.

"It's good to properly meet you," Jace said. He shook Oliver's hand. He had a firm grip, which also surprised Oliver. "A passing hello at the police station isn't the same thing, if you ask me."

"No problem. I didn't realize you would be in Mulligan during our stay," Oliver admitted. All clients were asked to disclose pertinent information. That included their travel companions.

"When the merger got complicated, Nigel called me in," he answered. "I hadn't planned on staying, but given recent events, I feel I should be here to support him."

They were standing in the kitchen, Oliver next to the back door with a clear sight line to the front. Nigel was still upstairs in his study with his lawyer, Stan, while Grant was stationed outside the door. Oliver had sent Thomas to rest as soon as he had come through the door, considering the new recruit hadn't slept yet.

"Nigel," Oliver repeated the name. Had he been informed wrong? Was Jace a stepson and not the millionaire's blood relation?

"He doesn't like when he's referred to as Father in a work setting," Jace answered with an apologetic smile. "He doesn't want anyone to think he's partaking in favoritism. So we keep to a first-name basis when working, but I guess it's become a general habit."

Oliver supposed that made sense. He didn't call Nikki by her first name in front of the new recruits or clients, but that was more of a show of respect. Members of Orion earned the right to be familiar with the head honcho by doing a good job and remaining humble. Nigel having his son call him by his first name might make sense, but Oliver couldn't deny he didn't like the informality of it. If he'd ever called his dad by his name, Jacob Quinn would have been fast to correct him.

"So you work at Charisma?" Oliver asked when it was apparent Jace wasn't leaving the kitchen anytime soon.

He sat down at the island and faced Oliver. "It's the only place I've ever worked," he said with notable pride. "I oversee the company's support specialists and deal directly with the more complicated clients, walking them through every part of the investment process. With this merger going through, however, I'm hoping to make the move up in the ranks. But now, with this…" He looked up at the ceiling and shook his head. "I just hope it all gets taken care of before it does any damage to the company."

Oliver couldn't help the raise of his eyebrow or, he was sure, the look of slight disgust that contorted his face. If Darling had been in the room, she would have flown right off the handle at how crass the millionaire's son was being. She would have pointed out in no uncertain terms that he was referring to a human being who had been murdered and that finding justice for her was much more important.

But Darling wasn't there.

"Hopefully it will be sorted out," Oliver offered.

Jace nodded, oblivious to Oliver's thoughts. "You know, I told Nigel he shouldn't have even come back to Mulligan for the merger. I could have handled it and stayed in the city, but he's getting stubborn in his old age." He frowned, and his brow creased. "If he had listened to me, this whole ordeal could have been avoided. But he loves this place, the small town he came from and the people who love him. I wonder, though, if they'll love him after all of this."

Oliver didn't have an answer to that.

"I should get going now. This merger won't happen by itself." Jace grabbed a water from the refrigerator and started to leave. "In case Nigel didn't tell you or your boss, my mother will be here by the end of the week."

"No, I haven't been told that yet," Oliver said, already cursing in his head.

"This family is all about supporting one another," Jace

said. "You accuse one of us of murder, you accuse all of us of murder." He said it with sarcasm, meant to be an offhand joke, but Oliver saw the irony in it. Jace's parents were, in fact, the top two suspects.

For the next three hours, Oliver did the more boring parts of bodyguard work while his mind kept running. If a thought wasn't about his current client, it was undoubtedly about a petite, sandy-haired woman with more attitude than even she probably knew what to do with. Darling Smith was incapable of ignoring what was wrong in the world. It was an infuriating and endearing quality that he hadn't realized he missed.

He moved through the first floor, scanning his surroundings with tried interest. Oliver liked to memorize each piece as if he hadn't done it the previous day. That way, if something was off—if something had changed—he'd be more likely to notice.

The smaller details often ended up making the most impact.

THE LONGER DARLING stared at the note, the harder she willed it to explain itself.

"Who wrote you?" she asked it for the tenth time. "And why?"

Like the nine times before, the note didn't answer. Instead, it stayed frustratingly still against the top of her desk, its red ink blaring across the surface.

You already did the right thing, Darling. Now stop.

There was no denying the message had been intended for her.

So, Darling had gone back to her car with the hairs on the back of her neck standing at salute, also confused.

She had driven back to Acuity and pulled the newspaper clipping with the first note out to compare the two.

The handwriting and color had matched perfectly.

Whoever wanted Nigel's affair out in the open was not only was watching Darling but also had taken her camera. Why? The cops had seen everything in that room plus more once they had gotten there.

Darling growled to her office.

It felt like a threat.

Had Nigel caught wind of her case against him, or had he figured it out like Oliver had? But then why give her the pictures of Nigel and the red-haired woman, and urge her to turn them in to the police? And why tell her to stop?

Stop what?

Darling cast a long look at her empty coffee cup. It was nearly five, and she had put off calling Derrick for hours. Just as her resolve to disclose everything began to dissolve, her phone chirped to life with the name Liz across the screen.

"You're very hard to get a hold of," Darling greeted her, no humor in her voice.

Elizabeth didn't waste an excuse.

"We both know I'm a suspect in this murder. I'm having to cut my vacation short while recording my recent movements to send over to my lawyer. All under the ever-watchful eye of my mother. Be thankful I was finally able to step away from her."

"Does she not know about your case with me?"

"No. I love my mother, but I don't love her tendency to run her mouth. Give her enough wine and she'll tell you every secret she's ever been told." Elizabeth was tired, that much Darling could tell. She pictured the woman's impeccable posture slightly bent, makeup pulling double duty to hide the stress in her face. "Have you told anyone about our case yet?"

"No, ma'am. I wanted to at least talk to you first." There was a silence, and Darling used it to her advantage. "Did you hire another private investigator to trail Nigel before me or after me?"

"No," Elizabeth responded. "Truthfully, hiring you was a last-minute decision. The less people know about my plans to leave Nigel, the better. That being said, I want you to go to the police and tell them everything."

Darling had to take a beat to process that. "About the case?"

"About the case, the reason why I hired you, what you've found, everything." There was a change in her tone. Elizabeth had moved from tired to determined in a breath. She brooked no argument with her words. "Give them total disclosure. I don't want them looking at me as a suspect. I didn't hire anyone to kill that woman, and I don't want anyone to think I did. I will ask, though, if you think the police could keep my desire for a divorce on the private side of the investigation?"

Darling thought this over. "I can't promise anything, but I think they would. Nigel has denied knowing the woman or even seeing her, so right now, I think they are just trying to figure out who she is. I don't think they would take the time to publicize your marital problems."

"Good. Then, please, could you tell them everything while still trying to keep it from Nigel?"

"Yes, I can do that." Darling wanted to exhale in relief. Elizabeth didn't know it, but if she hadn't called before six, Darling would have told Derrick everything anyway.

"Great. Now, one last thing," Elizabeth said before her

voice dropped to almost a whisper. "I don't care how you do it, but I want you to find out who that woman is. My husband may be a cheat, but he's no killer. Something isn't right, and now my family is suffering for it. I will not stand for that."

Darling didn't doubt for a second that anyone who crossed Elizabeth Marks would regret it. She just hoped Jane Doe hadn't been one of those people.

Darling accepted the job, though she didn't tell Elizabeth she had already decided to pursue the woman's identity. She marveled at how straightforward Elizabeth had been. It was refreshing in a way. She wasn't sugarcoating anything, and she wasn't trying to get Darling to lie about their involvement. No, she knew she was in a compromising position and was trying to get out of it. Full disclosure to the police. That hadn't been what Darling had expected, but she was happy to comply. Grabbing her coat and cell phone, she began dialing Derrick's number as she closed up Acuity for the night.

The sun was setting, leaving a light glow hanging around the parking lot. It was serene and almost calming. A feeling Darling tried to hold on to as she approached her car and saw the door was cracked open. On the driver's seat was a paper bag.

In it was her camera.

Chapter Eight

Darling's body went on high alert. She turned her head from side to side, scanning the parking lot for her mystery figure. Her hair slapped her cheeks at the movement, and a chill found its way into her bones.

She was alone.

"Hello?"

Darling was so startled she nearly threw her phone. She had forgotten she had called the deputy.

"Hey," she exclaimed into the phone. Her nerves pushed her voice into a high octave. She tried to tamp down her fear. "We need to talk again." She checked the back for any unwanted passengers, then climbed into the driver's seat. Her grip on the phone had gone tight, as if talking to a police officer made her instantly safe. She knew this was not the case.

Derrick said some not-so-nice words before answering.

"More evidence, I'm guessing."

"Something like that," she hedged. "I'm coming to the station now."

"Unless you know for certain the identity of either the deceased or her killer, can we meet at Carter's? I'm just now going off duty and haven't had a lick of food since this morning."

At the mention of food, Darling's stomach let out a loud growl.

"That actually sounds good, but you think you could pick me up from my place? I'd like to change. It's getting cold." Even as she asked, Darling started her car and backed out of her spot. What had been a cute outfit that morning was now feeling like a poor choice. April in Maine might have warmer days, but its nights could get nasty quickly. It helped that her apartment was midway between the station and Carter's. The return trip would also have them passing by her place on the way to his work.

Plus, she was hoping he'd be chatty when boxed inside a car.

Derrick agreed, and within fifteen minutes Darling was dressed in a long-sleeved royal blue sweater and a heavier coat. Her ankle boots were swapped out with a pair of black boots that laced up her shins, keeping her calves warm. She didn't bother with refreshing her makeup or checking her hair. Impressing Derrick was nowhere on her list of things to do.

Darling lived in a large house built in the 1900s that had since been converted into four apartments. Hers was apartment number three and tucked away on the left side of the second floor. In her years of living in Mulligan, she had found she loved the two-bedroom, one-bathroom dwelling. She jogged down the community stairs and wondered if Oliver would like her home.

It amazed her how complicated life could become within two days.

"Whatever you're about to say or ask, I'd like you to hit your pause button until we've sat down and at least have drinks in front of us," Derrick said when Darling had situated herself in his Jeep. So much for Chatty Cathy. "A man can only take so much on an empty stomach."

OLIVER PULLED ON his beer, looked around Carter's Bar and Grill, and wondered what it was like to live in Mulligan. It was such a small town compared with most places he had visited through the years. A giant leap different compared with Dallas, especially. The fact that Darling had settled in Mulligan made him question the town even more. Was it that great a place, or had Darling's need to distance herself from her old life driven her to settle for the exact opposite?

Now off the clock, Oliver took his time finishing his beer. The noise level in the restaurant had risen considerably. He turned to survey the new crowd. Should he get a table or stay at the bar?

"Evening, Deputy," he heard one of the waitresses call. He cast a quick glance toward the door and was surprised to see Deputy Derrick holding the door open for none other than Mulligan's private investigator. The couple didn't see him as they were seated.

Couple.

Darling had already told him—of her own accord—that she and the deputy were no longer an item. Either way, it wasn't Oliver's business. He had been in town for only two days and had spent no more than an hour or two with her during that time. Feeling a connection that wasn't there was a distraction he didn't need and one he was sure Darling didn't want.

When he'd left home—and Darling—eight years ago, he had been firm in his decision. What Darling didn't know wouldn't hurt her...at least, he had hoped it wouldn't, not forever. He had watched the younger Darling change into an independent, clever young woman within the year they had spent together. She'd had so much potential at such a young age. He had never doubted her future would be bright. His, however, had always been in question. When he left Darling behind, he hadn't ever planned on returning to her.

He laughed to himself.

Now he was in Maine, sitting a few feet away from the same woman and her ex, the deputy.

In a way, Oliver was glad she had dated Derrick. He hoped that, even though it hadn't lasted, she had been happy. He hoped she had opened up to Derrick—or to some other man—letting him in to her carefully guarded world. Because even though he had purposely broken her heart, Oliver had hoped it would one day mend.

He watched as Derrick pulled out her chair, and the two settled into their seats. Darling had changed clothes but kept her yellow daisy earrings in. She had always loved daisies.

"Want another?" the bartender asked, pulling Oliver's attention away. He was thankful for it. He needed to give Darling and her life the privacy they deserved.

"Yeah. Can I also get a menu?"

The bartender tossed a laminated menu over and slid him a replacement beer.

"Our steak dinner is a favorite," he said, pointing out the item listed under Entrees before going to tend another patron. Oliver didn't keep looking. George had said the same. If a Mainer praised it, then that had to mean it was good, right?

"It's a lie."

Oliver sloshed his beer in surprise at the new voice to his left.

Darling was amused.

"A lie?" he questioned, regaining his composure.

Darling took the menu from his hands and set it on the bar. "The steak dinner is good but not amazing," she continued. "You'd be disappointed."

"Your friend George the Gate Guard would beg to differ."

Darling snorted. "Well, George is a liar. Didn't we already establish that yesterday?"

It was Oliver's turn to laugh. "We didn't, actually."

Darling waved her hand through the air as if to shoo off such trivial thoughts.

The bartender made his way back over, but before Oliver could put a word in edgewise, Darling had caught his attention.

"Hey, Benny, Oliver here will take one of your fantastic lobster rolls," she said. "And can you send it over to our table?" She pointed back to where Derrick was seated, talking on his phone. Bartender Benny nodded.

"Well, looks like I'm eating some lobster, then. And not alone."

"You can't just come to Maine and not have one of its best dishes. Plus, if I remember correctly, you're a fan of fresh seafood." Oliver nodded, conceding that. "And as for the whole eating-alone thing, that's just sad." There was a teasing tone in her voice, but when she spoke again the humor was gone. "I need to tell Derrick something about the case. I have a feeling I'll cross your client's path again before this is all over. I'd rather keep you in the loop." She held up her hand to silence any questions Oliver was about to ask. "But first, I also *really* need a drink."

Chapter Nine

Derrick greeted Oliver with a nod that picked up enthusiasm only when he saw the beer Oliver had gotten for him. The past two days had been long for Darling, but she knew they were nothing compared to what Derrick was having to deal with.

"I hope you don't mind dining with an out-of-towner," Oliver said. He took the outside seat next to Darling. It wasn't a long booth, and their thighs touched as he got settled.

"Listen, as long you don't go on a killing rampage before we get our food, I'll be fine."

"I'll see what I can do," Oliver responded.

Derrick had stayed true to his plea to keep shoptalk out of the picture until he at least had a drink. He and Darling had done almost no talking on the ride over to Carter's. Then she'd seen Oliver sitting alone at the bar after they were seated. The act of including him had been impulsive.

Why? she wondered.

She waited as each got his fill of his respective drink. Darling found that her lips wanted to remain shut, also, until her drink arrived.

"So, how are you enjoying Mulligan so far?" Derrick asked.

"Well, aside from the Marks residence, I've only had the pleasure of visiting a few places." He tipped his beer toward Derrick. "The police station was my favorite, by the way. I'm a sucker for being colder inside a building than I am outside it." Derrick let out a laugh. It seemed genuine. "But Mulligan has its charms. I don't know if I'd be singing the same tune year-round once the snow comes in, but for now I can see the appeal."

"The appeal. You've traveled around the world and you think Mulligan is appealing?" The deputy held up his beer. "That's mighty generous of you." They clinked their bottles together, and Darling rolled her eyes.

She listened to them talk a bit longer before her drink arrived. She had readjusted her attention to the small glass between her hands.

"Is that milk?" Oliver asked, peering at the cream-colored drink.

"This, my friend, is another part of Maine you should partake in." She took a long sip. The creamy goodness of Allen's Coffee Flavored Brandy mixed with milk created one of Darling's favorite after-hours drinks.

"It's cheap and delicious," Derrick supplied. "This one here can only take so much before she turns into a puddle of giggles."

"A puddle of giggles?" Darling said. "Is that even a thing?"

"I think I get what he means," Oliver defended the deputy. He turned his attention to Derrick. "Right before her eighteenth birthday, Darling got ahold of the key to her father's liquor cabinet and called me after she did a few taste testings. She laughed for almost the entire conversation. I caught maybe one or two words the whole time."

The two men laughed, and even Darling found herself smiling. In the time that she had met and fallen for Oliver, a lot of bad had happened in her life. However, when she was able to step back from her pity party, she could remember the good times, too.

"Okay, so I may turn into 'a puddle of giggles' when I drink a little too much, but at least I don't cry or yell!" As if they had planned it, the two men shrugged. "But, just in case, I think I better go ahead and talk shop." Darling took a large gulp of her drink and dove in.

"Elizabeth Marks hired me last week to get proof—pictures—of Nigel with another woman while he stayed in Mulligan. She believes he's been having an affair for quite a while." None of this information fazed either man, so she continued right along. "She planned her trip to the Bahamas with her mother for the duration of his stay because she thought the fact that there was no way she could accidentally catch him might entice him to philander."

"That's a different spin on reverse psychology if I ever did hear one," Oliver observed.

"The Markses have a prenup that—in the foolish throes of young love—Elizabeth signed without question. If she divorces him now, she forfeits money she thinks she deserves, including the funds she actually made herself."

"But if he cheats and she can prove it…" Oliver started.

"Then that prenup is void, and she's free to take, at minimum, half of everything he owns," Darling finished.

Derrick leaned forward. "Which gives her one hell of a motive to hurt both her husband and his mistress. This is the kind of thing you tell the police who are investigating a murder," the deputy bit out.

"We both know you already checked her alibi, and it's as clean as Nigel's. I knew from the start where she was and that she couldn't physically do it."

"Did you see her in the Bahamas?" Derrick pushed her. "Do you know for a fact that she actually went?"

Darling sighed. "Derrick, I had Dan keep an eye out at the hotel just in case Nigel stopped by, and that's exactly what happened. Nigel spent the night with Jane Doe. Dan saw him. We both know that now Nigel's lying about even being there. We also both know that Elizabeth Marks was checked in to her resort at the time of Jane Doe's death."

"Then why are you telling me this now? Why not keep it to yourself if you think it's not a big deal?" Darling knew Derrick was angry with her for withholding information. She didn't blame him for it, either. If she had been a cop, she would have been angry, too.

"Elizabeth wanted me to disclose everything to you because she realizes she's a top suspect. She wants me to tell you everything we've talked about and everything I've found," Darling explained.

"Just like that?" Oliver asked, clearly impressed.

"Just like that. Sure, she wants discretion—if Nigel finds out she's wanting to divorce him, he could do it first and leave her with nothing—but she isn't stupid. Hiring a private eye to follow your cheating husband and then running off to the Bahamas for an airtight alibi? Yeah, she's smart enough to know how that looks."

The men thought that over, and Darling used the silence to take a few more sips of her drink.

"Have you had any luck with figuring out who Jane

Doe is?" she ventured when they appeared too involved in their own drinks. "Any new leads?"

The deputy rested his bottle on the table. He began to thumb the label off as he answered. He seemed to be considering each word he spoke.

"We have hit a few...snags."

"Snags?" Darling and Oliver asked in unison.

"We're still searching several avenues in an attempt to identify her, but as of right now, we're no further than we were when you found her." Derrick wasn't much for sighing, but his body sagged with the weight of frustration. "As far as we can tell, no one has reported her missing. We've sent her picture and description out to other departments to see if anything catches, but so far it's been one dead end after another. We even checked with cab companies and car rental agencies since we still can't locate the car she went to the hotel in. If we don't find something soon, we'll have to take this to the media."

Darling shifted in her seat, as if she could move away from the bad information.

"Has anyone reported on the death yet?" Oliver asked. It was a question that Darling hadn't answered, either. Meaning to buy a newspaper wasn't the same as actually buying one.

Derrick shook his head and pulled a long strip of the beer label off. "Nigel's name might be in the clear because of his alibi, but word has already started to spread that he was possibly at the hotel with Jane Doe. Covering a story, even without his name directly in it, is still getting too close to insulting Mulligan's golden child," he said. "I don't expect that to last much longer, though. The chief has a meeting with a local reporter first thing tomorrow morning." He shot a look at Darling. "Rebel Nash."

Darling let out a whistle. Rebel Nash was a Mulligan transplant who was the embodiment of unwavering determination and absolute stubbornness. If anyone was going to break the story *with* Nigel's name in it, Rebel would be the one to do it.

"From the little I know about her," Darling explained to the out-of-towner Oliver, "Rebel values the truth more than the consequences of losing Mulligan's hero. Which, I have to say, I like about her right now."

Oliver smiled. "Just what everyone needs, another you in a different profession."

Derrick laughed and Darling picked up her glass. "I'm going to take that as a compliment, thank you."

"I knew you would," Oliver replied with a smirk.

The food arrived shortly after, and their conversation all but died. Well, the one in which Darling was included. Derrick and Oliver went back and forth, sharing their war stories about law enforcement and personal protection before switching gears to sports. Darling watched her exes with interest as she sipped away her drink.

When Derrick was tense, it was hard for him to ease up. Finding the humor in a case, if only for a brief stretch, was a task in itself. Darling knew that emotionally, it was hard for him to get out of his head long enough to enjoy his surroundings.

Oliver, on the other hand, knew when to laugh and did it with no issues. He was lighthearted but could slip into a more serious tone when needed. She watched as he laughed and slowly began to remember all of the sweet moments they'd had together. Sure, age had changed Oliver—he was more confident and there was no denying he had more muscles beneath his shirt—but Darling still could see the boy she'd once loved.

Darling let out a laugh at the thought. Both men paused their conversation but didn't comment. She ordered another drink and thought back on the case.

"What about the ledger?" she asked suddenly. She'd interrupted the men, but Derrick knew what she was talking about.

"We didn't think about looking until this morning," he said with obvious disapproval. Whether it was of himself or the other deputies, she didn't know. "When we went back, someone had torn out the last three pages. We grabbed it for prints, but nothing so far."

Darling brought up the pictures on her phone and slid it over to Derrick. "I took these yesterday, after I found the body." Derrick's eyes went wide. "I swear I would already have given it to you had I remembered," she hurried on. "But with everything that has happened, it slipped my mind." The real reason being the mysterious letters. It had knocked her off her game, along with the amber-eyed man sitting next to her.

"You took a picture of the check-ins from the night Jane Doe checked in?" Derrick wanted clarification, but with his free hand he was already waving over the waitress.

"Yes. I wanted to use it as evidence against Nigel that he was having an affair. At the time, I didn't realize Jane Doe would stay a Jane Doe."

"Check, please," Derrick called to the waitress. "And you haven't searched these names yet?"

Darling shook her head. "I didn't even think about them until just now."

"Send me this picture. I'm going to go back to the station and run them."

Darling took her phone and did as the deputy said.

"I'll take care of the food," Oliver chimed in. "You go ahead and get outta here."

Derrick might have reconsidered had he not been given a new lead, but instead he just left.

"Looks like my snooping comes in handy sometimes, huh?" Darling said after she'd sent the picture. Oliver laughed and gave the waitress his card when she came back. "You don't have to pay for me," Darling added.

"Consider it a reward for your snooping."

"I'll finish my drink to that."

And she did just that.

Oliver not only paid for dinner but also extended his gallantry to offering Darling a ride home. They settled into his rental, each pushing through the cold of outside, before Oliver started the engine and its heater.

"I have to say, Mulligan keeps on surprising me," Oliver said.

"Do you mean Mulligan or its murder mystery?"

"Both," he admitted.

"I still can't believe that no one can tell us who Jane Doe is," Darling dove in. Her lips were a little loose and her body was a little warm, and not from the heater.

"Yeah, you would have thought that the cops would have found a witness by now. Even someone who had seen her at least driving through town." Oliver clapped his hands together. It made Darling jump. "On the way in from the airport, I only passed one gas station," he said, eyes bright. "I'm assuming that on the other side of town there's a gas station leading into Mulligan?"

Darling thought for a moment, then nodded.

"So there's a chance she might have stopped at either one of these gas stations, depending on which direction she was coming in from? We even checked with cab companies and car rental agencies since we still can't locate the car she went to the hotel in."

"That's a slim chance, but yes."

"Why don't we go check it out, then?" He started the car, suddenly energized. "A slight chance is better than anything you have right now."

He was right about that. Even if Derrick was able to identify her, getting video of Jane Doe could make all the difference in the case.

"Okay, so let's assume she did drive in but not from the city side."

"Why not?" Oliver asked. He had his hand on the gearshift, ready for direction.

"If she was already in the city, why would Nigel *and* Jane Doe drive out here to Mulligan to meet? I'm sure there are plenty of places they could have done it there," she reasoned.

That was all Oliver needed. He backed out of his parking spot.

Once again, they were a team.

Chapter Ten

The clock read nine fifteen when Oliver cut the engine in the parking lot of Zippy's Pump & Pour. Its two pumps were positioned in what they hoped was the front security camera's range.

"Okay, that's Connor-something," Darling said, pointing through the windshield to the clerk inside.

"Looks young. How do you know him?"

"Just from getting my gas here on occasion." She gave him a quick wink that made him wonder if she was feeling her two drinks yet. "They're the only place in town that carries the candy bars I really like."

"Do you think he'll let us see the security footage?"

Darling bit her lip as she thought. Oliver couldn't deny it stirred up some feeling within him. He readjusted in his seat.

"Maybe," she answered. "I don't know enough about him to make that call yet. We're going to have to find out."

Oliver nodded and they entered the station. It was small, and Connor was undeniably bored. When they walked to the counter, he stood from his stool and smiled.

"Hey, hey," he greeted them. His eyes slid over them, stalling on Darling. "Whoa! You're the private eye."

Darling's cheeks tinted red, but Oliver didn't know if that was another aftereffect of brandy or surprise at Connor's obvious admiration.

"Private investigator, but yes," she said with a smile. "That's me."

"Awesome! I was telling my buddy the other day I wouldn't mind doing what you do," Connor said, excitement only mounting. "You wouldn't happen to be hiring right now, would you?" He lowered his voice and leaned closer. Oliver and Darling leaned in, too. "Because working here kind of sucks."

Oliver couldn't help but chuckle.

"We aren't actually hiring at the moment," Darling said. Connor looked supremely disappointed. "But you might be able to help us now if you're not too busy."

Connor's disappointment was short-lived. He smiled, and it was downright mischievous.

"I'll do anything you want!"

Darling cut a quick smile to Oliver. "Well, great!"

Oliver wondered how the private investigator was going to approach the topic at hand. If he was a betting man he would have put his money on the honeypotting approach. Being sweet to lower the boy's defenses, getting information with a nice tone and even nicer words. Or would she try to trick him into giving up what they needed to know? He leaned against the counter and watched with interest.

"Were you working here two nights ago, by chance?" Darling asked.

"Oh, yeah, I've worked night shift for the last week and a half." Connor lowered his voice. "My boss is out of town 'on business,' but I think that's a load of crap." He made finger quotes to show what he must have thought was a lie.

The private investigator took a beat before responding, no doubt noting the employee had some obvious disdain for his employer. "That's gotta be a drag." She let her body droop a bit as she said it. Oliver realized it was because she wanted Connor to feel as if they were on the same page as him. It was an approach somewhere between honey-potting and straightforward. She wanted to be relatable.

"I told him I'll quit if he keeps me closing every single night. I mean, I can do it once and a while, but I have a life, you know?" Oliver nodded in unison with Darling. A different thrill than the one he'd felt in the car filled him as he realized they were in secret cahoots, working together toward the same goal without any friction from their past breaking in. He wondered if she felt it, too. They had always made a good team.

"I don't blame you," he said to show his empathy further. Conner nodded again, giving them both a look that clearly said he liked them. Darling must have realized it, too. She straightened slightly. She was going in for the kill.

"Well, the thing is, two nights ago, a woman might have stopped here." She paused and pulled out her phone. She scrolled to one of the pictures she'd been given of Jane Doe and Nigel. "This woman. Do you remember her, by chance?"

Connor squinted at the phone's screen for a few seconds before snapping his fingers.

"The redhead, yeah! She was here." Oliver and Darling shared a look. They had gotten supremely lucky. "She didn't come in, but I remember her getting gas."

He winked at Darling. "I don't forget a pretty face, especially a new one in town."

"Do you remember if anyone was with her? In the car?"

"No, she was alone," he answered, brow wrinkled as he thought. "Why? Is she in some kind of trouble? Is she a criminal?"

Darling raised her hands and laughed. "No, no, she's—" Oliver could tell she was looking for the right thing to say.

"We're worried about her, is all," he interjected. "She came to town for a visit but hasn't checked in for a few days, and we thought she might have stopped by here."

"She isn't from around here, so we're really worried," Darling added. "You said she didn't come in, but that camera outside would have seen her, right?"

Connor was emphatic as he answered. "Oh yeah! You two want to see it? We still have tapes from a week ago." He lowered his voice again. "I may have fallen behind on changing them out, but, hey, it's not like I get paid out the yin yang to keep up with it all." Oliver raised his eyebrow at Darling as Connor ushered the two of them to the back room. Oliver couldn't tell if he was being so lax with security because he seemed to dislike his current boss or if he was trying to show off for the woman he wanted to be his new boss. Either way, after throwing around several VHS tapes, the clerk popped in the right one and hit Play.

"You can fast-forward as much as you want," he said as a ding sounded from the front door. "There's no sound—the boss is too cheap, ya know—but everything else works okay. I'll be back!"

"We seriously lucked out that the boss isn't around,"

Darling whispered, already hitting the fast-forward button. She kept her eye on the time stamp in the corner of the screen. "I think we also lucked out that our Jane Doe stopped here.

"Good call, by the way. I hadn't even thought about the possibility of her coming here." Darling turned to give him a quick smile. It made his breath hitch for a split second. When they were younger, sometimes Darling would look at him and the world around him would slow. A candid moment from the woman that reminded him how beautiful she was in every way. It caught him off guard as he realized that all the time that had passed hadn't changed that feeling.

Her lips turned up, her cheeks rosy, her eyes unrelenting as they searched for the truth. Darling Smith was determined, and Oliver knew nothing would get in her way.

"Just trying to get the town PI on my side," he ribbed her.

She turned her attention back to the television monitor with a laugh.

They quieted as the footage's time ticked by, leaned in and focused. The footage wasn't in color and, at best, only a step up from unrecognizably grainy.

Oliver pointed to the pump farthest from the security camera. Partially hidden by the pumps was a young woman exiting the driver's side of a car. She disappeared behind the pump before reappearing to put the nozzle in her gas tank. Her hair was shoulder-length and wavy. Wearing dark pants and a light button-up blouse, she rubbed her hands together before walking to the trash can between her car and a van closer to the building. An older woman stood against it as she waited for her vehicle to fill up.

"Is that her?" Oliver asked, still uncertain. Darling's eyebrows drew together, her eyes squinting at the screen.

The woman in question was all smiles as she caught the older woman's eye. Her mouth began to move, but without sound, they couldn't hope to decipher what the two were saying.

"Yes," Darling answered. "That's our Jane Doe. Her smile is identical to the one in the pictures. Working on the assumption that the woman in those pictures *is* our Jane Doe. Which is what I'm doing."

Oliver continued to watch as Jane Doe held a conversation with the older woman at the neighboring pump. There was no denying she was happy about something, almost bouncing as she talked. The conversation didn't last long. Both women finished their pumping and paused to say goodbye to each other before getting back into their respective vehicles. Jane Doe drove off first. Darling paused the tape as soon as the car was out of view.

Oliver kept silent as she rewound the tape and they watched it for a second time. The van at the next pump and the angle of the security camera made the scene difficult to decipher. Only the driver's side door and seat, and the back end of the car where the gas tank was could be seen around the van and pump. The color of Jane Doe's car was dark, but aside from that, the black-and-white footage didn't give anything away.

"It's clearly a four-door, and a smaller one at that. I'd say it's an older model, too." He scooted closer as if that could help him figure out what the model was. The new proximity didn't help. "I'm not a car guy, so I can't make this call. Pause it as she drives off."

Darling did as he said, but the picture was blurred.

"They may have a security camera, but it sure isn't that high-tech," she muttered.

"The boss is a lot of things, including cheap," Connor said from the doorway. Darling jumped.

"Sorry, we just need to figure out what kind of car this is." She put her finger up to the blurred spot that was Jane Doe's car. If Zippy's had had a camera at the pumps, they would have been able to see the make and the license plate. But that wasn't the case.

"Ew, yeah, sorry about that." He, too, squinted at the footage, as if that could suddenly make it clearer. "The farther away from the camera you are, the worse it comes across on the tapes."

"Do you remember anything about the car she was in?" Oliver asked.

The question turned Connor's cheeks red. "No," he said with the shake of the head. "I wasn't really focusing on anything else after I saw her." There were no perverted or salacious undertones in his statement, just honest appreciation for the woman's beauty. It earned a sincere smile from the private investigator.

"Connor, would you mind if we borrowed this?" she asked. "I'd like to take a closer look at it."

The clerk shrugged but nodded. "You can keep it for all I care," he said. "The boss man doesn't ever look at them unless we've been robbed."

"Great! Well, if he does happen to find out and isn't happy about it, tell him to give me a call. I'll set him straight."

"Yes, ma'am."

"This was surprisingly productive," Darling said when they were back in the car.

Oliver gave her a questioning look at her new level of excitement. He was betting she was definitely tipsy.

"Because we know where she was the night before she was killed?" he asked.

Darling laughed. "No," she exclaimed with a grin. "Because for the first time, we have a witness who talked to Jane Doe."

THREE OF THE FOUR names from the hotel ledger checked out. Derrick guessed the fourth was a fake. Darling could hear the stress in his voice as he said he would be tracking down the other three people to see if they saw anything at the time of check-in. Even though he was sure he had already questioned each the day the body was found. Darling had been hesitant to give their new information over to the deputy, but Oliver had urged her on. Plus, she supposed she owed it to the main investigator on the case.

"And you're sure it's her?" Derrick asked.

"Yes, but we can't figure out the make of her car," she said. "But, if you let me, I can track down the woman she spoke to and ask her tomorrow if she saw anything…"

She waited for the backlash from suggesting she help in the murder investigation, but it never came. With an exhalation so loud that Oliver chuckled in the seat next to her, Derrick relented.

"I'm only saying yes because we're swamped…and I know how crafty you can get." Darling smiled at the windshield. Being called crafty was a much nicer descriptor than what private investigators were usually given. "Call me if you get something, and try not to do anything illegal."

"He acts like I do illegal things all the time," Darling said once the call was over. Oliver raised his eyebrow.

They were still seated in his rental, parked at the curb outside her apartment. "I don't, I should add."

"Of course not." A wisp of a smile trailed across his lips, suddenly bringing her attention to his mouth. His lips were thick, yet entirely masculine. And, when pressed against hers, made the world feel whole. Darling cleared her throat and reached for the door handle at the thought. Fantasizing about the bodyguard in any way was dangerous. Considering there was a murderer on the loose, there was enough danger for all of them without reigniting old feelings. A monumental distraction that could cause either one of them to slip up at their jobs.

"Well, I guess I should turn in for the night," she said, hoping her heated cheeks weren't visible in the darkness of the SUV. "I have a feeling tomorrow's going to be a long day."

Oliver nodded and started to get out, too.

More heat ran up her neck. Did Oliver want to come up to her apartment? There wasn't much they could do other than watch television, talk or get *reacquainted*. However, Oliver didn't seem to care about any of that.

"I'm going to walk you to your door, if you don't mind," he said, coming around to her side. "Mulligan is a little too surprising for my liking at the moment."

"And it's appealing, too, right?" she teased.

He cast her a sideways look as they walked up the sidewalk and to the front door. "It has its perks."

If she hadn't been blushing already, she would have blushed then. Or maybe it wasn't a blush at all. Maybe it was the alcohol. Either way, she led him into the foyer and up the stairs to the left. When they stopped in front of her door, she turned with every intention in the world to say good-night, but he had stopped much closer to her than she had realized. Having to tilt her head up to meet his eyes, Darling's thoughts scrambled.

The world became quiet. It didn't make a peep as she held Oliver's gaze. She imagined the feel of his lips against hers—soft yet rough, full of desire and passion—and almost rocked up onto the pads of her feet to close the space between them. The rest of her body tingled in anticipation of such a bold move.

The bodyguard had been in town for two whole days. Almost a decade spanned between now and their past. Even though they had gotten to catch up on the major life changes they had gone through, they were still swimming in a sea of unknowns.

Yet at the same time, Darling felt as if they had picked up right where their old lives had ended. Fitting together without resistance like two pieces in a large, complicated puzzle. Could it be that easy? And if it was, did that mean they *should*?

Darling felt weight settle in her feet, declaring they weren't going to support her pushing up to make an impulsive decision. It was time to break the news to her brain that kissing Oliver—although almost every part of her wanted to—wasn't going to happen.

"Thanks for coming with me tonight," she said, almost whispering. She took a step backward and grabbed the doorknob. "I should probably get some sleep now." She unlocked the door and opened it wide, breaking eye contact for a moment so she could cool slightly. "Thank you for dinner, too. Next time is on me."

Oliver blinked a few times before simply nodding. He didn't hesitate as he turned and headed for the stairs.

"Let me know if you need anything," he called over his shoulder. But he didn't stop, and he certainly didn't turn around.

Chapter Eleven

Harriet Mendon lived in a tiny yellow cottage surrounded by one hundred or so other tiny, brightly colored cottages. Darling parked at the curb and waved to a mother and her young girl who were walking past. They smiled and waved back, their minds already returning to the beautiful day.

Darling wished she could follow suit. Not have to worry about talking to a stranger about another stranger who had been murdered. She could—get back into her car, drive to the coast and relax next to the water—but she was too invested in Jane Doe's case to stop now. Finding her body had somehow given Darling a sense of protectiveness over the case, deeply investing her into the pursuit of truth in what had happened. Sure, getting into the car and leaving would have been easy, but it wasn't an option her heart could reason was good.

The cottage's front door was baby blue and sounded thin as Darling rapped her knuckles against it. After taking the security tape from Zippy's to Acuity—and watching it a few more times—Darling had plugged Jane Doe's pump mate's license plate number into her computer. Using a private investigator database she paid for monthly—a tool that often came in handy when searching for a name—Harriet Mendon had been the result. In a town as small as Mulligan, it wasn't hard to find her address thanks to a stack of old telephone books Darling's former boss had left behind. Now, waiting for Harriet to open the door, Darling wondered if she should come up with an alternate story for how she'd tracked the woman down. One that sounded less calculating.

As far as broaching the topic of Jane Doe, Darling wasn't going to dance around the reason for her visit. She was going to ask Harriet to tell her about her conversation with the young woman and hope it was enough to identify her. Or damn her killer.

However, Harriet didn't come to the door. Darling knocked again and listened for any noise from inside the house. It remained quiet.

"Great," she muttered. She took out one of her cards and quickly wrote a note across the back before placing it into the jamb next to the doorknob. Hopefully Harriet Mendon's interest would be piqued enough to call.

Darling drove back to Acuity with her mind somewhere else entirely. The day might have been beautiful, but the temperature was already dropping. She wondered how Oliver was faring with the chill but then decided it wasn't safe to think about the man. Thinking of him in any capacity—no matter how innocent—pushed thoughts of his lips and their almost-kiss right between her eyes. Would it be a familiar feeling or some new sensation since the last time their lips had touched? Her parents would get a kick out of how, after everything they had said and tried, Oliver Quinn had found his way back into their daughter's life after all.

The thought of her parents brought on another set

of memories she needed to stay away from, but it also helped her trail back to what was important.

Jane Doe had tangoed with the wealthy, too.

She just hadn't survived the dance.

Darling recalled her silent laugh and jovial attitude when talking to Harriet at the gas station. "I need to find you, Harriet," she said aloud. "I will find you."

A handful of cars were parked in the lot behind Acuity, all of which Darling recognized as belonging to the strip mall's tenants. Still, she kept alert. It was best to not forget about her mystery note writer and the fact he or she had been watching her. With caution, Darling swept her eyes all around her as she went to Acuity's door. Her mind dropped to the next task on her mental list. She wasn't the most patient person. Waiting for Harriet to see her calling card was beyond Darling's current capabilities. She was going to have to find her at work and go from there.

All she needed was to search a little longer on the internet until—

"Whoa."

Acuity's front door was cracked open, the top window pane broken out. Through the hole, Darling could see shards of glass littering the lobby floor. Her hand went to the doorknob on reflex, but fear caught up to her. What if the culprit was still inside? She pictured Jane Doe wrapped up in the tub.

Maybe she needed to call in some backup.

Nigel was acting strange. There was no doubt about it.

"Are you okay?" Oliver asked when the businessman came down from his office. He was visibly shaken. Eyes too wide. Face taut. Oliver glanced up the stairs where he knew Thomas stood guard next to the office door. Grant wasn't on the clock for another few hours. Oliver had rotated between perimeter checks and standing guard at the two entrances to the house's main floor. He'd looked out at the gatehouse each time he made an outdoor pass but kept his distance from it. He appreciated the loyalty George had for his job, but he didn't want to get caught up in a conversation with the man. Aside from the three bodyguards and their client, Oliver knew they were alone. The lawyer and Jace were at the new Charisma branch's office. Which was why his concern was so acute. There was no reason Nigel should look as off-kilter as he did.

Nigel blinked several times, clearing his throat when the words still didn't come.

"Yes. I just got off of the phone with Deputy Arrington." His voice wavered as he answered. It put Oliver on even higher alert. Why would Derrick call Nigel if Nigel alibied out? What was the point? "He told me how the young woman was killed. I don't think he believes I had nothing to do with her death." He gave Oliver a weak smile and went to the refrigerator. Unlike his son, instead of a water, he went for a beer. "I didn't kill her, but that doesn't mean I don't feel sympathy for her…" He dropped eye contact for an instant. "Bludgeoned to death with a hammer seems barbaric."

"A hammer?" It was the first Oliver had heard about it.

"Yes."

"Seems cowardly."

Nigel gave Oliver a look that questioned him and agreed simultaneously. The older man wanted to say something—Oliver could feel it—but he didn't. Instead he nodded and made his trek back up the stairs.

A few minutes went by before Oliver decided to check

in on their client. Thomas was standing in the hallway next to the door. When he saw Oliver, he shook his head.

"What?"

Thomas lowered his voice to a whisper. "I don't know what you said to him down there, but he's really upset." Oliver raised his eyebrow and the younger bodyguard shrugged. "I heard a weird noise and looked in and he was crying."

"Crying?"

Thomas nodded. "He stopped when he got a call but, man, I hope he doesn't do it again. I wasn't trained to handle all of that."

Oliver didn't know what to say to that, so he left the bodyguard to go back downstairs. He didn't know if he should feel sympathy for the man. Had he been crying for the loss of Jane Doe? The woman he claimed to not know?

His phone started to vibrate in his pocket. When he saw it was Darling, he knew she'd find the information interesting.

"Quinn," he answered.

"Oliver, can you come to the office right now?" she asked in a rush.

"Why? What's wrong?"

There was worry in her voice. "I—well—the thing is…" She sucked in a deep breath before another gushed out with her words. "I think someone broke in to Acuity and might still be here but I don't want to call the cops just yet."

"Wait, where are you now? You aren't *in* there, are you?" He could imagine the spunky private investigator hiding in the office bathroom as the culprit went through her things a few feet away.

"Of course I'm not in there! I'm sitting in my car, watching the door from the parking lot," she defended herself. "If they are still inside and decide to leave, I'm going to catch them on film." Again, it wasn't hard to imagine Darling sitting in her car, looking through the lens of her camera at her office.

"You need to call the police, Darling. This isn't some kind of game." As he said it, he was walking upstairs to Grant's temporary room.

"I know it isn't a game, but the police have a lot on their plates already. I'm not going to call them until I've personally assessed the damage. If you can't come, though, I'll wait a few more minutes before going in myself." Every word held a stubborn edge.

"No. Don't go in." He knocked on Grant's door. "I'm headed that way now."

If Grant minded stepping in for Oliver while he "attended to a personal matter," he didn't show it. Oliver didn't like up and leaving during his shift, but he took solace in the fact that Nigel planned on working from home for the rest of the day. Just in case, though, he paused at the gatehouse as he was leaving.

George took his time coming out. He looked ruffled, as if he had been caught napping. Oliver didn't have time to admonish the guard for sleeping on the job. Not when he was leaving in the middle of his own shift.

"Hey, George, I'm running out for a bit," Oliver said. "Until I get back, call Thomas if anyone shows up here. Okay?"

George nodded, and Oliver left before the man could get a conversation going. He had a private investigator to worry about.

Minutes later, he pulled into the strip mall's parking

lot, next to Darling's car. He was relieved to see her face bob into view when he walked up. True to form, her camera was in her hands.

"No one has come out," she said in lieu of a hello. "I didn't hear anything when I first was at the door, either. I just wanted to be on the safe side."

"Caution isn't a bad thing," he pointed out. "You stay here and let me go check it out. If you hear anything, take off and call the cops." He could see an internal battle wage across her face. Why had she called if she was going to argue about him going inside without her? She must have been really nervous.

"Okay," she agreed after a moment.

Oliver adjusted his shirt to keep his gun covered as he walked to Acuity's entrance. He didn't often carry it— Orion's bodyguards used nonlethal weapons as much as they could—but it was never too far away from him, either. If someone had broken into Darling's office—in his opinion—that showed malicious intent for her. Oliver wasn't about to go easy on someone who had shown that level of disregard for the investigator. Especially when she was in the parking lot, yards away.

The door was cracked open. Whoever had broken the glass had snaked a hand through the window to unlock the door. He wondered if anyone else in the strip mall had heard the break. Pulling his gun out, he quietly pushed the door open enough to get a good look at the lobby. No one was inside. He moved into the room, gun raised and ready. Whoever had broken in was either being really quiet or wasn't inside anymore. Oliver moved slowly to Darling's personal office. The wood was splintered; the door was ajar. He paused to listen again for any movement.

Nothing.

Using his foot, he nudged the door open. Anger flared within him. He stood alone in the office.

It had been tossed.

Desk drawers were on the floor, the filing cabinets had been toppled over and pried open, papers were scattered around and—the detail that made Oliver's blood run hot—every framed picture on the wall had been smashed.

He went back out into the lobby and made sure to check the small bathroom before going outside to wave Darling in. She was more than ready and hurried over. Oliver returned his gun back to the back of his jeans and frowned.

"I hate to say it, but someone trashed your office," he told her before she could move through the lobby to her personal space. Oliver didn't like watching her face fall at the news.

"Is it bad?"

"It's not pretty."

He followed her back into the small, disheveled room. She stood in the doorway for a few seconds, eyes roaming over the mess. Then, like a switch had been flipped, she hurried to the other side of the desk and started to move through drawers on the floor and their spilled contents.

"It's gone, Oliver!"

"What's gone?" But before she could answer, it dawned on him. "The security tape."

Darling nodded, clearly upset and stood straight again. An overpowering urge to comfort her pushed him forward. He put his hands on her shoulders, making her look up into his eyes. The moment from the night before played back into his mind.

She was close enough to kiss.

"Oliver, there's something I need to tell you."

"Yes?" his voice dropped low. Her green-eyed stare could stir up a drove of feelings in mere seconds.

"I think I know who did this," she whispered. "And you aren't going to like it."

"YOU SHOULD HAVE told someone—told me—about this note writer, Darling," Oliver fumed. He hadn't liked her story about the warnings—plus the mention of her parents and the news article—she'd received from her anonymous stalker one bit. He'd already called the station and talked to Derrick directly, recounting everything she had told him.

The doubt she had harbored that the note writer was trying to help had left the moment she'd seen her office and found the security tape gone. She wasn't dealing with a third-party player anymore.

Darling believed they were dealing with Jane Doe's killer.

Oliver paced back and forth in the lobby, face reddened with emotion. His words were angry, but she knew he was worried. However, that didn't mean she liked being scolded by Oliver, of all people.

"You can't keep making these decisions," he continued. "It's reckless and stupid."

"Stupid?" Darling asked, voice pitching high.

"Yes, stupid." He put his hands out wide, exasperated. "How am I supposed to protect you if you don't give me all the facts?"

In the back of her mind, Darling knew it was concern that made his tact disappear, but it triggered the deep-rooted pain Oliver Quinn had left all those years ago in her heart. Their camaraderie from the night before vanished.

"Protect me?" She laughed. "News flash—I don't need you to protect me, Oliver. I've taken care of myself for the last eight years just fine. Thank you for coming over here, but I realize now that it was a mistake." Once she said it, she felt a twinge of regret, but her pride wouldn't let her back down. "So, if you don't mind, go back to work and protect the person who actually wants it."

She walked to the broken door and held it open for him. The sound of a car door shutting derailed whatever he was about to say. They both looked out to see Derrick walking toward them.

"Darling, I—" Oliver started.

"Please, just leave."

"But I wanted—"

Darling heard the strain in her voice as she pleaded one last time with him. "Oliver, you owe me that much."

The bodyguard's brow creased, but he didn't have time to answer.

"I have some words for you," Derrick called, coming closer. He looked exhausted.

"Oh, I know," Darling said, trying to sound annoyed rather than wounded. "Mr. Quinn was just leaving. He has to go back to work now."

"Yeah, I guess I was," the bodyguard said, not meeting Darling's gaze. Instead he looked to the deputy. "But first, can I grab a quick word with you?"

Derrick must have liked Oliver, because he didn't give him any snark about the request, but Darling was done with the fair-haired man. She excused herself to the bathroom and took a long look at herself in the mirror.

How could one man make her feel so crazy?

THE SKY WAS dark by the time Oliver decided he couldn't take it anymore. His shift had ended an hour earlier, but he had stayed on the house grounds, going over Elizabeth Marks's itinerary. She was set to be in town in two days, which meant Oliver and his team would have to scout out routes and try to foresee any vulnerabilities that their trip to pick her up might cause.

Vulnerable.

What Darling had looked like when she had told him to leave.

He balled his fist.

He didn't want to leave her side, but she had been right. It wasn't his job to keep her safe. He had given up that privilege eight years ago when he'd left her without so much as a backward glance.

The idea that someone had been watching, following and threatening Darling put fire through his veins. Despite their past and her present wants, Oliver wouldn't have left her side had Derrick not convinced him she'd be safe.

"Listen, we're at a point in this case where we're waiting on results and information to come in," Derrick had said when Oliver had pulled him to the side at Acuity. "Whoever is messing with Darling won't get away with it. I'll make sure of it."

Derrick had promised he'd keep an escort outside her house that afternoon and through the night. Until they caught the culprit, he wasn't going to let her be alone. Oliver might have been wary of the deputy when he'd first come to Mulligan, but now he was grateful for his presence. It was true they weren't currently dating, but that didn't stop Derrick from being zealous about keeping his friend safe.

Still, Oliver couldn't ignore the worry that ate at him.

He would at least check in with Derrick, even if Darling didn't want his concern.

The temperature had dropped considerably since the sun had gone down. He wondered how he would handle Mulligan's true winter. Just the thought of the massive amount of snow made him turn the heat on high. By the time he pulled up outside of the old house, he was downright toasty.

It was a feeling that didn't last long.

All lights were off in Darling's apartment, from what he could tell. In fact, the entire building was dark save for the foyer light, which could be seen through the front windows of the common area. It was there on the front steps, in the faint glow of that light, that Oliver saw the outline of a body.

He swung his car into the parking lot between a police cruiser and Darling's car, all feeling of warmth gone from his body. For the second time that day, he grabbed his gun from his console. This time, though he didn't pretend to not have it.

No one sprung from the cruiser as Oliver hurried from his rental, gun in clear view. But he wasn't expecting anyone to. If they hadn't seen the body from this close, chances were no one was in the car.

The body belonged to a man lying on the top step and porch. He was on his side, face away from the parking lot. Oliver pulled out his phone and used the flashlight to see that the man was Derrick.

Blood was caked on the back of his head, and his left leg was bent at a weird angle. Oliver checked for a pulse. It was weak.

Adrenaline began to pump through him. Dialing 9-1-1,

he ran through the entryway and took the steps two at a time to Darling's door. It was shut but not locked.

"Darling?" Oliver called into the apartment. He didn't bother knocking, and he didn't worry about her privacy when no one responded. He quickly searched each room, gun raised. There was no sign of struggle inside.

Oliver ran a hand through his hair and went back to the front door.

"What's the nature of your emergency?" the operator finally answered.

"Deputy Derrick Arrington was attacked and needs immediate medical attention," Oliver bit out. He was angry at himself. "And private investigator Darling Smith has been kidnapped."

"What is your location?"

Oliver repeated the address as he checked the door. It wasn't broken, and there were no scratch marks to suggest someone had tried to pick the lock. He kicked the bottom of the door. Pain exploded in his foot, but he didn't care. He shouldn't have left Darling in the first place. He pulled his fist back this time, ready to let the door know the anger and regret flowing through his blood when he noticed a piece of paper sticking out from under the doormat.

He moved it out of the way, careful not to touch the actual paper. Its neat red writing made Oliver growl in absolute anger.

One more strike and you're out, Darling.

⟶ Chapter Twelve

Cold.

Seeping, slithering, unrelenting cold.

It didn't just push against her body. It invaded. Twisting and turning around every inch of her skin. Darling repeated her first waking thought.

"Oh, my God."

She was sitting outside in what was a clearing, as best she could tell. Whether it was night or early morning didn't matter. She couldn't see a thing. Darkness and the freezing air had combined and were currently conquering her. In the back of her mind, she calculated the normal temperature after the sun went down. It could drop to anywhere between forty to fifteen degrees. She certainly felt as if it was more like fifteen.

And that's when she realized why she felt the chill so acutely.

She was naked.

Fear, panic and slight hysteria rose up into a small scream that bubbled from her lips. With shaking hands, she clamped her mouth shut, afraid that whoever had put her here was still around. That's when the pain around her neck registered. Between deep breaths, she recalled her last memory of walking out of her apartment.

And then strong hands wrapping around her neck and squeezing until darkness came.

Before she could even replay the memory again, she had to entertain a new, terrifying one first. Tenderly she got to her feet and focused on the lower parts of her body. She nearly cried with relief when she found there was no pain or soreness south of her waistline. Whoever had tossed her into the freezing unknown without a stitch on had at least not taken advantage of her in such a horrible way.

It was enough of a silver lining to put a little light back into her dark situation.

A breeze picked up, and Darling wrapped her arms around her chest. Closing her eyes, she listened.

Deafening silence.

No noise from the town. No cars. Nothing.

A picture of a territorial moose or bear happening upon her made Darling's eyelids flutter back open. She prayed right then and there that her demise wouldn't be by some hungry animal. Though dying of exposure also wasn't fun. Before her mind could fill up with images and stories of lost hikers and stranded civilians who couldn't outlast the cold, Darling put one foot forward.

Standing still wasn't going to save her.

She walked in small strides, feeling dead grass and dirt between her toes before putting her weight down. Mulligan was a small town surrounded by enough rural land that she could have been anywhere within the town's limits. That included a stretch of land south of the town center that was reserved for hunting. Just as Darling didn't want to be eaten, she didn't want to stumble across an old hunting trap.

What if she was no longer even in Mulligan?

Minutes crept by and nothing seemed to change. Just grass and dirt—no trees or asphalt—pressing against feet she was slowly losing feeling in at each new step. Worry and panic, which Darling had decided to push clear out of her head when she took her first step forward, were using a battering ram to get back in.

Someone had knocked on her door. Thinking it was Oliver, she had flung it open, ready to fight. Yet no one had been there. Curious, she had moved down the stairs and out to the front porch. That's when she had seen Derrick.

Darling's heart squeezed as she remembered him sprawled on the steps. Had there been blood or any obvious wounds? She hadn't found out before someone had decided to choke her out.

Darling let out a humorless chuckle.

With its battering ram taking another charge, panic got one step closer to getting in.

What felt like ages later—though realistically she bet it had been only an hour at best since she had awoken—Darling's steps faltered. Her body ached and shook from the cold. Her mind had become blank. Slowly she angled her gaze down to question the change in her walking. A cloud must have finally passed by, because the blessed moonlight broke through and created a hazy glow around her. For the first time since she had opened her eyes, she could see. Pale skin stretched downward—too pale—and a dark spot that looked suspiciously like blood covered the grass next to her left foot.

Panic hadn't given up. She felt it hoist its battering ram back up for one last attempt to break down her emotional barrier.

Darling bent to investigate but lost her balance and

toppled over. She repositioned herself into a better position and felt a thrill of happiness that she could still feel anything in her almost-numb limbs. Pain meant she was still alive. The moment she couldn't feel at all was the moment she would lose it.

The blood—because it was blood and not her imagination—was coming from her foot. Her left one, to be exact. She wiped at the cut on her sole, but more blood replaced what was now smeared across her hand. There was nothing in the cut and nothing in her immediate area that looked sharp. Yet as she wiped another layer of blood off, the wound kept bleeding at a good clip.

How could she not feel the large gash in her foot?

The answer didn't matter. Panic took three steps back before rushing the door that was made to keep her sane and rammed it clear off its hinges.

Darling Smith finally hung her head and let out a sob. It shook her body more than the cold.

"WE'LL FIND HER. I promise you that," the chief said.

Chief Sanderson was a tall, thin man in his fifties with cropped gray-white hair and a clean-shaven face. His badge and gun were visible on his belt, but it was his demeanor that spoke of authority. He and Oliver stood outside Acuity's office, retracing Darling's steps for the second time. Looking for anything that might lead them to who was behind her disappearance.

Her phone was off—all calls going straight to her voicemail—and no one from her building or the strip mall claimed to have heard or seen anything out of the ordinary.

Oliver wanted to believe the chief was right—needed to believe him—but it had been hours since he'd found the empty apartment and the injured officer. Derrick had been alive but hadn't woken up before his surgery. Chief Sanderson had said that even though he temporarily was out of the woods, they wouldn't know the extent of the damage from his head injury until he was conscious. They didn't know if the same hammer that had killed Jane Doe had been used, but they did know the same method had been.

Hit from behind to knock them out of commission.

Though it looked as if Derrick hadn't gone down without a fight. His leg had been broken in two places, and his knuckles had been bloodied.

Oliver hoped Darling was putting up a better fight.

"This case…it's all theory and no conclusive, hard evidence. This note writer, a possible affair and now our own kidnapped private investigator," the chief ground out. "We're missing something big here."

"Whatever it is, I think Darling must have gotten close to it."

"It's time we get closer. Excuse me." The chief stepped away to answer his phone.

Oliver had been surprised when the chief had personally accompanied him in an attempt to find out what had happened. He could have sent other deputies but hadn't hesitated in getting his hands dirty. Oliver was finding he liked Sanderson just as he liked Derrick. Both men were fond of Darling and, instead of seeing her as a nuisance because of her profession, seemed to respect her. Sanderson wanted her to be found. It helped that the popular opinion had changed about the connection between Derrick's attacker and Darling's note writer.

Which also meant the chances were high that the mystery person was directly connected to Jane Doe's murder.

Oliver's stomach dropped as his mind jumped to the worst possible outcome for Darling. He needed to find her. Whoever was behind this couldn't have been this careful. There had to be a trail he could follow somewhere.

Like water to the face, Oliver knew for certain there *was* one person who knew more than they did.

Nigel.

Pulling out his phone, he scrolled through his contacts and went straight to the number of Orion's senior technical analyst, Rachel Delvough. Although he'd brought Grant and Thomas up to speed on the situation, he hadn't yet made a call to Nikki. As far as he was concerned, they were still doing their job correctly with the other two members still protecting the client.

The client he was about to target.

"Hello?" Rachel answered after a few rings. It was almost ten in Dallas, but she didn't sound as if he had woken her. Though he wouldn't have cared if he had. Darling's life was more important than being polite.

"Rachel, it's Oliver."

"What's wrong?" Orion operated with a handful of people. Everyone knew everyone else. Rachel was more connected at times than the rest, considering she handled all the behind-the-scenes affairs of each agent.

"I need a favor," he said, turning his back on the chief. "And I really need you to do it, Rachel." He wasn't as close to the quiet analyst as he was to Nikki, but he liked to think she'd help him out. Even if what he wanted was illegal.

"Okay…what is it?"

"Can you remotely look through someone's phone?" Nikki had hinted that Rachel's technical background might not have been wholly on the up-and-up. She hadn't used the word *hacker*, but he was taking a shot in the dark.

"Look through? Anything specific?"

"The incoming and outgoing call logs."

Nigel was lying about not knowing Jane Doe. If Oliver could see the numbers he had called or been called from, maybe he could find out who Jane Doe was. And if Nigel *had* hired someone to kill her and take Darling.

"Yeah, I can do that. But Oliver, it's illegal."

Oliver's fist balled. He wasn't angry at Rachel but at himself.

"Listen, I wouldn't ask unless it was absolutely important," he said.

There was hesitation. "Do you need it tracked, too?"

"No." He knew Nigel was still at his house.

"Whose phone?"

"Nigel Marks's."

More hesitation. Rachel knew exactly who Nigel was. She knew he was Orion's ticket to keeping afloat.

"Does Nikki know about it?"

"No," he admitted. "Listen, I wouldn't ask unless it was necessary. Please, Rachel."

He could hear movement on the other end of the phone.

"I'll have to head back to the office. I'm assuming you need this now?"

He let out a breath of relief. "As soon as humanly possible."

"I can do it. And Oliver? I won't lie to Nikki." Her voice was resolute. He didn't blame her. Everyone at Orion respected their boss. "But I won't bring it up to her unless you do."

"Deal."

The called ended, and Oliver was left feeling helpless. His job was to protect people, and yet he was invading the privacy of the client he had been hired to guard and had let down the only woman he had ever loved.

Oliver blinked.

Was that true?

And did he love her still?

Chapter Thirteen

Debrah and Andrew Smith had both come from money, but that didn't stop them from wanting more. They took to the business world, becoming a force many respected. Debrah and Andrew were inspiring. The perfect role models for a child with a growing mind like Darling.

So when Darling's childhood friend Annmarie Moreno's father accused the tycoons of running a string of Ponzi schemes, everyone including Darling couldn't help but not believe him. It was absurd, she had thought, but Annmarie's father didn't back down.

So Debrah and Andrew made sure to prove him wrong, in a very public way. A newspaper article and a televised interview painted a picture of their innocence, and their accuser's jealousy and greed.

It ruined his career and social standing in the community. He left the city with Annmarie and life returned to normal.

Until Darling received an anonymous email claiming the evidence that her parents were lying was about to be thrown out. She was given an address and told what to look for, and less than thirty minutes later, Darling's entire world had changed.

That was also the first time she had ever met Oliver—

standing in a Dumpster, holding the first clue in a series that would prove her parents had lied.

And destroyed a man's life because of it.

Since then she'd gone down the rabbit hole and found nothing but corruption. Bold-faced lies that built up until the moment she realized they would travel great lengths to ensure their fame and fortune were never threatened. That was the moment she asked Oliver to run away with her. Little did she know as she stood there watching him walk away, tears blurring her vision, that within the month, she would be on a plane to Maine, to a small town named Mulligan.

Now, as Darling pressed her hands to her cheeks, unable to feel her tears, she mused how her end felt intrinsically connected to the beginning of her adulthood.

Corruption.

Despair.

Oliver.

The last point—the man with golden hair—didn't hold the same dark weight as the first two points. Even if he had denied her all those years ago, she couldn't find the heat behind her anger for it. In fact, she realized the anger wasn't there at all anymore. She liked the life she had made since. She liked to think she had made a difference and left a mark in the lives of those she had met and helped through the years.

All Darling felt now was a needling of regret.

She should have kissed Oliver when she had the chance.

Thinking of kissing him replaced an ounce of cold with an ounce of warmth. She hoped she could hold on to it for a long while.

Darling closed her eyes, took a deep breath and stood.

It wasn't the most graceful of movements, and she did struggle, but in the end she was back on her feet.

The moonlight hadn't waned while she had reveled in her breakdown. She let her eyes adjust and started to turn in a circle to see if she could make out anything else. She stopped halfway through the cycle.

She was in a field of short, dead grass. A tree line darkened the distance, giving her no bearings for where she actually was. However, it was the hunk of black metal to her direct right that made her heart flutter. Without the moonlight, she might not ever have seen the car.

With an extreme amount of caution, she dragged her heavy feet and closed the space between her and her possible savior. Darling wasn't sure if she wanted someone to be in the car or not. Her rising grief and fear had kept the idea of her attacker being nearby from her mind. What if this was her attacker's car? But why would the attacker still be here? If her body hadn't been numb, she would have felt the hairs on the back of her neck stand as the idea of someone staying behind to watch her crept in.

No one jumped out from behind the car to grab her as she neared it. She circled it anyway. Better to see the attacker now than drop her guard and be surprised later. It wasn't as if she had much of a chance to defend herself either time, though. When she was satisfied she was alone, she peered into the car to find it was empty save for some clutter in the front seat floorboards. She tried the driver's door handle and let out a shaky breath. It was locked.

The other doors also wouldn't open. Scouting the immediate area, she found a rock that fitted in the palm of her hand. Squaring her shoulder, she approached the backseat's right window.

She threw the rock and watched as the window only cracked.

"Co-come on!"

She scooped the rock back up and threw it again. This time it missed the window completely. Trying to aim when you couldn't feel your throwing arm or hand was definitely difficult. The third time she was able to widen the crack. At this rate she would freeze where she stood.

I can't feel my face, she thought with a new sense of determination. *I need to get into this car.*

This time she gripped the rock and took a deep, shuddering breath.

Go through the window.

The sound of glass shattering cut through the silence.

She dropped the rock, ignoring how the new cut across her hand dripped blood, and unlocked the back door. Reaching around the front seats, she hit the unlock button for the rest of the doors. It felt like so much work, but she finally managed to sit behind the wheel with a slight feeling of accomplishment.

There were no keys in the ignition or anywhere else in the car, as far as she could tell. Her inner optimist hung her head. The center console had CDs in it, and the glove compartment was filled with napkins. Food wrappers littered the floorboard. A silver watch stuck out from under one. but Darling had little use for that. The small hope that she would be able to drive away or, at the very least, turn the heater on, withered away as the rest of her search turned up empty.

She would have to wait it out until the sun came up. The car was a few degrees warmer than outside. If the wind was kept at bay, she might survive the night. In a last-ditch effort to find something to save her, she hit the button that popped the trunk. Once more she pushed back out into the cold.

The trunk contents didn't give her any relief. A bag of tools and a greasy, balled-up hand towel. Darling cursed but grabbed the towel and, after a quick thought, the yellow-handled hammer. She settled back into the driver's seat and locked the doors. She pulled her knees to her chest and rested her head on top, draping the hand towel over her shins. It didn't warm her, but at least it was something.

A few minutes went by. Exhaustion was trying to drag her into sleep.

Leaving her naked in the cold Maine darkness sent a pretty clear message. Someone wanted her to die but didn't want to get their hands dirty.

Darling just hoped she could make whoever that was regret it. She might have been naked, hurt and as cold as a Popsicle, but she wasn't dead. Debrah and Andrew Smith had passed on the drive that kept Darling from cracking again.

With a small smile, Darling formed a thought so clear she wondered if she had actually said it out loud.

You should have killed me when you had the chance.

OLIVER WAS SECONDS from calling Rachel for the third time when the chief jogged over to him. There was no mistaking he was excited.

"We tracked her phone!"

"What?" Oliver followed him to the cars when he didn't stop. "I thought you couldn't if the phone was off."

"We can't. It just came back on." Oliver's mouth opened in surprise.

"I'll follow you."

He left no room for the chief to mistake his statement as a request. For the first time since he had met the man hours before, the older man laughed.

"I knew you would."

Chapter Fourteen

Oliver drove, white-knuckled, in a convoy to the point where Darling Smith's phone was located. The sun was starting to rise, creating a crisp blue landscape without a cloud to blemish it. Under different circumstances, he would have called it serene and even beautiful. However, his heart was in his throat, terrified of the possible outcomes when they found Darling's phone.

In front of him was Chief Sanderson in his four-door pickup. Bringing up the rear was a deputy named Casey Heath in her patrol truck. Oliver raced along the asphalt between them with no worry about what the cracked road might do to his rental. Finding Darling had become his top—no, his only—priority the second he'd found Derrick unconscious. Everything else was on the back burner.

The chief braked for a second. The action bit into Oliver's nerves. They didn't need to stop. They needed to keep going until they found her. After a few beats, Sanderson flipped on his left turn signal and drove off-road. Without hesitation, Oliver and Heath followed.

He made a left onto the new road, and they whizzed down it, away from town. He didn't slow until they had gone past trees on either side. He braked, and Oliver followed suit. They were on a dirt road, dense tree lines surrounding them.

"It's coming from around here," Sanderson called after he swung out of his truck. His hand rested on the top of his piece, a silent gesture that Oliver didn't miss.

His security experience had already tensed up his body but not enough to hinder the fluidity of his movement. He didn't have his gun out, but he didn't think he needed it, either. His adrenaline was too high. He would use his strength to overcome whatever obstacles the unknown was about to throw at them.

"Spread out," Sanderson barked. They all fanned out. "Darling?" he called.

Silence.

Less than a minute later, Deputy Heath yelled.

"Over here!"

The phone was on the ground just inside the tree line a few feet from their cars. It was on but unattended. Deputy Heath shooed Oliver's hands away when he went to grab it and instead threw on a pair of latex gloves.

"We don't know who has been touching this," she said.

"Check the recent calls and texts," Sanderson ordered. Oliver looked over her shoulder.

"The last call she made was to me yesterday when she found someone had broken in," he confirmed.

"And the last text…was from a week ago." Heath quickly browsed the last few pictures. They were of the photographs she'd received at the start of the case.

Heath pulled a plastic Baggie from her pocket and dropped the phone in.

"The phone was placed here," Chief Sanderson said when the bag had been returned to the patrol truck. Oliver agreed.

"It wasn't thrown from a car when they realized she had it. It wouldn't have landed like that," he said. The phone had been on the other side of a tree. "It was purposely placed here."

"But why was it turned back on?" asked Heath.

"For us to find," the chief said at the same time Oliver said, "So we'd find it."

Silence didn't have time to fall around them. Oliver bet that the same sick feeling had exploded within the chief.

"We need to find her," Oliver said, voice hard. "Now."

"Agreed. Heath you go through there," the chief said, pointing to the trees behind them. "Just in case." Heath went back to her truck and pulled her rifle out and did as she was told. "Oliver, follow the road in your car until you are on the outer perimeter of these trees." He held up his hand before Oliver could complain. "We know we won't find her in the direction we just came from. If she was on foot, there's a chance she came out on the other side. Darling doesn't seem like the kind of woman who would hide. Follow the tree line. If you see anything, call my cell." He reached in his pocket and produced his card.

"But if she's in there—" Oliver started. He didn't get far.

"Deputy Heath and I know these woods. You come, you'll slow us down." There was no more discussion as Chief Sanderson began his trek. Oliver saw the reasoning, but he didn't have to like it.

The road extended south for another mile before the trees thinned and open fields replaced them. A quick scan showed no sign of people. Oliver cut the wheel and took his rental off-road. He followed the outside of the woods as the ground sloped uphill and down, but he did so at a slow clip.

An emotion he couldn't quite place clung to his mind and body like a second skin. Fear and longing. Regret and anger. They were mixed in with the unfamiliar feeling, causing a calm before the storm. It was the only way for him to stay focused.

Oliver slammed his hand against the steering wheel.

He had hoped beyond hope that Darling would be with her phone. Being the stubborn woman she was, he'd hoped she had taken down the bad guy and would be waiting for the cops to come. She'd make some wisecrack about Oliver being a day late and a dollar short, and then life would become simple again.

Finding Darling's phone—one that had most likely been purposely placed there—without the private eye at its side brought on a flood of thoughts Oliver didn't want to entertain.

He focused on the trees that he drove past, occasionally scanning the land to the left. He was so intent on the woods he almost missed the spot in the passenger's side mirror. Slamming the brakes, he turned and looked through the SUV's back window. A black car sat a few yards from the woods, its hood angled away from view.

Oliver threw the SUV in Reverse and sped toward the car. He put the SUV in Park and dialed the chief's number. The chief picked up on the first ring.

"I followed the tree line and found a car in the middle of nowhere. Going to check it out. Hold on," he said, not giving the chief room to respond. Oliver's body was even more tense than before. If caution was a tangible material, it would have been dripping off him by the bucketload. He slipped the phone, still on, in his back pocket and approached the car from the rear.

The car was an old Mazda and seemed to be in good

condition minus a dent in the fender and a broken back window. The tires, as far as he could tell, weren't deflated, either. So why was it out there?

Oliver snatched his phone out and yelled into the receiver.

"It's Darling!"

He didn't hear if the chief responded. He had come around the passenger side of the car and had seen her through the windshield.

She was curled up in the driver's seat with a small towel around her feet. Blood was streaked across her face and, he realized with anger and concern so poignant he almost stumbled, she was completely naked.

Oliver pulled on the door but it didn't budge. It was locked. Darling didn't stir. He ran back to the open window and unlocked it before opening the door and unlocking all doors from the passenger side. Then he was back at Darling's side.

She was leaning against the back of the seat but slumped over toward the center console. Her knees were pulled against her chest, her arms slack at either side. Her cheek was pressed against the top of her knee. She was pale.

So pale.

"Darling?" Oliver's voice came out in a whisper. A harsh yet faltering sound. He placed his hand on her blood-stained cheek. He felt the cold all the way in his heart.

A feeling he would never forget.

"Darling, please..."

With his free hand he pressed his fingers to check her pulse. For one horrible moment there was nothing. Then, like a storm in the distance, Oliver felt a soft beat.

He backed up and tore off his jacket. It wasn't thick or long, but it fit around her front easily enough. Oliver put one hand around her shoulders and the other under her knees. There had been a time where an entirely naked Darling in his arms would have made him happy in every way possible, but as he pulled her limp body against his chest, Oliver felt no glee.

"Keep beating," he whispered, as if her heart could hear him.

"Okay."

Oliver looked down, wide-eyed, at the woman in his arms. She tilted her head back and gave him the smallest of smiles.

"God, you're beautiful," he said.

Her smile didn't disappear.

"You found me," she whispered.

"You bet I did."

She made a noise that almost sounded like a laugh, but she didn't speak. Oliver cast a quick glance back into the car. There was no blood on the beige seat, he was happy to see.

"Are you hurt?" he asked anyway. He turned, trying not to jostle her too much, and walked toward his rental.

"No," she answered, voice still low. "I'm cold."

Oliver held her tighter.

"How long have you been—" He was cut off by the sound of a vehicle approaching. Darling tensed so quickly that Oliver had to look down to make sure she was okay.

"Who?"

"Chief Sanderson," he answered as the four-door raced toward them. Deputy Heath wasn't far behind.

"Keep me covered," was all she said.

Oliver angled his body to the side so the chief couldn't see Darling's skin that wasn't covered by the jacket. It was an absurd thing to worry about in the moment, but she sounded so weak. The protective side of him needed to do this for her. It was his fault he hadn't kept her safe in the first place.

The chief kept his truck running and jumped out. He waved Oliver over and flung open the back door.

"It's quicker to drive to the hospital than to wait for an ambulance," he said. Oliver nodded and realized there wasn't a way to shield Darling's body from the older man.

"Could you step aside for a sec?" Oliver asked, a few feet from him. Sanderson sent him a confused look.

"We don't have time to waste," he shot back.

"I'm naked," Darling spoke up. The chief's eyes went skyward at the news. Oliver hurried to get her into the backseat, repositioning the jacket after setting her down. He was thrilled to see she was able to sit up on her own.

"I found her in that car—driver's side—unconscious," Oliver said. "I need to go with her."

The chief nodded his approval, and Oliver slid in next to Darling, shutting the door behind him.

Deputy Heath ran up to the truck and was given quick instructions. Sanderson was inside the cab seconds later, already reversing and heading back to the road.

"Any serious injuries?" the chief asked, eyes not moving to the rearview mirror.

"She says no, but there's blood on her face."

"My foot," she replied. "I cut it."

"And your hand." He caught her wrist and followed the dried blood to her palm. Her skin was still so cold.

"Were you outside all night?" the chief asked.

"Yes," Oliver answered for her when she nodded. His

anger almost boiled over at the realization. In one fluid movement, Oliver took off his shirt.

"Let's put this on you," he said, already moving her to face him.

"No," the chief cut in. "Put her against you."

Oliver raised his eyebrow. "What?"

The chief was all business when he answered. "She'll warm up faster from your body heat. Just putting your shirt over her—although it's a kind gesture—won't work fast enough. Sit her on your lap and let her hug your bare chest. Your warmth will become her warmth."

Never did Oliver think he would see the day that a cop told him to hug a naked Darling, but it wasn't time to marvel. Darling didn't argue. She must have been a lot colder than he'd thought. She didn't resist as he pulled her onto his lap. She slowly moved her legs around him while he helped guide her arms into his jacket to cover her back.

Oliver made sure to keep eye contact with her as he wrapped his arms around her torso and pulled her down until her bare skin was pressed against his.

Darling's eyes fluttered closed for a moment before she returned the embrace. He waited as she settled her cheek against his shoulder. There was no denying she needed the warmth. Her skin was as cold as ice.

"How long to the hospital?" Oliver asked when Darling relaxed against him. Absently he began to rub her back beneath the jacket.

"Ten minutes. You still with us, Darling?"

Oliver felt her nod against his shoulder.

"What happened to you?" Oliver didn't want to push her, but he also needed to know. Whoever had done this was still out there. "I went to your place and saw Derrick on the ground and you nowhere to be found."

"Derrick okay?"

"Just a nasty bump on the head is all," the chief supplied. "He'll be back to it in no time."

Darling nodded into his shoulder again. As her cheek moved across his bare skin, he had to repress a shiver.

"Someone knocked. I thought it was you," she said, voice a bit louder than before. "No one was there. I went downstairs and then—" She let out a shuddering breath. Oliver looked down to see tears shining in her eyes. She tilted her head to the side, and Oliver cursed.

"What?" Chief asked.

Oliver let out another string of obscenities before he answered.

"Someone choked her," he bit out. "There are marks on her neck. I don't know how I missed the bruising before."

"I didn't see a face," she said after the chief also voiced his anger. "Flat chest. Male. Then woke up outside."

Oliver returned his hand to her back, satisfied she hadn't been hit over the head like Derrick.

The cab of the truck became silent as their individual thoughts formed faster than their mouths would let them. Oliver was trying to keep his growing anger under control. To put hands around Darling's neck until she had passed out, and then to strip her and leave her in the cold to die were two acts that painted an unsettling picture of a man with nothing but bad intentions. The idea that he had been watching Darling and waiting for her to leave her apartment was one that crawled under Oliver's skin and simmered. But at the same time, a thin yet strong layer of guilt covered it.

He shouldn't have left her alone after someone had ransacked her office. Even if Derrick had consoled him with promises of her staying safe.

Darling sighed, and Oliver felt the movement go from her chest to his. Despite the fact that she was completely naked—and pressed against him—Oliver noted that the overriding emotion he felt was protectiveness.

Sure, he could admit that what he had seen of her today was all woman and all beautiful. Her curves, her breasts, her hips, her legs. But instead of overpowering feelings of lust and desire, he had instantly felt the need to keep that body safe.

To guard it with his own body.

In that moment, Oliver realized the only person he wanted to be a bodyguard for was wrapped up and shivering in his arms.

Chapter Fifteen

The chief took charge of the entire hospital when they came in. He barked orders no one questioned. That included giving Darling privacy until she was placed in a room with a nurse, a doctor and a gown.

"We need you to step out of the room for now," the nurse told Oliver after he'd made sure she was situated on a bed. He started to argue, but Darling silenced him.

"It's okay," she tried to assure him. "I'm safe."

He didn't want to point out that she'd thought that before. Instead he kept his mouth shut. She'd been through enough.

"Heath found something," Chief Sanderson said, bustling over. "Call me if you learn anything new or she remembers anything. Give me your keys and we'll have someone bring your car over."

"Thanks." In truth, he hadn't even thought about the rental.

"And tell Darling we'll get the bastard who did this."

"You bet your ass we will," Oliver responded. The chief gave him a quick nod and was gone.

Now that Darling was safe, Oliver was able to think about the rest of the world. Grant and Thomas were having to stretch themselves thin to cover Oliver's day shift, but he couldn't see a way around leaving Darling.

He let out a long exhalation and slumped against the wall. There wasn't enough time to rest.

"You look tired."

Standing next to him in a black pantsuit and matching heels, Nikki Waters was the last person he had expected to see. At least, not this soon.

"It's been a long twenty-four hours," he said. Nikki didn't smile.

"How is Miss Smith doing?"

He glanced back at the shut door.

"Cold," he said. "Scared, but won't admit it. I don't think there's any permanent or life-threatening damage."

"I'm glad to hear that."

"How do you even know about all of this?" He motioned around them.

"Thomas told me about the break-in when I called for a status update." She shrugged. "With all these unknown variables continuing to come into play, I thought it best to jump on a flight and come out here." She was waiting for Oliver to say something, but he didn't want to start a conversation he knew wouldn't end well. Nikki must have realized this. She turned her body toward the empty room across from them. "Can we talk in private a moment?"

Oliver followed without complaint. He moved himself so he could see over Nikki's shoulder to Darling's room. If anyone who wasn't hospital staff tried to get to her, they'd soon find out they would have to go through him.

"I don't know where to begin, really," she started. Her posture was stick straight, her arms across her chest. "But I suppose I'll start with this. What were you thinking,

Oliver? You asked Orion's senior analyst to *hack into an active client's phone to take information*." Disbelief and blatant disappointment blanketed each word. "Do you have any idea how much trouble we would be in had I not stopped Rachel when I called to tell her I'd landed?"

Oliver was taken aback.

"It was necessary—it still *is* necessary—to find out what Nigel's hiding," he said, frustration pouring out. "Nigel is connected to all of this. We have to know how, and that call log could be the key."

"Then let the police get a warrant for it," Nikki snapped back. Her cool composure cracked. "Did it ever occur to you that getting evidence illegally would hurt your case more than it would help it? Courts would dismiss whatever evidence you found. Plus, what makes you so sure he's involved with that woman's death or Darling's abduction? You told me yourself that in your gut, you didn't believe he killed the unidentified woman. What changed?"

That gave Oliver pause. She was right. Oliver knew in his gut Nigel hadn't had anything to do with the death. When he didn't come up with a good answer, she continued.

"Just because there isn't another obvious suspect doesn't mean you should jump on one of the only suspects you *do* have. This is one bad judgment call I can't overlook, Oliver. You didn't just jeopardize Rachel. You jeopardized us all. Every agent—their families—and every person we ever would protect in the future. You put us all—including yourself—in danger."

Oliver was about to protest. Finding a kidnapped Darling didn't compare to the remote possibility that Orion could be held accountable for the breach in security. He had already decided that if it came down to it, he would shoulder all of the blame. However, Nikki didn't give him a breath to say any of that.

"All of it—all of this—could have been avoided had you just come to me directly," she said, voice cooling. "Instead you went behind my back, asked an analyst to go against her ethical code and broke the law. You should have come to me, Oliver."

"You'd already made it clear I wasn't supposed to get close to Darling," he reasoned, thinking back to his first day in Mulligan. "I thought you would have shut me down and then out. I didn't want to take that chance."

"That chance? Oliver, I started Orion because I believe that every life deserves the basic right of safety, no matter that person's financial situation. For three years I have busted all of our collective asses to make sure we offer virtually free services and every client who comes to us can rest a little easier. What makes you, Oliver Quinn, think that I wouldn't have done everything in my power to help when I knew a woman's life depended on it?"

Oliver's mouth slid open, but no words came out. Like a fish out of water, he stared at her. She had him there.

"I—I wasn't thinking straight," he admitted. "I'm sorry, but I couldn't take the chance."

"And *that* is why I'm taking you off this case and sending you home." Whatever anger had been within her was seeping out. Her resolve, however, was absolute. There was no reprieve to be had. As he responded, he hoped she could see his level of intensity, as well.

"She's more than just a friend. I can't leave her, Nikki. Not until this is all put to rest," he said, voice low, unyielding. "I won't leave her again."

For an instant Oliver thought he saw Nikki's body sag. She let out a low breath and shook her head slowly.

"Then I'm afraid I'm going to have to ask for your resignation."

"HE TOOK MY EARRINGS."

Darling rubbed at the smoothness of her ear lobes. They were warming up, as were her fingers, but she didn't feel any yellow daisy earrings beneath them. "Doesn't that seem oddly personal?"

"Excuse me?" Nurse Jones looked up from the end of Darling's hospital bed. Her glasses slipped to the tip of her nose.

Darling shifted her weight. The readjustment moved her foot, which earned her a glare from the nurse. She put her hands around the top Darling's foot to hold it still.

"Never mind," Darling said.

Nurse Jones finished her evaluation in silence. Considering she was inspecting the stitches on the bottom of her foot, Darling didn't want to annoy the woman. Even though she had been one of the handful of people who had seen Oliver carry her in wrapped around him naked, she hadn't questioned Darling about the situation when they were alone.

Not that she felt the need to talk to the older woman about it. Darling still had to sort her through her own thoughts.

"Okay, looks like your little stunt didn't tear open your stitches," Nurse Jones said, standing with her hands on her hips. She was a stern woman in her fifties and didn't care for any excuses. So Darling didn't give her one.

"Next time I need to get to the bathroom, I'll hit the

call button," Darling promised. "And not try to get there without my crutches."

Nurse Jones nodded and turned her attention to the rest of her patient. "And how do you feel now?"

It had been almost an hour since she had been passed off to the doctor. Hot water bottles and blankets had been applied to her body in an attempt to make her warm as the cut across her foot had been stitched. The doctor had confirmed she was suffering from hypothermia but, lucky for her, taking shelter from the wind had helped her more than anything. Also, Oliver's body temperature had begun to put warmth back into hers on the ride to the hospital. It was a great starting point, the doctor had exclaimed.

Some of the warm water bottles were still placed across her stomach and thighs while Darling kept buried beneath three thick blankets.

"I wouldn't say cozy, but I'm not cold anymore," she answered. Darling held up her bandaged hand. "This doesn't hurt anymore, either."

"And your throat?"

On reflex, Darling's hands flitted to her neck. She could still imagine the strong grip that had brought her to unconsciousness wrapped around her.

"It doesn't hurt as much when I talk," she admitted.

Nurse Jones wrote on the clipboard in her hand without commenting. The woman showed no signs of sympathy. The nurse had obviously seen a lot working in a hospital. Darling wasn't going to hold it against her that her bedside manner was lacking.

"Okay, I'll have to get the doctor to sign off on it, but I think you're good to leave just as soon as that young man brings you your clothes. You still need to take it easy, though." The nurse tapped Darling's big toe. "No pressure on this for four or five days. We'll set up a time for you to come back and get the stitches removed." She pointed to the set of crutches leaning against the bed. "Use those. Understand?"

"Yes, ma'am."

"Good."

The nurse left without another word. Darling let out a long, deep sigh and pulled the top blanket up to her chin. She imagined the cloth was a nice, hot bath. Her body submerged in water that would stave off any cold the night could bring. Scented candles along the lip of the tub, all combining in the epitome of a relaxing atmosphere.

"Should I come back later?"

Darling jumped and turned to see Oliver standing in the doorway. A duffel bag thrown over his shoulder, a smirk attached to his lips.

"Sorry. You looked like you were enjoying your thoughts."

Darling laughed. "I was actually dreaming of a bath," she said. "Cheesy, right?"

He walked over and put the bag next to her. "After what you've been through, I'd say you have every right to a bath. Heck, I'd even go so far as to say a bubble bath."

She followed that with another laugh but cut it short. Something seemed off about the bodyguard. He was smiling, but the expression didn't reach his eyes.

"What's wrong?" Darling asked with such intense concern it almost moved her. Oliver looked surprised.

"What do you mean?"

"Your smile doesn't reach—" She stopped herself and then amended, "Your smile seems off. Fake."

He crossed his arms over his chest. His eyebrow rose. "My smile seems fake," he repeated with obvious mockery.

Darling felt a flare of frustration lick to life inside her. When would Oliver realize that she could read him as easily as he could read her?

As if on cue, Oliver's face softened, and his voice lost all contempt. "I'm tired. I haven't gotten much sleep recently."

It was Darling's turn to soften. She reached out and took his hand. She had thought her skin had warmed considerably since she had been brought in, but where Oliver's hand touched hers, there was nothing but brilliant heat. Instead of pulling away, she squeezed.

"Thank you for finding me. I didn't get a chance to say it earlier."

Oliver squeezed back.

"Thank you for not freezing to death," he replied with a new tilt to his lips. Together they laughed and dropped hands. The moment passed, and Darling opened the duffel.

"Now, the question is, are you as good at finding a decent outfit?"

"If your idea of a good outfit is a white tank top, skin-tight jeans, and a red thong…" Darling's face heated before she could stop it. "Then that's not a good outfit. And on that note, I'll leave you to change." He started to leave but paused to add, "Unless you need help?"

"No, thanks. I think I can do it."

He shrugged and closed the door behind him. It wasn't as if he hadn't seen *and* felt her naked body only a few hours before. Heat flared up her neck and into her cheeks.

Oliver had picked out a sweatshirt, jeans and tennis

shoes. It meant he had grabbed the first thing he'd seen in her closet and chest of drawers. As for undergarments, thankfully he had gone sensible and picked a no-lace beige bra and a pair of black cotton bikini-cut panties. Darling spent the time putting on each item trying to recall what all he had seen when going through her underwear drawer. He had to have seen every type of underwear she owned. From the see-through special occasion lace to the long, unattractive pieces meant for a Maine winter. Within the past few hours, she had lost a lot of privacy points with the bodyguard.

Nurse Jones came back in just after Darling had wrangled on her pants, taking care not to disrupt the stitches on the bottom of her foot. Dr. Williams had signed off, and she was officially being discharged.

"Will the young man outside be taking you home, or do you need a ride?" the nurse asked after she had put some ointment on Darling's foot and wrapped it up. "It's the end of my shift, so I could drop you off." She shrugged to show indifference, but Darling smiled. Apparently the nurse wasn't completely apathetic.

"Thank you for the offer, but I suppose I'm with him."

Nurse Jones mimicked her smile for the first time. "That's not a bad lot to have."

"I suppose not."

Darling turned down a wheelchair to help her to the car and instead put a crutch beneath each arm and began an awkward gait down the hallway. Oliver carried her bag and kept close. He still seemed off somehow, but she was going to believe it was because he was tired. She couldn't deny she was in the same boat. The sleep that she had gotten in the car hadn't been sound or comfortable.

And she hadn't been too sure it wasn't the beginnings of death by exposure.

"Should I go see Derrick before we leave?" Darling asked. "The nurse said he should be waking up soon."

"It might be a better idea to let him rest for now," he answered. "I checked in on him before I went to your apartment, and he was still sound asleep. I think it's his pain meds."

Darling nodded. Guilt outlined with a sad edge cut inside her. If Derrick had not been watching out for her, he never would have been attacked. If she had only listened to Oliver and taken his offer to help protect her... Darling paused in her thinking. Whoever had taken her was determined. Hospitalizing an officer was a great testament to that fact. If Derrick hadn't been there but Oliver had, then it would have been Oliver hurt. Or worse.

Her guilt ebbed away.

Another feeling tore through her at the thought of a horrific fate befalling the bodyguard. She glanced sideways at him. When the chaos around her died down, she would have to think about why her heart and mind always seemed to clash when the topic of Oliver Quinn was put on the table.

Chapter Sixteen

The bathwater stopped running, and a few seconds later, a splash sounded.

"You okay?" Oliver couldn't help but call out.

They were back in Darling's apartment. To celebrate, Darling had indeed drawn herself a bubble bath.

"I'm fine," she answered through the door. "You can stop hovering now!"

Oliver fell into the couch when he was finished with another security sweep. He settled his back against the armrest so his sight line to the front door wasn't obstructed, a habit. The conversation with Nikki started to replay in his head.

He was no longer a bodyguard.

All to save Darling.

He hadn't fought Nikki after she had asked for his resignation. It was a choice he didn't resent. Funny, he thought, how once upon a time he had left Darling to protect her, and now he was staying to do the same.

Why was it so easy to sacrifice everything for a woman who would never trust him again?

"Oliver!"

In a flash he was off of the couch and standing at the bathroom door. "Are you okay? What's wrong?"

"I'm fine! I was just going to see if you were hungry?"

"Hungry?" he repeated, his adrenaline on the brink of spiking.

"Yeah, I haven't eaten in—" She stopped. Oliver almost opened the door all the way to make sure she was okay. "Breakfast yesterday, I suppose. So, I thought we could maybe order something? There's a pizzeria on Main Street that delivers. Unless you need to go back to work?" She had hesitated before her last question had slipped out. It made Oliver wonder if she knew about his conversation with Nikki. He pushed that thought away.

"No, I can stay," he answered. That was a conversation he didn't want to broach through a partially opened bathroom door. "And pizza sounds good."

"Wonderful," she almost sang. "I don't have anything here to eat. There's a magnet on the fridge with the number. Order whatever you want. Just make sure there's a lot of whatever it is."

Oliver shut the door and did as he was told.

Instead of sitting back down to swim in his deepest thoughts, he looked around the living room. Like the rest of the small apartment, it was filled with character. He found he liked it more than his apartment.

The bathroom door opened.

"Need any help?"

"No," she replied, frustrated. "But I sure do hate crutches." They clinked against the hardwood floors as she started to go for her bedroom. That gave Oliver an idea.

"Wait, are you dressed?" he asked, though he was already moving.

"Yeah, why?"

He held up his finger to get her to wait and walked

past her into the bedroom. Going straight for her mini-office in the corner, he grabbed the chair and rolled it back into the hall.

"It's no wheelchair but, really, isn't it a chair with wheels?" He cracked a smile and Darling laughed. She wore a long-sleeved white robe that fell to her ankles and tied around the middle. Her hair was wet and wound up into a bun atop her head. It was the first time in eight years he had seen her without a lick of makeup on, and he had to admit she was still as beautiful as ever.

He helped her angle herself into the chair and placed her crutches against the wall.

"Where to, madam?" he asked with little bow. She laughed again. He liked the sound.

"I heard the couch is all the rage this time of the year," she said playfully. "A five-star destination second only to the kitchen bar."

"Then that's where we'll go." He did another quick bow and began to roll the chair toward the living room. He kept an eye on her foot, careful not to jostle it. They reached the living room, and without letting her stop him, he lifted her from the chair and placed her on the couch, her back against the armrest and legs stretched out. He sat on the edge of the coffee table right in front of her.

"Are you comfortable?" he asked.

"My foot is sore, but I guess that's normal for having it split open and stitched back up. I didn't get it wet in the bath. I was too afraid," she admitted, rotating her ankle. As she spoke, Oliver's gaze went to the bruises on her neck. "It doesn't hurt that much," she whispered, tone changing with her mood.

Oliver couldn't help it. He reached out and traced

the skin around the bruise on her right. It made Darling shiver. He stopped but didn't pull away.

"I thought you were dead," he breathed. "When I found you in that car…for a moment I thought you were—"

"But I wasn't," she interrupted, voice soft. Her hand covered his. They sat still, both caught in a moment that couldn't be summed up in words.

Oliver leaned in. "I'm glad," he whispered.

Darling searched his face, but he only had eyes for those lips. Careful not to spook her, he slowly closed the space between them, giving her plenty of time to move away. His heartbeat sped up when he realized she wasn't going to.

The kiss was soft and warm. A ribbon drenched in sunlight. He wanted it to continue—to get lost in a moment that could be so much more—but he let it end.

After everything that had happened, Darling was vulnerable, whether she wanted to admit it or not. And he couldn't deny he wasn't in the best spot, either. He didn't want to take advantage of her. He was finding that she still meant too much to him.

He pulled back and smiled. The private investigator's cheeks were tinted red, her lips a shade of dark pink.

"Better than I remember." As the words left his mouth, Oliver feared he had overstepped their relationship by bringing up the past. However, Darling didn't seem to mind it. She mimicked his smile and opened her mouth to speak. Her response was cut off by a knock at the door.

"If that's not at least a large pizza, I'm going to be so upset," she said instead.

"I did you one better. I ordered two." Darling thrust her fist in the air in victory, and just like that, they returned to normal.

Ten minutes later, they were seated at the kitchen bar, plates covered in pizza slices and minds set to work. The question about who they were together was put aside for a time when one of their lives wasn't in danger.

"You know what I don't get?" Darling asked after putting down another large bite. "Why take me in the first place? I mean, I realize that stripping me down and dumping me in the cold is a pretty clear way to kill me without having to actually kill me, but why *take* me?"

"You must have gotten too close."

"But why not warn me instead?" It must have been a question she had been wondering about for a while. She put down her food and angled her body to face him. The top of her robe opened a fraction, giving him an uninhibited view of the top of her bare chest. She didn't notice his glance downward. He tried to refocus. "I get a folder of pictures of Nigel and Jane Doe with a note telling me to do the right thing—plus the article with my parents—and I follow those instructions. Then I go to get my camera with pictures of the hotel crime scene and there's another note, warning me to stop snooping. The camera is returned before I go to the police, but this time with no note."

"Then we take a trip to the gas station, confirm Jane Doe was there and get the security footage. You find out the woman Jane Doe talked to was Harriet Mendon. The next day Acuity is ransacked and the security tape is gone," he continued.

"But *with no note*." Darling said this with a punch, as if it held more importance than all of the rest.

"Yes, but then you come back here and get taken. There's a new note with a threat saying you have one more strike left. Though you didn't see that note." Anger began to build within him once more. He pictured her sitting in that car again, motionless.

She kept on, not noticing the tension. "Right! One more strike. Implying that I hadn't yet crossed whatever line had been drawn." Darling lowered her voice. "So, I ask again—why take me less than two hours later, and why not leave the note at Acuity?"

"Whoever it was, they got sloppy."

"You're right," she exclaimed. "*They* did!"

"Wait, what?" Oliver tried to follow the train of thought she was already on but came up short.

"Oliver, I think we're dealing with two killers. Hear me out," Darling began. "Two people are trying to frame Nigel. Note Writer enlists my help to make the case seem more valid. He—or she—is observant, smart. He knows what to say and when to say it. He's careful. But then he trashes my office without a note? Then *kidnaps* me? What's the point in leaving a threat on my door and then taking me after I clearly hadn't left the apartment or done anything else on the case?"

"You think that like all the good crime-fighting and crime-committing teams, one of them is the brains and the other one is the hothead," he finished for her.

"What's more, I don't think they're communicating all that well, either. I think the brains wrote the last-strike threat without knowing about Acuity being ransacked or vice versa. The note writer wanted to scare me. The other one wanted to hurt me."

"If this is all true, then our problems just doubled. What's worse than one killer? Two."

Chapter Seventeen

Darling was trying to put all the clues back together but couldn't help but see them now as two separate lines, running sloppily parallel next to each other.

"Two people would make killing and cleaning up after Jane Doe easier," she said aloud. "A rich man like Nigel wouldn't have a problem finding a killer for hire with his wealth."

Oliver didn't skip a beat. "I know you are keen on thinking Nigel is behind this, but I'm telling you, it's not him. Thomas caught him crying yesterday, just after Derrick called to tell him about how Jane Doe was killed." He knew now that had been an attempt to shake whatever truth Nigel had about the woman free. "Do you really think Nigel Marks would cry over a mistress he'd killed? If it's anyone in that family, I'd bet it's the wife. They share the wealth. She just as easily could have fronted the money for a contract killer."

Darling held in her rebuttal. Her desire for Nigel Marks to pay for all of his indiscretions was great, but she was finding the idea of him being behind Jane Doe's murder didn't quite sit right with her anymore. Although she wasn't ready to point the finger at Elizabeth, either. She still believed the older woman was too smart to do something so stupid. And if she really thought about it, if Elizabeth was going to kill anyone, it would probably be her husband.

"We need to figure out who our Jane Doe is," Darling said instead.

A booming knock sounded at the front door. It was so unexpected that Darling almost fell off her stool. Oliver's reflexes were a lot more productive. He was off his stool and standing in front of Darling, using his body as a human shield. He had even reached back to help steady her.

"I'm not expecting anyone," Darling whispered. "If you were wondering."

Oliver nodded and reached over the bar to the kitchen counter. He pulled two of the steak knives out of their wooden holder next to the toaster. He passed one to Darling and brandished the other. She grabbed the handle of her knife and watched wide-eyed as the bodyguard silently crossed the room and sidled up to the front door.

The knock sounded again. Oliver waited for it to stop before calling out.

"Who's there?"

Darling marveled at how controlled he was. He looked like a man about to go to war. Calm, calculating and also ready for whatever what was about to happen.

"Chief Sanderson!"

Darling relaxed, but when Oliver didn't, she tightened her grip on the knife handle. Slowly the bodyguard cracked open the door. He must have been okay with what he saw. He straightened his back and opened the door wide. The knife in his hand remained there, but the chief didn't seem to mind it as he looked between them.

"Sorry to intrude, but I have some new information

I'd like to talk to you about," Chief Sanderson said. Darling hadn't been too focused on the chief when she had ridden in his truck that morning, but now she could see as clear as day that he hadn't been getting much sleep, if any. Dark circles hung beneath each eye, and there was a droop to his shoulders as he moved to the chair next to the couch. Darling swiveled her stool around to face him while Oliver took point, standing between the two.

"Is it about Derrick? Is he okay?" Darling asked out of the gate. If anything happened to Derrick, it would be her fault. Derrick was one of the few friends she could claim as her own. She might not have been in love with him, but that didn't mean she wasn't loyal to him.

"No, he's fine. Sleeping last time I checked in," he assured her. "You two expecting company?" The chief looked at the knife in Darling's hand. Heat rose in her neck, and she put the weapon back on the counter. Oliver relaxed his hand but didn't put his knife down.

"We weren't, and that was the problem," he said with a nonapologetic smile.

The chief let out a chuckle. "Better safe than sorry," he said.

"So what's the news, Chief?" Darling asked. For him to personally visit was out of character.

"Well, we finally found what we believe to be Jane Doe's car."

"That's wonderful," Darling exclaimed. Surely they could find out who she was now. That was a break they all needed. The chief, however, didn't seem as enthused. She shared a look with Oliver. He didn't understand the chief's current emotion, either.

"The car was stripped. No plates. No insurance."

"Then how do you know it belongs to Jane Doe?" Oliver asked.

Chief Sanderson's face was absolutely stony when he responded. "We found the murder weapon on the front seat. A blunt object that fits the indention in Jane Doe's skull with trace amounts of blood on it."

"So—if you can get her prints—you should be able to ID her now. At least faster, I hope, than sending her blood off?" Oliver supplied.

The chief shook his head. "She isn't in the criminal database, so unless she's been printed at some point in her life, it'll still be difficult to see who she is. The system isn't perfect and sometimes, no matter how hard we try, it doesn't work." He cracked a smile. It wasn't happy. It was downright malicious. "So we're going to get Nigel Marks to tell us who she is."

That surprised Darling.

"Why?" Oliver asked.

"We found evidence that suggests Nigel was in that car recently, which means he knew our victim. Not even his fancy lawyer will be able to deny it. He's now physically connected to her."

Darling couldn't believe it. "What is the evidence?" she asked.

"I can't disclose that information." Before Darling could complain, he held up his hand. "But I'm sure if you think really hard about it, you'll remember."

"What do you mean, I'll remember?"

"You were in the same car, too."

Darling felt her eyebrows slam together.

"Wait a second." Oliver held up his hands. "You mean the car we found her in this morning belongs to Jane Doe?"

The chief nodded.

"Oh, my God," she said, drawing both men's attention her way. "The watch! It was Nigel's watch? It *did* look expensive. I didn't really think too much about it, given the situation."

"Well, some people should think twice before they get their names inscribed into their accessories."

"And the hammer," Darling exclaimed, realizing what the blunt object the chief was referring to was. "It's the murder weapon." Darling's raised her eyebrows when the chief nodded. She looked down at her hands and cringed. "I picked that up. It was in the trunk and I—I wanted a weapon! Did I mess up the evidence?"

The chief gave her a sympathetic smile. "No," he said. "We were able to tell the older blood versus the blood left from your hand. As for her prints, I'm betting the hammer will be wiped down like the car, save for yours. But I'm trying to remain optimistic."

"What about Nigel's alibi?" Darling asked.

"It still holds. We're just accusing him of hindering a murder investigation now. He's lied to us, and now we have physical evidence that ties him to the victim. It's enough to hold him until we get some answers. I'm sure his lawyer is already earning his keep right now." The chief stood to signal the conversation was over. "I also came by to make sure you were okay." He didn't smile, but she could hear the concern in his voice.

"I'm much better, thanks," she replied. "I would have been worse had you two not found me."

"Don't look at me," Chief Sanderson said. "Blame this guy. If he hadn't been so concerned about you, we wouldn't have gotten to you when we did."

Darling turned to Oliver. He shrugged, trying to look indifferent.

"Well, I need to get back to it. I'm going to have an officer stop by later to take down your official statement and also take your prints so we can know which are yours in that car." The chief turned to Oliver and put out his hand to shake. "Thanks for not giving up. Not everyone can keep their cool in these situations. I suppose I'll see you and your boss around the station since we have Nigel in custody now."

Oliver shook back. An emotion that Darling couldn't place flared to life across his face.

"Actually, I'm no longer on the case," he said, surprising Darling. "I might have said and done some things I shouldn't have when I couldn't locate Darling. I personally don't regret it, but professionally it wasn't the best call to make. Though I can't complain at the moment." Oliver looked pointedly at Darling.

"I can't, either," the chief agreed.

The chief said another quick goodbye and left. Darling waited until she thought the older man was out of the building before she turned on Oliver.

"You were taken off the case?" she asked with concern. "What does that mean? Does Orion lose the money now?"

"No, my team is still working with Nigel. Only I was taken off." He sat back down at the counter. Darling held her hands wide in question. "Though I don't know if even they will be working on it now that Nigel has actually been linked to Jane Doe. He might not be guilty of killing her, but this new evidence will make Nikki take a long second look. Do you think he'll admit to the affair now?"

Darling decided to put a pin in the issue of him getting dropped from the case and instead went along with this thoughts. Because, truth be told, the new information hadn't made the case any easier. Every clue was another layer of confusion. It was as if they were looking over a map and everything was a fraction off. They needed a key that would show them the correct way to decipher it all.

"I would imagine Nigel will either come clean about everything or give an alternate version. Something that covers him," she answered. "Elizabeth should be in town soon, right? To admit to the affair now would ruin everything for him. He's a smart man. He has to know he's got his back up against the proverbial wall."

"Nigel *is* a smart man." Oliver was looking at the wall, but she doubted he was seeing it. Concentration mixed with confusion were two expressions she could pick out with ease. Darling knew the feeling well. "So, why would he leave a watch with his name in his mistress's car?"

Darling had already picked up on that thread of thought.

"It could have been an accident." She didn't feel the certainty in it as she said it.

Oliver cast her a questioning look. "But…"

"But, I can't get over the fact that I was the one who found the car. Me being taken and then left to find it couldn't have been a coincidence, could it?" Like with the car, Darling tried to recall with new attention the moment after waking up in the darkness until her trek to the car. "If I hadn't had walked that way, it's true I might not have found it, but now that I think about it, there was no other place for me to go."

"What do you mean? You could have walked off in any direction. You just lucked out and happened to go the direction the car was already in." Darling knew Oliver was playing devil's advocate now. She knew the idea of her finding the car being a coincidence wasn't sitting well with him. However, he wanted her to work for her side of the argument. He was challenging her as he always had. Normally it would have made her angry, but she realized it was helping her work her own thoughts out, as well. Oliver Quinn, annoying her into being a better person.

"No, I think that was the only place to go," she said. "I heard the chief tell the doctor at the hospital that he guessed I had to have been left a few yards away from the Pinketts' property line." She envisioned the aerial shot of the land she had once seen framed in the police-department lounge. It, along with other land reserved for hunting, was show-cased in the room. "If that's true, then if I had decided to walk in the opposite direction, I would have run into their woods." Without meaning to, she shivered.

"Okay, so you could have walked into the woods."

"But I wouldn't have. Not with its hunting traps and animals galore," she rebutted. "Plus, it somehow felt creepier to be trapped among the trees instead of out in the open."

Oliver's frown deepened. He made to grab her hand but then changed tactics and put his own around his cup instead. Darling felt a twinge of sadness. Whatever moment they had had earlier seemed to have been lost in the muck of all the questions regarding Jane Doe's fate.

"You wouldn't go into the woods, but that doesn't mean whoever took you knew that. What about the road that cut through it all? If you had found that, you could easily have missed the car."

She didn't have a response for that. If she had found the dirt road Chief Sanderson and Oliver had come in on, she *would* have followed it one way or the other. She never would have seen the car. Maybe it *was* a coincidence. "Then why turn my phone *back* on?" she asked with a tilt of her head. "Why take my phone, turn it off, then turn it back on later so the car and I could be found?" Oliver didn't have an answer to that, either. She let out a frustrated sigh. "We need fewer theories and more facts," Darling muttered. "I'm so tired of guessing. What if we're just grasping at straws?"

"Well, let's look at the facts, then." Oliver got up from his stool and disappeared into her bedroom. Moments later he was back with a pen and one of her notebooks. He flipped it open to a blank sheet and started a numbered list. "Nigel Marks spent the late night and early morning at Mulligan Motel with Jane Doe."

"Which he denies having done."

"Jane Doe was killed while Nigel was eating with Orion agents. Giving him a valid alibi."

"Elizabeth Marks also has a confirmed alibi," she added. He quickly wrote that down.

"Jane Doe's fingers and teeth were removed, meaning the killer didn't want her to be identified, or maybe the killer wanted some trophies." Oliver hesitated before writing the last part down. Darling tried not to picture the body in the tub. "Then a mysterious person gives you pictures of Nigel and Jane Doe over the course of several months this year. Nigel's lawyer reasons it could be anyone or the images could be doctored. Without the original files to be tested, the cops can't keep him or get him to reveal her identity. You get another note saying to stop investigating, and they take your camera only to return it. Acuity gets ransacked, you get another note and then you're taken. You find Jane Doe's car stripped car with Nigel Marks's watch in it."

When he was done, she looked down at the short-hand list.

"I feel like we're just talking in circles now," she breathed out. "We're missing something."

They lapsed into a thoughtful silence. Maybe it was time to leave the case alone. Maybe they were hurting it instead of helping. It was already her fault that Derrick, the lead investigator, had been hospitalized. If she hadn't kept digging...

"Oh, my God, that's it," Darling exclaimed. Oliver met her wild stare with skepticism.

"What?"

"Let's stick with the theory that there *are* two people involved in the killing of Jane Doe. So far they've shown up whenever I discovered something new. The office was tossed looking for the security tape. They got it, so that should be it, right? But then they grab me two hours later? Why?" Before Oliver could answer, she beat him to it. "Because I found Harriet Mendon."

"Wait, what do you mean you found her?"

"Before you and I had it out at Acuity, I looked up where she worked."

Oliver's features seemed to reanimate.

"Oliver," she continued with new enthusiasm. "I think Harriet Mendon is our key."

Just as quickly as excitement at a new lead flashed across his face, a darker emotion replaced it. When he spoke, it made the hair on the back of Darling's neck stand up.

"Then we'd better find her before they do."

Chapter Eighteen

Darling found the number of the boutique where Harriet Mendon worked and left an urgent message with the owner, a friendly woman named Barb. She also left a new message on Harriet's home machine. One way or the other, she wanted to cover all her bases.

"Okay, it's time I change out of this robe," Darling said when she was done. "Make yourself at home."

Oliver looked around the living room with a new perspective after she went to her bedroom. He imagined his recliner in the corner, the picture of his parents next to the one of Darling and friends on top of the bookcase, his shoes tossed off next to the front door and the fight that would always come from him leaving them there.

Holiday get-togethers, quiet nights spent in, loud meaningless arguments that would never last long and makeups that would certainly last longer. There they were, moving around the small space without an ounce of regret or anger or guilt.

He pictured the two of them finishing something they had started when they were basically kids.

And loving every moment of it.

"It just isn't my week," Darling said a few minutes later, interrupting his thoughts.

"What happened?"

"Do you want a list or a long-winded sentence?"

He gave her his full attention. "Let's go long-winded sentence this time."

She took a deep breath.

"Elizabeth called because she's at the police station with Nigel—who apparently finally realized it was a good idea to tell the truth about knowing Jane Doe. But Elizabeth wouldn't say the name—and because of everything that happened, she terminated my contract," she said in a rush. "Finding Jane Doe's killer isn't her top priority anymore."

"Or she wants the police to handle it since you were *kidnapped* and left for dead by the same person or people," Oliver pointed out. Darling frowned and sent him a pointed stare. He held up his hands in defense. "It's guilt, Darling. She doesn't want to deal with it if something happens to you while under her orders." His thoughts turned to Nikki. "It has nothing to do with your job performance."

"I know," she admitted. "But the way she spoke…" Darling's brow furrowed and she sucked on her bottom lip, thinking of the right words. "She didn't sound upset at all. I guess I just assumed that finding out the identity of her husband's mistress might hit a nerve, even if she already knew about the affair." She shrugged. "Either way, I've been fired, so the case doesn't matter anymore."

The private investigator tried to look nonchalant. She leaned on her crutches in the doorway of her bedroom, gaze going through him as she focused on some thought in the distance. Oliver didn't point out that neither of them was ready to let the case go without getting justice for those who had determined Jane Doe's fate *and* hurt Darling. He crossed his arms over his chest and waited. It didn't take long.

"Who am I kidding?" Darling exclaimed. "Like being fired is going to stop me."

Oliver clapped. "That's my girl!"

Darling smiled. He could see how tired she felt.

"But first, coffee?" he suggested.

That earned a bigger smile. "That sounds wonderful, Mr. Quinn."

"DEPUTY HEATH, I never got a chance to thank you for helping to find me."

They had already gone through an entire pot of coffee waiting for the deputy to show up to take Darling's statement.

"It's no problem," she replied, wasting no time in getting down to business. She pulled out her printing kit, and Darling offered her hand. The older woman looked as if she also needed some coffee. "I can't wait until we catch those sons of b—"

"Those?" Darling interrupted. A wild kind of excitement crossed her face. Oliver bet she was ready to call out every clue she had that connected to two killers rather than one. "As in more than one?"

Oliver watched as the deputy's cheeks tinted pink. "I *meant*," Heath said, "whoever is responsible. We have a very promising lead and I—personally—am confident we'll have this case closed up soon."

The private investigator held her comments back while Deputy Heath finished the prints. Her gears were turning. That much Oliver could tell from his seat at the kitchen counter. With a bit of distance between them, he tried to look at her from an objective viewpoint.

Tired yet determined. Hurt yet unperturbed. Curious yet cautious.

"I can't disclose that information right now," Heath said after everything was done. "Give us tonight, Darling. Everything will make much more sense in the morning."

Oliver was ready to point out that after what Darling had been through, she deserved at least the name of Jane Doe, but the investigator shot him a silencing look. Neither pressed the issue as the deputy left.

"A sane person would probably take all of this—" Darling waved her arms around "—as a sign to change professions, huh?"

Oliver came around and took a seat next to her. "I don't know if you've noticed, but you aren't like most people." He patted her knee on reflex. She didn't pull away.

"I guess you really dodged a bullet back in the day."

Oliver tensed. Whether it was an off-the-cuff remark or a pointed comment about him rejecting her, he didn't know. What he was sure of was that he didn't like that she seemed to be blaming herself for what had happened. He cleared his throat.

"Darling," he started, but he was cut off when she touched his hand with hers.

"I don't want to talk about it," she said, voice resolute. "What you've done in the last week is more than most would have done for me. You saved me and it cost you. I'm sorry for that, Oliver." She meant to pull her hand away, but he held it fast. Darling's green eyes were calm as they searched his.

"Don't you dare apologize to me after what I've done," he said, voice filled with grit. "And I'll never regret what

I did trying to find you. Never." Unlike their kiss earlier that day, the atmosphere darkened. There was lust—he was certainly feeling it—but there was also pain. Had he gone too far when he left her? Had he changed her life for the worse instead of for the better? These thoughts pushed Oliver off the couch as if he had been burned. Darling let go of his hand, eyes wide. He didn't miss the flush across her cheeks, either.

"Well, thank you," she said in a rush, also standing. "I—uh—think I'm going to dry my hair." She reached back and took her crutches leaning against the couch. Oliver didn't respond. Guilt and regret were slamming against his rib cage. He shouldn't want her—shouldn't imagine a life with her—after deciding to cut ties with no explanation. She had a life. She deserved better than him. Always had, always would.

He watched as she awkwardly began her walk back to the bedroom. The crutches clinked in the silence. However, she didn't make it far. Oliver was in front of her in an instant.

Her eyes were red, tears waiting on each rim. His last image of the younger Darling had been with tears in her eyes, but his mind didn't connect that vulnerability or memory to the woman standing in front of him. He didn't connect it the day she found out what her parents had done, and he didn't even think to compare it to the cold, naked woman he had held in his arms that morning.

Bringing his hands up, he cradled her face and moved closer.

There was the difference. Between his fingers and the heat of her skin was an electricity he couldn't ignore. It coursed through each of them before crashing together. Rapid, shocking, sensational.

And it was begging him to not let go.

Before the world could catch up to them, his mouth covered hers.

Chapter Nineteen

Hunger. Passion.

Pain. Lust. Desire.

Everything exploded in the kiss. Darling didn't know which thought to rest on as Oliver's lips pushed and pulled at more than just her body. There were a million reasons they shouldn't be intertwining and yet she couldn't recall a single one.

Darling's eyelids fluttered closed, and she let herself enjoy the moment. Oliver's lips pressed against her with an undeniable hunger that ate its way right into hers. Her crutches clattered to the ground as she wrapped her arms around his neck, seeking a new anchor. A new lifeline. His tongue found hers, and they tasted each other for the first time in eight years.

Their painful past melted away. They were finding their way back to each other. Back to the home they had made all those years ago. Darling moaned against his lips. She had missed this.

Oliver deepened the kiss, moving his arms around her and pulling her flush against him. It forced a new proximity that woke up every part of her body. She arched against him and he grabbed her hips. She felt him push against her and a new thrill began to pool below her waist. Another moan escaped against him. Oliver silenced it with his own. Instead of raw hunger, Darling could feel the control in it. He deepened the kiss only to break it off a moment later.

Darling looked up at him, confused and breathless.

His face was flushed. His lips red and swollen. Those amber eyes searched her face in the quiet. For once, Darling dared not speak.

There weren't a lot of things in life she felt she absolutely needed.

But right then, she knew she needed Oliver Quinn.

"Darling," he whispered, voice husky. Another shock of pleasure pulsed through her at the sound. He closed the space between their lips again. It was a soft kiss that burned slowly.

He didn't speak again.

With one quick movement, he picked her up and put her legs around his waist. Darling gladly hugged his body back, not breaking their connection. Then they were moving down the familiar path to the bedroom.

Though as she began to unbutton his shirt, she realized that where they were going was a place neither had visited before.

THE SOFT CARESS of cotton against her bare skin.

The mattress that molded against her every curve.

The warmth of a man around her heart.

A wisp of a smile trailed across Darling's lips.

She stretched out, feeling for her bodyguard beneath the sheets. Her hand found the edge of the bed instead. Slowly her eyelids opened.

Fear made her heart beat against her chest. For one awful moment, Darling thought she was back in the clearing, naked and in the dark. However, as panic tried to claw its way through her, common sense blocked its path.

She could feel the bed beneath her, the sheets around her. She smelled the citrus that had attached to her skin after her bath. The scent of Oliver's body wash that mingled with it.

No, she wasn't in danger here.

She waited as her vision adjusted to the low light of the room. From where she was, she could see out into the hallway and to the stools at the kitchen counter. Light filtered across the floor from the TV. She closed her eyes again, still tired. She couldn't lie there and think about what had happened between them *and* keep her eyes open. There wasn't enough energy to sustain both acts.

So she burrowed back beneath the covers and let her smile widen. When she was younger, she would often imagine what it was like to be with Oliver. Would he be gentle? Would he be rough? Or would he be a man who walked the line in between?

It was as if she had been holding her breath for years, waiting for Oliver. Now that she had let him back into her life, into her home and her bed, she felt she could let that breath out.

She drifted back to sleep, thinking of the bodyguard, only to wake up a while later, looking at him.

"Hey there," he said.

Darling stretched and smiled. "Hey back." She glanced to her alarm clock to see it was still late. Before she could ask what was going on, Oliver answered her.

"They're running a news story about the murder. I wanted to make sure you saw it, too."

That made her sit up.

"Yeah, I really do want to see it."

Much like before, Oliver carried her across the apartment. The heat of his bare chest against her was a welcome reminder of that afternoon. However, this time, once they reached their destination, he set her down and let go. She marveled at how badly she wanted to stay in his arms—to be wrapped up in his touch—but told her brain to focus.

Which wasn't hard when she looked at the television. On its screen was a local news reporter standing in front of the Mulligan police station. A spotlight from her camera crew was positioned on her face, trying to keep viewers' attention on her and not the crowd behind. Even in the dark, Darling could make out reporter Rebel Nash and a handful of others in a semicircle around Chief Sanderson and a few of his deputies behind her. The woman who filled the screen, however, looked excited about whatever story she was reporting on. Oliver turned up the volume on the TV.

"—a corporate conspiracy that is connected to the death of a Jean Watford, found dead in a bathtub at the Mulligan Motel. One of Charisma Investment's board members and its interim CEO, resident Nigel Marks, has refused an interview at this time. His attorney issued the following statement—'My client cannot confirm or deny at this point in time that Ms. Watford was guaranteed a top managerial position within the company, but she was being seriously considered. The fact that this could have been the cause of her death is abhorrent, and the Marks family wants nothing more than to see those responsible brought to justice.'"

A picture of a red-haired woman—apparently their Jane Doe—popped up in the corner next to the reporter's head.

"Jean Watford, age twenty-three, resided in Miami, Florida. She was visiting Mulligan on business."

Her picture was replaced by an image of two men talking to each other by the side of a building. They stood in the shadows and didn't seem to be aware someone had been taking their pictures. Darling didn't recognize either of the older men but knew by their outfits alone they were high-level businessmen.

"CFO Lamar Bennington and executive assistant Robert Jensen are being held for questioning after an anonymous tip led to the discovery of controversial emails about Ms. Watford, including one that contained information pertaining to what police believe to be the murder weapon. Both men are currently denying these charges."

The reporter changed gears and gave viewers some background on Charisma Investments and their merger, which was almost complete. Darling already knew this information. She muted the television and gave Oliver a questioning look.

"So, Jean Watford wasn't a mistress?" she asked. Her entire investigation had been based on that one assumption.

"I suppose he—" Oliver's phone began to ring, cutting him off. "I don't know who this is," he muttered before answering. "Oliver Quinn here," he answered. Darling watched as his face hardened. He held up his finger to ask her to wait and headed to the bedroom for some privacy.

Darling sighed. She wished the police would give her phone back soon. Surely there would be no reason for forensics to keep it now that they had men in custody. She didn't like being without it.

The local news cut to a weather segment, so Darling turned it off. She reached for her office chair and hopped into it. Pushing herself with her good foot, she went to the kitchen counter for a pen and paper. Before she could forget the two men's names, she wrote them down. There was no need to pen Jean Watford. Now that she could put a name to the body in the tub, she knew she'd never forget either for the rest of her life.

"Well, looks like we have more of a story to go with," Oliver said when he came back into the room a few minutes later. "That was actually our friend Deputy Derrick. He's fine, by the way. Should be discharged in a few days." He grabbed the arms of the chair and rolled Darling over to the couch, sitting in front of her. He placed his hands on her thighs as he continued. "He was brought up to speed right before the news segment aired. He figured we were watching or, at the very least, deserved a bit more than what they had to offer."

Darling knew that the only reason they were getting the special treatment from Derrick was that the case had become personal for the three of them. Once he had been attacked, Darling had been taken and Oliver had helped save them both, Derrick had mentally put them on the same page. A task he wouldn't have done otherwise.

"Tell me," was all Darling could manage. Something akin to hesitant excitement had started to flow through her. The case felt as if it was almost over, even if it had taken a turn she didn't expect.

"Nigel admitted that he had been seeing Jean in secret for the past year. He met her at a business conference when he was in Miami and was impressed. Apparently Jean was a very smart cookie. Nigel was beginning to finalize the merger but wasn't happy with the people who were going to be in charge. He wanted some new blood and decided to start grooming Jean in secret."

"Why in secret?"

"He was afraid that if he publicly acknowledged he was about to restructure the new business, stocks would suffer and he'd have to deal with unnecessary backlash. No one was supposed to find out until the end of the month, but apparently word got out somehow."

"To the CFO and the assistant?"

Oliver nodded. "Nigel told the chief that the CFO had formed not-so-beneficial friendships with those who worked for him. He didn't care that they weren't doing their jobs anymore."

"And Jean was going to take one of their jobs at the new company?"

"Bingo. Nigel wasn't sure why the executive assistant was involved. He only guessed Bennington offered something in exchange for his help. They had emails about the rumor that Jean was going to replace someone, and the CFO was furious about it. They flew in the day before Nigel, and neither of their alibis can be confirmed for the time of death."

Darling leaned back, trying to take it all in.

"Robert, the assistant, also can't provide an alibi for the time Derrick was attacked and you were taken," he added, voice dropping to a whisper. "But they found a long blond hair on his jacket that the chief thinks might be yours."

The excitement she had been feeling at shutting down a case left in an instant. She recalled the picture of the two men, trying to place a face with the body that had choked her. Oliver took her hands in his and rested them against her legs again. It was enough to ground her emotions and make her able to ask another nagging question.

"What about the murder weapon? Surely they weren't stupid enough to *email* about it?"

"Bennington asked the assistant if he had some tools they could use for a secret project."

"The hammer!"

"He didn't ask for one specifically, but he did mention they needed to make sure they had pliers."

Darling's mouth dropped open. "To pull out her teeth," she said, horrified. "They put all of that in emails?"

Oliver shrugged. "Derrick said the chief thought Bennington was under the influence of some narcotics when they picked him up, so that definitely could have made him sloppy. Plus, I think this is a man who usually gets what he wants. Having a loyal follower—like Robert Jensen, who had access to Nigel's entire schedule, emails and probably calls—helped him pull off the murder without leaving anything behind."

"If all of this was business related, then why didn't Nigel just tell the cops about it all when Jean was found?" Darling didn't understand why the man had preferred to look guilty rather than coming clean in the first place, especially if the link would be easy to make when everything was out in the open.

Oliver's eyes lit up. "Get this," he almost sang. "He thought his wife was the one behind it. That she had hired someone to take care of a woman she thought was his mistress."

Darling didn't speak for a moment. "Wow. If they stay married, they definitely are going to need some counseling about trust."

Oliver agreed. "That's all Derrick knew. They were getting search warrants to go through each man's hotel room and belongings, but the way it sounds, both men are in trouble."

Darling nodded. "So, it's over, then?"

"It looks that way. The killers are in custody, and Jane Doe now has a name." Oliver squeezed Darling's hands. "No more looking over your shoulder. Unless I'm walking behind you and you just want to see all of this." He motioned to his chest and abs. A smile had stretched his lips, changing the mood from dark to playful. He felt relieved, and she knew it. But did she feel it, too? The motive, means and suspects made sense even though she had never even known about them until now. Logically, everything had fallen into place. However, her gut felt as if something was off.

Oliver brought his hand up to her chin and pulled her face forward.

"I know that look," he whispered, an inch from her lips. "You took the entire day off, remember? That means the night, too." He brushed his lips across hers, sending a wonderful thrill from her stomach downward. "That means no overthinking."

"But that's what I'm good at," she defended herself with no real weight behind the words.

He passed his lips across hers again, pausing only to speak. "Not tonight, my Darling."

Chapter Twenty

Everything felt so right.

Darling opened her eyes and didn't want to move. She could feel Oliver's even breathing against her back. His arm was thrown over her, pressing the warmth of their naked bodies together.

It was perfect.

She didn't want to leave the bed, but her mouth felt dry and she desperately needed to use the bathroom.

So, as carefully as she could, Darling slipped out from underneath his arm and grabbed her crutches discarded on the floor. Oliver didn't move once. It made her wonder how much sleep he'd skipped the past few days.

Once she was up and moving, Darling decided to go ahead and start the day. It was almost ten in the morning and she felt wildly energized. She knew that was greatly due to the naked bodyguard in her bed. With each step she took, her body reminded her just how close they had become the night before. Though in the light of day, she wondered what that meant for their future. Did they have one, or had it been a one-day event?

The bodyguard had promised to stay by her side as long as the threat of her kidnappers was still out there. Now that they had been caught, she didn't need protection. Why would he stay in Mulligan when his life—his home—was two thousand miles away?

She tried to push the troubling thoughts from her mind as she took a quick shower, awkwardly hopping around to avoid putting too much pressure on her foot. It took the attention from the potential heartbreak she might have to endure again from her fair-haired bodyguard.

Darling managed to dress herself without falling over. She chose a red, long-sleeve top that plunged low to show some cleavage, and a pair of dark jeans that hugged her nicely. It was a more flirty outfit than she usually wore but, as she looked at Oliver's still-sleeping form, she had the urge to break out of her boring wardrobe habits. Not that he seemed to mind when she was and wasn't dressed up.

Oliver stayed asleep throughout the next half hour as she got ready and made breakfast, confirming her suspicion that he had been seriously lacking sleep. She tried to be as quiet as possible but found that when her food was gone, a restlessness was beginning to replace her feelings of contentment. Her gut was back to telling her something was off about Jean Watford's death. But what was it?

"Do you really think Nigel Marks would cry over a mistress?"

Darling snapped her fingers as Oliver's words replayed in her head. That was it.

She went back to the bedroom and grabbed her laptop, putting it in a bag so she could avoid dropping it while using her crutches. Moving to the living room, she powered it on with new vigor. Working on a hunch, she opened an internet browser and searched Jean Watford's name. After some digging, she found the young woman's public social media profile. It had all the information Darling needed.

She did some quick math and typed in a new search.

A few minutes later she found a picture that nearly confirmed her hunch. The picture was from the early '90s and showed a young Nigel Marks at a Christmas party. He stood tall—and rather handsome—amid a large group of people. The quality wasn't the greatest, but Darling got the break she needed when she saw the name of each person printed across the bottom. It didn't take long to find the last piece of the puzzle.

Standing next to Nigel was a red-haired woman with a giant smile.

Her name was Regina Watford.

Darling's mind began turning at such a fast pace she almost felt dizzy. This was why Nigel hadn't admitted to knowing Jean. He *did* have an affair. It was just twenty-three years and nine months earlier.

If Darling was right, she was looking at the night the businessman had strayed from his wife of twenty-six years with the red-haired woman at his side and produced a child—Jean.

Darling thought about the pictures she had been given of Nigel and Jean from the past year. Everyone had thought the two happy people were having an affair, but that was because the daughter angle had never entered their minds. Now, the pictures of the two laughing, hugging and dining in public fit the scenario of a father and daughter meeting. Had they been seeing each other in secret for years or had they just reunited?

Before she could talk herself out of it, Darling went back to the bedroom and grabbed Oliver's phone. She went into the bathroom and shut the door. Scrolling through his contacts, she found Nigel's personal cell phone number.

For some reason she couldn't quite place, she needed to confirm the truth. She hit Call and waited with bated breath.

What was she going to say?

"Nigel Marks's phone," a man answered after two rings. "This is Jace Marks."

That put a kink in Darling's plan. Did Jace even know about his half-sister?

"Um, hi," Darling stuttered out. "This is Darling Smith. I, uh, just had some information for Nigel I thought he might like to know."

"Darling Smith? The woman who was kidnapped?"

"Yeah," she responded, uncomfortable.

"How are you?"

Surprised at the concern, she answered on reflex. "I'm okay. My foot is sore, but I'm alive."

"That's good. It would have been another senseless tragedy had that bodyguard not found you."

"I'd have to agree there." She cleared her throat. "Is there any way I can speak with Nigel, though? It won't take long."

"I'm sorry but no. He's currently unavailable. The best I can do is pass along a message."

"No," she said a little too quickly. She tried to sound calm as she continued. "It's personal. I'd really like to talk to him myself." She wasn't about to announce the real reason behind the call.

"Hold on, then," he said. She didn't hear anything on the other end of the line and looked at the phone to make sure the call hadn't dropped. "We're about to leave the police station and head home. You can meet us at the house, but we have to ask that you keep this meeting and whatever information you have private until Nigel has talked to you. This family has had enough false accusations and rumors started lately."

"Sure thing. I completely understand."

"Thank you. We'll see you soon."

Darling ended the call, shocked at how easy it was to get a meeting. She supposed it made sense that the Markses wanted to go ahead and squash any remaining gossip within the town or general public. Charisma Investments was going to suffer thanks to the actions of Lamar Bennington and Robert Jensen. They didn't need any more bad press.

She returned Oliver's phone to the nightstand and watched as the bodyguard continued to sleep. He looked so peaceful, she decided not to wake him. She wasn't a child. The danger was gone. She could go tie up this loose end without him. Her kidnappers weren't out there to get her. She could be back within the hour.

Bending low, she pressed her lips to his temple. He didn't stir.

She wrote a quick note and left.

Laughing at the fact that the last time she had been at Nigel Marks's home she'd been arrested, she thrummed her fingers against the steering wheel as she drove. It was amazing how a week could change everything.

The gate to the Markses' house was shut, but Darling could see a car parked in the driveway beyond it. She pulled up to wait at the gate and rolled down the window. George Hanely had never been one of her favorite people. He might not even let her in.

However, he never came.

She sat up straighter to see into the gatehouse. No one was inside.

"Getting lazy, George?"

She put the car in Park and opened the door. Pulling her crutches from the backseat, she made her way to the window. George was probably lounging, watching one of his daytime soap operas or whatever it was the man did all day. She looked inside, ready to scold the gate guard but stopped short.

George was sprawled out on the floor, facedown.

Darling tried the doorknob and let out a breath of relief when it opened with no resistance. She knelt beside the unconscious man, almost falling in the process.

"George?" She felt for a pulse and was happy to feel the beat against her fingers. "Hold on. I'll call for help."

She got back up and looked to the phone on the desk. Oliver was going to be upset that she had yet again found herself connected with the police in such a short span.

"Don't move."

Darling froze, hand hovering above the phone.

Turning slowly, she felt her stomach bottom out.

George Hanley was not only coherent but also sitting up and smiling. A gun was in his right hand, pointed at her, but that wasn't what put ice in her blood.

In the palm of his left hand were her two daisy earrings.

"Just so you know how serious I am."

AN ANGRY CHIRPING pecked at the haze of sleep around Oliver until, finally, he had to make it stop. Rolling over, he grabbed his cell phone and gave it a stare that could kill before turning off the everyday alarm. It was meant to make sure he was wide-awake by noon, which, to him, was a time that no man should sleep past. Even on his days off. Although, given recent events, he had meant to deactivate it the night before. But then a beautiful private investigator had let him into her bed, twice.

All thoughts of the alarm and pretty much anything else had gone out the proverbial window the moment their lips and bodies met.

Afraid he had woken her, Oliver rolled back over, ready to laugh that they had slept in. He was disappointed her side of the bed was empty. The rest of the room was, too. In fact, he couldn't hear any movement in the apartment.

"Darling?" he called, swinging his legs over the edge of the bed. He stretched wide and noticed a note on the nightstand.

"'Tying up a loose end with Nigel. Didn't want to wake you. Be back by lunch,'" he read aloud.

He read it again as if it would make more sense. It didn't. Of course the maddening woman wouldn't give him more information than that. What loose ends were left?

Oliver picked his phone back up and went to his recent call list. He sighed and made a mental note to take her by the police station to get her phone back. Now there wasn't a way to reach her directly. He was about to put the phone down when he noticed the most recent call was placed earlier that morning. Darling had used to his phone to call Nigel.

It was a bold move. One she wouldn't have made unless she had a solid lead on something.

Suddenly Oliver's calm wasn't as resolute. A sinking feeling of apprehension slunk in.

He dialed the number again and put it to his ear.

It went straight to voice mail.

"Okay," he said to the empty apartment. "Time to get dressed."

Five minutes later Oliver was in his rental and driving toward Nigel's vacation home. He could have called Thomas, Grant or Nikki to let him talk to Darling if she was with Nigel, but after his talk with Nikki the previous day, it didn't feel right. Darling wasn't in trouble. He was just being overprotective. Jane Doe's, or rather Jean Watford's, killers had been caught. The men who had taken Darling were being held...or were they?

He rolled his shoulders back. The seed of doubt that had sprouted in his mind was growing, but there was no need for it, he tried to reason with himself. Yet it was a pill he couldn't seem to swallow. The closer he got to the vacation home, the more his nerves pricked. Why, he wasn't sure, but he knew he wouldn't shed the sudden restlessness until he set his eyes on a certain sneaky private investigator.

Oliver was sorely disappointed that no one seemed to be home when he arrived outside the gatehouse. No cars were in the driveway minus one he believed to belong to George. His aversion to calling Nikki was starting to ebb. He pulled his phone out just as it buzzed against his palm. It was a Maine number but not one he recognized.

"Oliver Quinn," he answered, getting out of his SUV to look into the gatehouse for its guard. He mentally snorted at its emptiness. He was probably goofing off somewhere, not doing his job.

"Hello. I think this is the number I was supposed to call. Barb said some people were looking for me?" a female responded, uncertainty clear. There was a blanket of noise in the background.

"Harriet Mendon?" Oliver guessed.

"Yeah, that's me! Now what's this about?" She didn't sound mad or scared. Only curious. An older Darling, he quickly mused.

"The woman at the gas station you stopped at on the way out of Mulligan the other night—the one with the red hair—was—" Oliver paused and changed where the statement had been headed "—she died the next morning." There was a tiny gasp, but she didn't interrupt. "There was a guy—a bad guy—who thought whatever it was you two talked about might have been something that could have hurt him. We just wanted to make sure if you saw him to call the police, but you shouldn't have to worry about that anymore. He's with the police now."

"Oh, wow, I leave Mulligan for the first time in ten years and suddenly it gets exciting," she answered after a beat. "I am sorry about that young woman, though. She was so happy and vibrant. Made me feel young again just talking to her. How did she die?"

"I'm not sure," he lied. Jean's death was probably already splashed across the local paper. Harriet would be able to read about it all when she got back. Oliver didn't want to rehash the details.

"What a tragedy. I can't imagine what the man thought she told me. We only talked for maybe a minute. Nothing out of the ordinary. She was just excited to meet up with her dad and relax for a few days."

Oliver stopped, his hand against the SUV door.

"Her dad? I thought she was in Mulligan on business," he said, recalling the reporter's words from the previous night's news.

"I don't think so. I remember her specifically saying she was going to spend time with her dad and enjoy some downtime," Harriet said. "She was smiling ear to ear. Does that sound like she was about to work to you?"

"No," Oliver answered. "It doesn't sound like work had anything to do with her visit to Mulligan after all."

Oliver didn't extend his conversation with Harriet Mendon past the new information. He also didn't question the validity of what the woman had gleaned from her chat with Jean. The security footage had shown a happy young woman, not someone about to dive into a stressful, secretive business world.

No, Jean Watford was about to go to meet up with her father.

She had been on the way to meet Nigel Marks at the Mulligan Motel.

All at once, the clues and lies made sense. The pictures of Nigel and Jean over the past year—meeting in secret—with the two of them enjoying each other's company without any sexual or provocative contact. The pain and surprise Oliver had picked up on when Nigel had been told about Jean's death.

In Orion's research on the Marks family, Oliver couldn't recall a single detail about a daughter. Half, step or otherwise. Jean Watford must have been one of the best kept secrets of Nigel's life.

That's what Darling was referring to as her loose end, Oliver realized. That's why she had called Nigel. She had figured it out, and the always curious Darling needed confirmation.

But where was she now?

Oliver took another look at the house. His feeling of unease had grown so strong, he felt as if it was a tangible object he could wield to cut open the gate. Had the entire story of Jean Watford joining Charisma Investments been a lie? If so, where did that leave the motive for her two supposed killers?

A new puzzle was coming together just as the old one was falling apart.

Oliver flew through his contacts until he found Grant's number. He hesitated and passed the name, going straight for another. He pressed Call next to Nikki's name, not willing to make the same mistake twice. Knowing her, she was still in town and would remain there for the duration of the contract. "Yes?" she cut right to the chase. Oliver could hear several voices in the background.

"Are you still with Nigel?"

"Oliver, you know I can't divulge information like that on a current—"

"Is Darling with him?" Oliver's voice had dropped to an almost icy plane of existence. Nikki picked up on it immediately.

"No. We've been at the new Charisma building since this morning." He could hear her moving away from the group of people next to her. She spoke louder. "Why?"

"She called him while I was asleep and then left a note saying she was coming here to talk to him. I'm at the vacation house now."

"Unless she called him before five this morning, she didn't talk to him," Nikki said with certainty. "He's been in board meetings all day, trying to clean up this mess. He literally hasn't left the room in hours. The room has a glass wall and everything. We've been able to see him at all times, and not once has he made or picked up a call."

"Could he have done that when you looked away?" Oliver reasoned.

"Here, he's coming out now. Let me just ask." He could

hear her annoyance at not being taken at her word, but Oliver needed to know what had been said during that call.

It could be nothing.

It could be everything.

Muffled voices filled his ear. It was a white noise that did nothing to break the silence of the outside world around him. He stood back from the gate and wondered if Darling had come here at all. If George hadn't been at the gate, she would have had to leave. Why wasn't George there to begin with? It was paramount he be at his station when the house was empty. To make sure it stayed that way.

Oliver went to the gatehouse and tried the door. It was locked. He cupped his hand and looked inside. Everything seemed normal.

"Oliver," Nikki said, bringing his focus back. "Nigel said he never talked to Darling. He can't even find his phone."

"He's lying, then," Oliver responded with grit. "My phone said the call was made." He didn't need to look again to know that was true. It not only was received but also lasted almost a minute.

"Well, Nigel didn't speak with her." Nikki kept talking, but Oliver didn't hear it.

"I need you to get Rachel to track George Hanley's cell phone," he ground out. Oliver tried the doorknob again, and when it didn't budge, he took a step back.

"What? Why?"

Oliver didn't answer as he threw his shoulder into the door. It splintered at the lock and swung open.

"Oliver?" Nikki's confusion was turning into anger.

"Because I'm pretty sure George Hanely took her."

"How do you know?"

Oliver had scanned and rescanned the gatehouse each time he had made a sweep while on duty. George was a neat person. Every item in the small room had always been in a specific spot and order. His DVDs all were stacked nicely next to his television, his books were ordered next to his security tapes, and even his chair had always been pushed beneath the desk when he was occupying it. Now Oliver saw a room out of order. A few of the books were strewn across the desktop, the chair was on the other side of the room and one of the DVD cases lay in the corner, cracked open. However, it wasn't the unusual state of the space that caught his eye. It was the set of crutches poking out from beneath the desk that coaxed a concerned Oliver into the gatehouse. The blood on one of the pads only threw fuel onto the burning fire within him.

"Her crutches are here. Nikki, I need you to track him now," Oliver repeated, more urgent than before. "Please."

This time Nikki didn't hesitate.

"Give me five minutes," she answered. Her voice had taken on the calm of the determined woman he knew her to be.

"Let me talk to Nigel," he added. Again she didn't even pause.

"What's going on?" Nigel asked a few seconds later.

"George Hanley took Darling," Oliver said. "I need you to tell me why."

"What? He took her?"

"Yes. Now, what the hell would he want with her?" Oliver was moving around the room, looking for something that might clue him in to where the gate guard had gone.

"I have no idea!"

"Come on, Nigel. I talked to the man. He seemed to worship you, said you two were great pals. Think!"

"You're mistaken," Nigel said hurriedly. "Mr. Hanley is close with my son, Jace, not me."

Everything stopped for a moment.

"Hello?" Nigel asked, bringing Oliver out of his icy thoughts. He only had one question left.

"Did Jace know that Jean Watford was your daughter?"

As if he was standing in front of the millionaire, Oliver could see the older man had reached the same conclusion as he just had.

"Oh, my God."

Chapter Twenty-One

It was a three-story building with cracked gray siding and a crumbling roofline. There was a workshop in the back, attached by a makeshift walkway that hadn't fared well against the weather. The several acres around each were untouched and gave clear sight lines to the road in the distance.

Darling took in all of these details as George drove up the long dirt drive. She had been to this abandoned house hidden near the heart of town before with Derrick who had said knowing its location might help with future cases considering the amount of criminal activity that happened there from time to time. It was dubbed the Slate House and hadn't been occupied in almost twenty years. The local teens really liked it as a location to drink in private, considering its next neighbor wasn't even in shouting distance.

A shiver ran up Darling's spine.

Perhaps that's why George was taking her there, as well.

"Why?" Darling asked the gate guard for the third time. Her chin was throbbing, but with her hands bound behind her back, she couldn't touch her face to assess the damage. She took solace in the fact that before George had managed to wrestle the plastic zip ties around her wrists, she had been able to do some damage of her own. Her crutch had made an excellent bat. The bleeding gash on his forehead was a testament to that.

George didn't slow the car until they were next to the workshop's outside door at the back of the house. He cut the ignition without answering her yet again. Never had she hated the silence more.

"George, why are we here?" she asked, expanding her earlier question in hopes he would answer. Instead he opened his door and got out.

For one wonderful moment, Darling thought he'd leave. That he would just walk off and give her enough time to figure out an escape route. But George didn't do that. He turned to the back door and opened it, and for the first time since he'd yelled at her to get into the car while simultaneously shoving her, he spoke.

"Someone wants to talk to you."

He reached into the car and grabbed for her. Darling tried to shrink away, but George was faster than he looked. He caught her jacket sleeve and tugged hard.

"Don't fight it, private eye," he snarled as he struggled to pull her out and up. "You brought this on yourself."

"What are you talking about?" Darling yelled. He shut the car door and held her by the tie on her wrists, bending her slightly so she couldn't stand at full height. Without her crutches, the weight she put on her foot made her wince.

"Have you ever heard of the story where curiosity killed the cat?" He started to walk to the door, pushing her in front of him. She stumbled and considered making a run for it, but no sooner had the idea popped into her head than she felt the gun poke into her back. If anyone would shoot her without warning, it would be George. Whatever anger he was harboring for her, it was malicious. He stopped in front of the door. "In this story, you're the cat."

George let go of her wrists long enough to open the workshop's door, then pushed her inside. Darling wasn't sure what she had expected to find in the tiny room, but she hadn't foreseen the lone two chairs and freestanding electric lights in the least. The chairs faced each other between the white peeling walls and the concrete floors. It felt cold and sterile.

And terrifying.

Whatever was about to happen, Darling was positive she didn't need to be a part of it.

George shoved her into one of the chairs and stepped back while she righted herself. He didn't take the seat opposite.

"You don't even remember me, do you?" he asked, voice pitching higher than normal.

Darling was confused by the question. Surely he wasn't referring to the trespassing incident that had just happened. Apart from that, she had seen the man only in passing. Nothing that would earn her the death stare he was giving her now.

"What do you mean?" she asked instead.

George laughed.

"Of course you wouldn't bother remembering what you did."

"Just tell me," Darling snapped. She was afraid, but she didn't want George to see it.

"Wow, you ruin a family's life and you don't even remember it," he said, surprising her. The gun in his hand stayed trained on her as he spoke. Darling glanced at the door they had just come through. If she managed to escape she would be out in the open. She hoped he wasn't a good shot, because he could hit her easily. But if she could somehow make it into the house, there was a chance she could find something to defend herself with or, at the very least, hide until Oliver found her.

Because he would.

He had done it before.

"Then tell me about it," Darling said. She wanted him to talk, get distracted and waste time.

The gate guard kept the gun pointed at her. Standing behind the chair opposite, he would not miss if he wanted to shoot her.

"You know, when you first came to Mulligan, I thought you were cute. Young, new, interesting." Darling searched her memory for George when she was new to Mulligan but was drawing a blank. Whatever memory he was in, she wasn't sharing it. "Even when I heard the rumor you were working for Jeff as an intern, I still thought that made you more interesting than the women I had grown up around. But then you stuck your nose where it didn't belong, and I realized you were no better than your scum of a boss." He waved his gun at her in a sudden burst of anger. Without meaning to, she yelped.

"My father skipped out on my family when I was a kid," he said. "My mother worked her fingers to the bone trying to give us a good life. When I graduated, she hurt her back on the job at the woolen factory. For the first time in years, she was able to take a break, and she deserved it." Recognition started to prick against Darling's memory. "So, I encouraged her to tell a little white lie and say she was still hurt. Have herself a little vacation."

Darling could almost feel the color drain from her face. George must have seen the change.

"Ah, you do remember me," he said.

"Workers' compensation fraud," Darling responded as if she was reading the file Jeff had handed her years ago. She hadn't put together that George had been Carmen's son. Their last names were different, if she recalled correctly.

"That's it."

"It was more than just a little white lie," she said with an even tone. "She was collecting it for a year and a half."

George grabbed the chair and hurled it into the wall. The echo it made rocketed Darling's fear skyward, but it was nothing compared to what she felt when she realized where the gun was. George held it level with her face. His hand was calm. His eyes were filled with rage.

"You watched and followed her like she was some kind of criminal when all she was, was a woman who worked herself into the ground to provide for her family," he roared. "She had to spend a year in jail and pay almost fifty thousand dollars! It broke her, it bankrupted us and it was all because you and your boss wanted to make a little cash!"

Darling wanted to say that, although she could sympathize with his mother, her actions had been illegal. Darling had done her job the correct way, observing an energetic woman with no issues and reporting back to the insurance company that had hired Acuity. But she didn't say anything. George was enraged. He had already cast the first stone and didn't seem to regret that one bit. Anything she said now would only fan the fire. She didn't want to give him any more reason to use his gun.

"All out of questions?" he spat when Darling still

didn't speak. Her back was ramrod straight. Her heart was racing.

"I wouldn't talk to you right now if I was her, either."

Darling gasped as a voice spoke from the doorway. She hadn't heard or noticed the door open, and she hadn't expected that particular man.

"You're too passionate, George. It's terrifying." Jace Marks smiled a perfect smile at the gate guard. His eyes slid to Darling's look of surprise, and he laughed. "After all of his obsessing over how bothersome you can be, I'm kind of shocked you didn't put the dots together much sooner."

He grabbed the discarded chair and set it up across from her. In the process of sitting down, he took the gun from George's hand and pushed the man gently aside. Darling watched the interaction with new attention. George was being obedient and took the spot behind Jace with obvious pride. She had never known the two even knew each other, yet the loyalty George was exuding for the younger Marks was concrete.

"The dots," was all Darling could manage at first.

"Yes, the dots." He crossed his legs and leaned back in his chair. As if they were in a meeting making small talk. "About Nigel's little secret. His tryst from younger years."

"You mean Jean," she said, finding her voice. "Your sister."

"Half-sister," he corrected. "*Secret* half-sister."

"But you knew?" Darling was going back over all the events that had taken place. This time she was inserting the two men before her. Finally what felt off about the arrest of Lamar Bennington and Robert Jensen made sense. "Nigel told you?"

"Of course he didn't tell me," he said. "Perhaps that

would have been the right thing to do, but Nigel doesn't always operate with the best morality."

"Then how did you find out?" Darling didn't know why he was opening up to her, but if it bought Oliver more time to find her—which she prayed he was already trying to do—then she'd keep the conversation going. Although she couldn't pretend that Jace confessing to everything was good for her health. Trying to tie up the loose end with Jean Watford's identity had turned Darling into Jace's loose end.

"A very inebriated family lawyer let it slip that Nigel wanted to make some changes to his will. At first I thought it was to give Mother and me what he had set aside for leaving this pathetic community after his death, but then Mother made an odd comment about Nigel's extracurricular activities. So I followed him, and there she was." Every time he referred to Jean, he acted as if it left a bad taste in his mouth. Darling didn't wonder which of the men had actually killed her. She would bet everything she owned Jace had been the one to do it.

"At first I thought it was an affair," he said, "but after watching them, I realized the affection wasn't sexual. That's when I really did some digging. I even went so far as to steal her hairbrush for a DNA sample to make sure, but when I went to get something of Nigel's, he caught me." He rolled his eyes. "He didn't deny it but had the audacity to ask me to keep it a secret until he could figure out how to tell Mother."

"And you did, didn't you?" Elizabeth hadn't known about Jean. Darling was sure of that. If she had, it would have been more than enough to get out of the prenup.

Jace shrugged as if keeping his father's illegitimate child a secret hadn't been a big deal. "It was just another job in a long list of jobs he had already given me. I really didn't mind the new development."

"But?" Darling wanted to know what had changed.

Jace smiled wide. It didn't last long. His words became low, dangerous. "But then he tried to give her money, and when she wouldn't take it, he promised her a job at the new branch of Charisma." He paused and uncrossed his legs. Moving his head side to side, he cracked his neck. The calm exterior of control he had been trying to exude was beginning to flake off. When he was ready to speak again, however, George put his hand on Jace's shoulder.

"He'll be looking for her soon, Boss," the gate guard said.

Jace didn't look as if he enjoyed being interrupted, but he shrugged the irritation off with a nod.

"Go," he commanded. "And don't waste any time. Shoot to kill, as they say."

It was George's turn to nod. He took the gun from his demented friend and began to leave.

"Shoot to kill? Who?" Even as Darling asked, she knew the answer. George left without a word. She turned her wide eyes to the man in front of her. "Who is he going to shoot?" she almost yelled.

Jace's smile came back. "Your bodyguard, of course."

Darling's breath went shallow. She felt her nostrils flare, and her eyes became slits. Every fiber of her being was warring between anger and fear.

"Why? He doesn't know anything," she ground out. "I didn't tell anyone. There was no need to, since the murderers were already thought to be in custody."

"Oh, Darling, we both know that Mr. Quinn won't stop until he saves you or avenges your death." A shiver shot up her spine at that, but she tried to hide it. "Either way, he's a problem, and I don't need any more of those."

Darling heard her car drive away, picturing it going around the side of the house.

"If we were such problems, then why even involve me in the first place?"

"You mean the pictures," he guessed.

"And the notes."

"When I realized my mother hired you to prove Nigel's infidelity, I checked up on you. With all that happened with your parents, I assumed you had some guilt I could use to my advantage. Plus, considering your relationship with the police here, I figured you'd want to do the right thing and turn in any evidence. The hope was that you being so adamantly against Nigel would help put a nail in his coffin." He made a *tsk* noise. "By the way, I must ask. After you got all of that evidence on your parents and their extracurricular activities, why didn't you turn it in to the authorities?"

Anger was starting to win against the fear she felt at being so vulnerable in front of a killer. She lifted her chin a fraction.

"I would think someone like you would understand," she answered. His eyebrow went up in question, so she explained. "Being the children of powerful people isn't easy, especially when you see how far they will go to protect themselves. Like you, I was afraid." It was the first time she had ever admitted that to anyone. In a small way, she felt a sense of relief at finally saying it out loud. It was a shame the admission was wasted on Jace Marks.

"I'm not afraid of my father," he spat.

"Then why do all of this?"

Jace cracked his knuckles. More of his calm fell away.

"I wanted to be a painter, once upon a time. Travel the world, find beauty in everything, set up shop in Europe and start a family with a woman with dark hair and an accent." His voice trailed off for a moment before clear anger started to shine through. "But Nigel already had plans for me. He had high expectations, and I wanted to meet them all. I graduated at the top of my class in high school and college—where I pursued a degree he picked out—and when it was all done, I went straight into Charisma. I didn't even take a break.

"I rose up through the ranks the right way. No special treatment from Nigel…and no appreciation or approval, either. I gave up the life I wanted to live for the only one I thought would make him happy. Not once has he ever given me a 'good job, son' or 'I'm proud of you.'" His fists balled. Darling readied herself for whatever outburst she was sure was coming. "Then Jean shows up after all of these years, and suddenly Nigel is laughing and smiling? Changing his will to include her even though she didn't want a dime? Giving her a job in the company without her having a college degree? All of it finally helped me come to the most important realization of my life."

Darling gave him a questioning look when he didn't continue. He opened his fists and rubbed his palms against his pants. A small smile lifted up the corner of his lips. He looked as if he had mentally checked out.

"I realized that I could never please my father. So, I found a way to hurt him instead."

Darling swallowed. The bravado she had started to feel stalled at the callousness in his words. "But she was your sister," Darling started.

Whatever thread of calm he had was severed at her statement. He stood so fast that his chair toppled over.

Less than second later he was in her face, hands on the arms of her chair.

"She was a stranger," he roared. Any facade of a sane man vanished as his anger reverberated off the walls, making its way around the small room. He was seething, chest heaving. It wasn't until that moment that Darling felt absolute fear. Jace managed to calm himself enough to keep talking. But when he spoke, his tone was nothing but ice. "And you're about to find out how little sympathy I have for strangers."

Darling didn't try to hide her new fear. Instead, she let it show clearly across her features. There was no hope for Jace. There was no turning back. He had chosen his path, and there was no doubt in her mind that he would kill her when his story finished. Though Darling didn't want the end of it to be the end of her. She also refused to let an angry gate guard be the end of Oliver.

Darling gave the man in front of her a quick once-over. She met his gaze when she spoke.

"You don't have a gun."

And then Darling threw her entire weight against the man who dared threaten her happiness.

Chapter Twenty-Two

Jace was taller and heavier than Darling, but she had the element of surprise on her side. He let go of her chair, and together they fell to the ground.

He let out a moan as his back met the concrete. With her hands still tied behind her back, Darling fell against his chest. She didn't want to lose her momentum, so she brought her knee up hard against his groin. He cursed loudly and swung up, his fist meeting her jaw. The blow was hard enough to make her see stars but also had enough power to push her off him.

Trying her hardest not to pass out, she managed to rock up into a crouching position and, using the wall, eventually stand. Jace wasn't fast to respond, still writhing in pain. It gave Darling all the time she needed to get to the door. She backed against the door and was thankful she could still move her wrists enough to grab and turn the doorknob.

"There's nowhere to go," she heard Jace yell out as she ran through the poorly made hallway to the next door that led into the house. With adrenaline pumping through her body, she opened the door and immediately backtracked to shut it. The task of throwing the deadbolt took precious seconds, but she managed it by getting on tiptoe to lift her hands up. She heard Jace laughing from the workshop but didn't let it slow her down.

The Slate House had three stories. The basement was dark and damp, and had one half bathroom in it. Its stairs were located next to the kitchen—the room she was currently in—but Darling refused to enter a room with only one exit. Without any lights on, the natural light that filtered in through the upper stories' windows wouldn't touch the lower level. The main floor, if she remembered right, had four rooms and no real place to hide since there was no longer any furniture. That left the top floor and its three bedrooms and attic space.

Darling had started to move through the kitchen when a shot rang out behind her. Unable to stop the scream that tore from her throat, she looked, terrified, at the bullet hole in the door she had just locked. Jace had a gun after all.

With more urgency than before, Darling hobbled down the hallway and turned at the stairs. Quickly yet quietly, she took the steps two at a time until she was at the landing. The pain in her foot was incredible, even though she was trying her best to only put pressure on the very edge of her foot, but she knew she had to keep going, If she could find a place to hide, maybe it would buy Oliver enough time to get to her.

She just hoped Oliver would see George Hanley coming.

OLIVER RACED DOWN the road, determination pushing him. The pleas from Nikki to wait for the police replayed in his mind, but he paid them no heed. This time he wasn't going to count on them to guide him to Darling. She had been gone too long. Every second counted now.

He glanced at the gun on the passenger seat. Rarely

did he find a good excuse to bring it out, but he couldn't think of a better reason.

Rachel had traced Jace's cell phone to a piece of land in the middle of Mulligan. George's phone had last been used at the gatehouse, so that had been a quick dead end. Oliver was betting that Jace believed no one else had figured out his connection to the murder or the kidnapping. He had the confidence of his father. Though when Nigel had come to the realization that his son was one of the two behind everything that had happened, Oliver could hear the man crumple.

He had no time to sympathize.

If Darling had been hurt or worse…

He crushed that thought. The private investigator was strong and clever. She wouldn't let someone like George or Jace end her life.

Oliver pictured the two men trying to hurt her, and anger instantly filled him. It took him a few seconds to realize his phone was ringing on his lap. Not recognizing the number, he answered on the second ring.

"Darling?" he asked, hopeful.

"It's Derrick," the deputy replied. "I heard you're going after her by yourself."

"If you're going to tell me to wait, you can—"

"I'm not," Derrick interrupted. "You're driving up to a house that's three stories. There's a front door, a side door that leads to the attached workshop from the kitchen, and a back door that leads off of a second sitting room." Oliver didn't stop the man as he continued to give him a quick layout summary. After detailing the rooms on the main and top floor, he said, "There's also no cover driving up to the house. Whoever is in there will see you coming a mile away. So I suggest you go in fast and hot."

"No problem there," he assured the cop.

"Good luck, Oliver. Backup should be there a few minutes after you."

They hung up without any more comments. Oliver visualized the house from the deputy's description, already forming a plan for entry.

Crash.

A car from the opposite direction slammed into the side of the SUV.

Oliver tried to keep the vehicle from going into the ditch, but the impact was too great. The SUV went to the left just as the airbags deployed, and the SUV flipped before he could do anything to stop it. The windshield blew out and an awful metal crunching sounded before the world stilled.

Oliver gasped, trying to suck in some air while getting his bearings. His seat belt kept him upside down but still in his seat. Below him he could see the ground where the windshield should have been. He tried to look out the driver's side window, but the door was too damaged. When he could catch his breath, he undid his belt. The fall to the car's roof wasn't graceful, but he was glad when he didn't feel any broken bones. Though his left shoulder didn't feel the best.

He tried to open the door, but it wasn't budging. As quickly as he could, Oliver crawled to the passenger's side door, grabbing his gun as he went. He wouldn't have left the vehicle without it. Whoever had hit him had done it on purpose. That he was sure of, at least.

He had been hit about five minutes from his destination, which meant that on either side of the road there was nothing but open fields with trees in the distance. That meant no cover. Oliver kept that in mind as he exited the flipped SUV and moved around its side to the back to get a view of the road he had just been on.

The car that had hit him was in the middle of the road, the front right side dented but mostly intact. Oliver checked his gun, wincing at the pain in his arm. It was Darling's car he was looking at, but it was empty.

"You're harder to kill than I thought."

Oliver spun around, gun raised.

George Hanley met him with his own raised gun.

"Where's Darling?" Oliver yelled. The gate guard was bleeding from his forehead and shoulder.

"Does it really matter?" he said with a smirk.

Oliver pulled the trigger and jumped to the side before George could do the same. The bullet hit the gate guard in the shoulder, and he dropped his gun in surprise. He hadn't expected Oliver to act that quickly.

George tried to bend down to get the gun, but Oliver wasn't through with him. He closed the space between them and punched the sleazy man for all he was worth. George crumpled to the ground.

It was an instant knockout.

"I don't have time for you," Oliver said to the unconscious man. He didn't give him any more thought before jogging back up to the road. The keys were still in the ignition of Darling's car. He hopped into the driver's seat and sighed in relief when the car started. Although the door didn't shut all the way and the window was gone, it did the job of turning around and speeding down the road.

George had been dispatched to take care of him, which meant that Darling was alone with Jace. It was a thought that kept his adrenaline running high.

Derrick had been right about the house being in the middle of nothing but open space. Minutes later, Oliver was speeding up its drive. Darling's car was quiet, but anyone looking out of the windows would see him. Pain went through his shoulder as he cut the engine and opened the dented door. He knew he'd feel more of the crash's damage as his adrenaline wore off and he was able to rest, but for now he needed to find Darling. Thinking of losing her tightened his chest. He pushed the feeling away. He needed to focus.

He hurried to the back door and moved beside it. It was locked. Derrick had said there were two more ways to get into the house. As much as he wanted to burst through the door, he didn't want to give up his location until he had a better handle on what was going on. If he went in, guns blazing, he might spook Jace into doing something he would seriously regret.

Oliver would make sure of that.

Following the wall closely, Oliver crept along its length until he turned the corner to see the workshop extension. He held the gun firm and listened for a beat. Nothing. He turned the knob. It opened with ease. With gun raised, he went inside.

There had been a struggle but thankfully no blood. Two chairs were knocked over and Oliver could see through the open door, down the walkway and into the kitchen. He imagined Darling running into the house and hoped his mind wasn't inventing a wishful scenario instead of a plausible one. He moved quickly through the windowless pathway and into the kitchen. The house wasn't as well-lit as he would have liked—shadows stuck to the corners—but Oliver was thankful the house was devoid of furniture. Only a random assortment of bottles and trash was scattered around. He sidestepped a glass bottle and moved into the adjoining room.

It was empty, and so was the room opposite.

"Here, here, little Darling," Oliver heard Jace taunt.

Oliver pushed himself against the living room wall, looking out through the double-framed archway to the base of the stairs.

"Come out so we can get this over with," Jace called in a singsong voice. "You can't hide forever."

Sweet relief swept through him. Darling was alive.

But where was she?

Oliver looped around the archway, and instead of going for the stairs, he went to the front door. He threw it open, making as much noise as he could, before retreating to the living room again. This time he positioned himself with his gun held high and steady.

Footsteps sounded against the landing and then the stairs as Jace ran down them. Oliver waited until the man was in his sights before he spoke.

"Don't move or I'll—"

Just as Oliver had done to George, Jace raised his gun and shot before Oliver could finish talking. The bullet hit the wall beside him, and he returned fire.

But nothing happened.

His gun jammed.

Oliver pulled back deeper into the room as another bullet struck the wall. He could hear Jace move back up the stairs in a hurry. Oliver cursed under his breath and ejected the jammed bullet from the chamber. Now that Jace knew he was in the house, he might get more desperate to find Darling. Oliver couldn't have that.

Readying his gun, he swung around into the hallway and started to run up the stairs. He didn't expect Jace to keep shooting blindly. Oliver had already made the judgment call that the younger Marks lacked courage unless he was confident everything was on his side. Less confidence, less control. Stepping out to gun Oliver down on the stairs would mean that he would have to put himself in a compromising position. No, Jace was probably already setting himself up in one of the hallway's corners, waiting for Oliver to step onto the landing. The question was, was Jace to the left or the right?

Taking a deep breath, Oliver stepped past the last stair and pointed his gun to the right. It was the wrong way. A bullet whizzed by his ear and shattered the top portion of an already broken window at the right end of the hallway. Another noise filled the air, but he didn't have time to register it before turning and shooting to the left. Jace ducked into one of the bedrooms to avoid the hit. That's when he realized the noise he had heard had been Darling's scream.

He turned his head back to the now fully broken window. Standing on the outside of the house—on what must have been the workshop walkway's roof—was his private investigator. She was bleeding across her chin and her hair was wild, but she didn't seem to be in any major physical distress. She watched him with wide eyes as he ran over to her. Had the bullet hit her?

"I'm okay," she answered his unasked question. "It scared me."

Oliver looked over his shoulder, expecting Jace to pop back out. He needed to get Darling out of the way. She must have been reading his mind again. She ducked to avoid a low-hanging shard of glass. Her hands were bound, so he helped guide her through the window until she was standing inside.

"Oliver!" she yelled before he could usher her to safety. He spun around, gun raised, but it was too late.

Oliver put his body in front of Darling's and felt an explosion of hot pain searing into his stomach. Only on reflex was he able to return fire. It put Jace back into the bedroom, giving Darling enough time to drag Oliver to the left.

"No, no, no," Darling chanted, putting her body under his arm to help him walk. The pain was excruciating. It took all he had not to fall to the floor. The bedroom was empty save for a dark oak bed frame in the middle. Darling guided him to the side farthest from the door. They all but fell to the ground next to it. "Oh, my God, Oliver."

He looked down at the bullet wound and winced at the sight. A bullet in the stomach wasn't good—though most bullets anywhere weren't—and he knew he was in a bad situation.

"You need to put pressure on it," she whispered. "I can't. My hands are tied."

Oliver put down the gun and reached into one of his pockets. The movement made him see stars.

"Lucky you," he said, pulling out his pocket knife. Darling turned and scooted toward him. He cut through the ties easily enough. As soon as her hands were free, she surprised him by taking off her jacket and putting it against his wound. He couldn't stop the yell of pain at the pressure.

"We need to get you help," she said, not apologizing.

"The police—" he said between his teeth "—will—will be here soon."

"You need them now."

Her voice shook as she said it. Oliver wanted to let her know everything was going to be okay, but the truth was, it wasn't. He looked down at his wound again.

He was losing too much blood, too fast.

He was going to pass out soon.

He dropped the knife and picked up the gun again. "There are ten shots left," he said, handing it to her. "Just pull the trigger if you see him."

If Jace thought Oliver was down for the count, he wouldn't hesitate in underestimating Darling and trying to finish her.

Oliver watched as a myriad of emotions crossed the woman's face.

"You shouldn't have jumped in front of me," she said, matching his tone.

"It's part of my job description."

"It's not," she whispered, "but thank you." Oliver didn't miss the red in her eyes. The pain in his stomach intensified. He was sure his own eyes were starting to tear, too. He reached out and took her free hand.

She was beautiful.

"I wanted to, Darling," he started, pausing once again to make sure he didn't hear Jace moving around. Maybe his bullet had also found its mark. Darling raised her eyebrow. He was happy to see she kept control of the gun in her right hand. She could defend herself if push came to shove.

"You wanted to what?" she asked.

"I wanted to run away with you," he continued. "When you asked me, there was nothing I wanted to do more, but—" Oliver sucked in a breath. Darling squeezed his hand.

"Don't."

The pain tripled from his wound. He couldn't hide it. Darling's face softened in acute concern. He needed to finally tell someone—finally tell *her*—the reason he had left the girl in the daisy dress all those years ago.

"I didn't want to hold you back," he whispered. "You would have given up everything for me, and I didn't want you to have to do that. I'm no good for you, Darling, but —" he took his hand from hers and placed it against her cheek "—I'm no good without you, either." His vision started to tunnel. He was on the cusp of unconsciousness. Before Darling could respond, Oliver let his hand drop. "Now focus. I can hear him coming."

Without much furniture in the house, Jace's attempt at stealth echoed off the walls and down to their room. Oliver half hoped he would leave them and make a run for it, but he knew the millionaire's son had too much to lose. In his mind, Oliver and Darling were the only two people who knew about his connection to Jean. Their deaths could ensure his continued freedom, especially since two men were already in custody for it. Although if Jace really stopped to think about it, he'd realize running was his best option.

However, he didn't.

DARLING FELT AS if she was having an out-of-body experience, watching the horrible scene unfold from somewhere else entirely. Jace was almost to the door—all caution apparently abandoned—and the life was visibly draining from Oliver. His revelation had touched a deep part of her, but it had also been terrifying. The bodyguard's breathing had shallowed. She knew he was giving it his all just to stay conscious.

Darling could feel the urge to distance herself and wait for the inevitable to happen. Wait for Jace to make it to them and finish the job while Oliver bled out. To give up and give in. She bit down hard on her lip. She didn't need to distance herself. Oliver needed her now.

She tightened her grip on the gun and took two deep breaths. Jace was nearly at the door.

"I love you, Oliver Quinn," she whispered.

And then she was up and shooting.

Chapter Twenty-Three

Darling was uncomfortable but trying her best not to show it. She was sitting in the hospital hallway with her foot propped in the chair next to her, waiting for Nurse Jones to come back out.

The older woman, along with the doctor on duty, hadn't seemed surprised when Oliver was rushed through the ER doors with Darling limping by his side hours earlier. The chief or Derrick must have given them a heads-up, which was fine by her. It had meant Oliver had gone into surgery almost immediately.

An ache had crossed her heart at seeing him go limp in the Slate House's bedroom. His state hadn't changed in the ambulance, either. There had been so much blood...

"I thought you might need this."

A woman with dark red hair, wearing a smart burgundy pantsuit, took the seat to Darling's left. She held out one of two coffee cups. Darling's eyelids fluttered closed for a moment. The coffee smelled like heaven.

"You must be Nikki," Darling responded once her coffee euphoria was over. The woman nodded and handed the second cup over. It warmed Darling's hands. "You came into town to fire Oliver."

Nikki let out a chuckle. "I've been warned you say

what's on your mind." She smiled. "I have to tell you, I like that in a person. But yes, that's why I came. I won't apologize for it, though. I have an obligation to protect all of my agents, even if it's from themselves from time to time."

Darling nodded. Oliver still hadn't told her what he'd done that was so bad when he was trying to find her, and she didn't care. He had saved her. Twice. She wasn't going to nitpick him about it.

"Which brings me to this point," Nikki continued, leveling her gaze with Darling's. Her expression softened as she spoke. "Thank you for protecting him when no one else could." It was an admission Darling hadn't expected. She bet it was a rare show of emotion for the founder of Orion. Especially with a stranger. "Starting Orion and trying to keep it afloat have left me little time to do much else. I have few friends, and Oliver is one of them. So, thank you."

It was Darling's turn to smile. "I don't know if I did the best job at protecting him. He did still get shot."

"Don't sell what you did short. You shot and then disarmed a man hell-bent on killing you both before the cops even got to you," Nikki pointed out. "If that's not protecting someone, then I don't know what is."

Darling replayed the moment after she had told Oliver she loved him. Jace had been right outside the door, and she hadn't taken any chances on him getting past it. Shooting through the wall, she had hit her target. She rushed him when she heard his gun clatter to the ground. Like Oliver, Jace had passed out from his injury. Unlike Oliver, Jace's wound hadn't been serious. He was currently handcuffed to a hospital bed on a different floor, surrounded by cops.

"I suppose I should listen to the owner of a bodyguard service," Darling said with a smile.

"You've got that right."

They lapsed into a mutual silence as they appreciated their coffees. Darling took the moment to marvel at the past week. It would be a while before Mulligan returned to normal. The gossip alone would carry them into the new year.

"You should let Oliver come back to Orion," Darling blurted after a minute had passed. "I can tell he really loves working there." She expected some kind of push-back, but Nikki kept smiling.

"I'm going to offer him his old job," she said. It made Darling happy and sad at the same time. She wanted to be greedy. She wanted to keep Oliver in Mulligan, to stay with him and live out the rest of their lives together. But she also wanted him to be happy. Orion was a big part of that. "However, I have a feeling he won't take it."

Darling raised her eyebrow. "Why wouldn't he?"

"Have you tasted this coffee?" Nikki shook her cup. "I wouldn't want to leave this place, either."

"The coffee is good but not *that* good."

"Something tells me Oliver feels differently." She paused, letting her double meaning sink in. Darling didn't want to smile, but she couldn't stop it. "On a completely unrelated note, since there is no issue with Nigel paying Orion for its services, we now have enough money to start expanding."

"That's great!" Darling was glad something good had come from everything that had happened.

"I'm thinking of creating a new analyst division. One that would cover finding and assessing threats, and building strategies for the more complicated cases. I wouldn't start it right away, but I do think creating a freelance position now would only help Orion in the long run. So whoever took the job could work from home. Wherever that might be." She winked at Darling. "It would only make sense that that someone would need to have a thorough knowledge of the group as well as an unwavering loyalty…"

"You know, I think I might know someone who fits that description," Darling said, already picturing a certain bodyguard wrapped up in winter clothes, grumpy at the Maine temperature. The thought warmed her heart. "But don't get your hopes up," she said more to herself than Nikki. "This person might be fine staying with his old job."

Nikki took a long pull from her coffee and smirked.

"I think we both know that isn't true."

"I CAN'T BELIEVE you crashed your rental."

Orion Zeta team lead Jonathan Carmichael, Oliver's closest friend, was shaking his head at Oliver. It had been a week since his surgery, and he was finally being okayed to leave the hospital. Oliver had been surprised when Jonathan had shown up instead of a certain private investigator to give him a ride. Though he wasn't going to question his friend. He knew the man had been worried.

They all had, including Oliver.

"I'm telling you, it wasn't my fault," he said. "There should be a clause in those contracts that says if a crazed idiot is trying to kill you by using a stolen car, then the rental place can't get mad at the renter."

Jonathan laughed and helped Oliver into the car. Although no long-lasting damage had been done by Jace's bullet, Oliver was still mighty sore.

"Nikki said the cops thought you had killed that idiot and left him on the side of the road," Jonathan said as he got behind the wheel.

Oliver smiled. It wasn't sweet.

"After what he had done to Darling, I would rather he rot in jail for years and years to come." George had been released two days before with a straight shot to jail. Jace Marks was right behind him. After Jace had awoken in the hospital, he had cracked under Chief Sanderson and Deputy Derrick's unrelenting questioning. Jace had admitted to murdering his half-sister as punishment for his father after convincing his old friend George to help. The two of them had tried to pin the murder on Nigel but hadn't expected the millionaire to have such a great alibi. Then, when Darling started to figure out Jean Watford's connection—which would have shown Jace had a great motive to kill her—they had panicked. George had jumped the gun and, instead of dropping Darling off next to Jean's car with evidence showing Nigel was lying, he had tried to kill her through exposure. It had just been a happy accident the private investigator had found the car. Another accident that ended up benefiting them was Jace's knowledge of CFO Lamar Bennington's and executive assistant Robert Jensen's drug addictions. Framing them was easy, especially when both businessmen were picked up under the influence of narcotics.

Now Jace and George were going away for a long, long time.

Nothing made Oliver happier.

Well, almost nothing.

"I still can't believe that girl of yours tackled a killer to keep him from getting to you *after* she shot him,"

Jonathan observed. "Sounds like you got a good partner in crime there."

"I can't complain," Oliver responded with a smile. Right before passing out in the Slate House, what he thought would be the last thing he ever heard had been Darling saying she loved him. He had been ready to die happy at those three little words.

However, now that he wasn't on his death bed, he was ready to make those words into something much more.

FOR THE FIRST time since Elizabeth had hired her, Darling had no trouble walking up to the front door of the Markses' Mulligan home. Since George was no longer on the payroll, and Grant and Thomas were still doing their Orion bodyguard duty until the end of the month, the front gate was left open, and the gatehouse was kept dark. All it took was one knock on the heavy front door and a smile to be welcomed inside the mansion.

"Which Marks invited you?" Thomas greeted her. He had met Darling while Oliver slept in the hospital. Both he and Grant had made sure to check that their former partner was okay.

"Elizabeth, but I'd like to talk to Nigel for a quick second if that's okay."

Thomas and Grant hadn't hidden their new respect and appreciation for Darling keeping their friend alive when she'd talked with them in the hospital. Thomas wasn't hiding it here, either. Without a question he led her to the second-floor office and through its open door.

"Sir, Darling Smith would like a moment," he said to the millionaire. His tone had gone almost stern, as if warning Nigel that declining her presence wasn't a good idea.

Nigel looked up from the papers on his desk and nodded. Darling bet the man hadn't slept well in days. Everything about him sagged. Only his eyes remained strong, no doubt holding the confidence he had garnered over a lifetime of experience.

"Thank you, Thomas," he said. The bodyguard left but didn't go far, standing on the other side of the open door. Darling wasn't afraid of any more attacks, but she was grateful for the watchful eye. "I'm sorry it's taken so long for us to meet, Ms. Smith. Life has been…" He ran his hand through his hair and let out a long sigh.

"I hadn't expected you to want to meet with me in the first place," she said honestly. From the brief phone conversation she had had with Elizabeth earlier that day, she knew the millionaire's wife had admitted to her husband that she had hired Darling to prove his infidelity. Beyond that, Darling didn't know where that left the couple. What was more, if Darling hadn't kept digging, his son wouldn't be in jail.

"I admit, at first I was angry, but then I realized it was at myself," he said, guilt ringing clear in his words. "I could list the things I should have done differently in my life, but there's no point now. My son killed my daughter, and the simple truth of it all is that it was because of me."

"When did you find out about Jean, if you don't mind my asking?"

"A year ago she approached me at a business convention in Miami. Her mother was a good friend of mine in college. Our paths crossed one night while she was on business. It was only a one-time thing, though I know that doesn't make it right—I was with Elizabeth—but I didn't see her again after that. She passed away a few years ago, and Jean decided to start looking for me. Her mother never told her who I was, and she certainly never told me who Jean was." His brow furrowed. "I would have been there for her growing up if she had." Darling had just met the man, but she felt in her heart he was telling the truth. Finding out he had a daughter had seemed to soften a big part of him. "When we met, I thought maybe she only wanted money, but the more time I spent with her, I realized she just wanted family."

"You tried to set her up with a job in Charisma?"

He nodded. "Her mother was sick for a while, and that drained almost all the money they had. Jean dropped out of school to take care of her but couldn't afford to go back. She was smart—very smart—and I told her that if she did well at her job, after a year the company would pay for her to get a degree. It was the only way she'd let me help. A lot of good it did in the end." Nigel averted his gaze, and Darling pretended not to notice his eyes rimmed with red. He was a strong man but, like everyone else, had a breaking point.

Darling cleared her throat. "I should go talk to Elizabeth now, but I wanted to stop by and give you this." She handed him the folder she had been carrying and stood. "I did a little more digging the past few days and found something that you should know about." Confused, Nigel held up the picture of a little girl that was attached to the file. "Her name is Isabella, she's five and I've been told she is a ball of energy." Darling smiled. "She's your granddaughter."

Nigel's mouth opened to say something but words never formed. He looked back at the picture of the red-haired girl.

"But Jean never said…"

"According to Jean's best friend—who is taking care

of Isabella right now—Jean was going to use this trip to tell you about her. She wanted to get to know you a bit before she included her. Just in case."

"She looks just like Jean," he whispered. Nigel's reddened eyes were now shining.

"I can't stand here and tell you that everything is going to be okay. That the little girl's existence is going to help make everything that has happened better," Darling said. "But maybe someday it will help."

Darling left Nigel with his new revelation without another word. There wasn't anything more to say.

LESS THAN AN hour later, Darling walked into Acuity in a much better mood. It only intensified when she saw Oliver lounging on the lobby's couch. She hadn't seen him since the night before, having visited him every day since he had been admitted. Though they had talked, neither had brought up the topic of their future.

"Well, don't you look better," Darling said as she sat down next to him. "I'm sorry I wasn't the one to pick you up, but Jonathan insisted he could handle you."

Oliver laughed. "That's funny, because he insisted that I couldn't handle you," he said. "He told me any woman with that much fire would just burn me up."

Darling smirked. "That doesn't sound too unpleasant, if you ask me."

Oliver's eyes widened. His smile grew.

"So, how did your meeting with Elizabeth go?" he asked, slightly defusing an escalating moment. A part of her didn't want to answer. Telling him about the last interaction she'd had with Elizabeth in a professional capacity, officially ending her case with the woman, cut the last thread that had in some way attached them while

Oliver was in Mulligan. She wouldn't need his help anymore. There would be no shoptalk left to hide behind to avoid talking about their future.

"Surprisingly well," she said almost reluctantly. "She started by telling me she didn't blame me for what happened to Jace. She understood he needed to be punished for what he'd done. Though you could tell she was hurt by it all. Who wouldn't be? She also paid me because, in the end, I proved that Nigel had an affair *and* I discovered the identity of Jane Doe." Darling left out the part where she had refused Elizabeth's money the first two times it had been offered.

"Is she going to file for divorce?"

Darling shrugged. "She wasn't too clear about that, and I certainly didn't push it. If she does decide to do it, I don't think it'll be for a while. They have a lot to talk about." Elizabeth had been upset—obviously—at what had happened but, as with her husband, there was strength holding her up. Darling was confident that no matter what happened in the future, Elizabeth Marks would be fine.

"So, it's all done, then?"

Darling didn't want to, but she nodded. Fear that she had misjudged their reconnection filled her. But it was only fear that he didn't feel the same.

Darling knew without a doubt that she loved Oliver. She hadn't *stopped* loving him, no matter how many years had gone by.

"Well, I guess it's time to get to work, then." He got up from the couch and walked to the lobby's lone desk.

Darling looked on, confused. "Work?"

Oliver grinned. "You're looking at Orion's first freelance strategy-and-threat analyst," he paused. "Well, I don't know if that's my official title, and technically it won't be live for a few weeks, but I figured I'd go ahead and check out the available office." He made a show of inspecting the desk.

Darling's heart filled with happiness.

"You're staying?" She stood, unable to contain the mounting joy.

Oliver's grin widened.

"Why would I leave?" He closed the space between them. Taking her chin in his hand, he tilted her head up so their eyes met. "Unless that's a problem."

"Not on my end," she whispered.

"Good, because there's nowhere else I'd rather be than by your side."

Before Oliver had a chance to say any more, Darling pressed her lips against his.

In that one moment, all of the pain from their past turned into beautiful hope for their future.

* * * * *

Look for the next book in
Tyler Anne Snell's miniseries,
ORION SECURITY, *on sale next month*
wherever Harlequin Intrigue books
and ebooks are sold!

WHAT HAPPENS ON THE RANCH

USA TODAY Bestselling Author
DELORES FOSSEN

Chapter One

Anna McCord figured she had committed a couple of sins, maybe even broken a few laws, just by looking at the guy in the bed. He was naked, so it was hard not to have dirty thoughts about him.

Drool, too.

Mercy, he was hot.

Thick blond hair all tousled and bedroomy. Lean and muscled. At least what she could see of him was muscled anyway. He was sprawled out on his stomach, his face cocooned in the fluffy feather pillows of the guest bed. He reminded her of a Viking just back from a good pillaging, minus the bed and feather pillows, of course.

But who was he?

Even though she should have bolted out of there the moment she opened the guest room door and saw a partially exposed butt cheek, Anna stayed put. Someone had obviously glued her feet to the floor. Glued her eyeballs to the hot guy, too.

She glanced around the room and spotted a clue as to who he was. There was a military uniform draped over the back of a chair and a duffel bag on the floor near the bed.

Anna didn't actually need more clues to know he was

an Air Force officer and likely a friend that her brother Riley had brought home. But she also saw the dog tags. The ball chain holding them was still around the hot guy's neck, but the tags themselves were lying askew on the bed like smashed nickels.

Maybe he sensed she was there, because he opened an eye, and the seconds trickled by before it must have registered in his mind that he had a woman ogling him.

He made a grunting sound mixed with some profanity and rolled over, no doubt because that was the fastest way he could reach the sheet to cover himself. However, the rolling over gave her a view of his front side.

Definitely more dirty thoughts.

"Sorry, I didn't know anyone was in here," Anna said, as if that explained the gawking. The drool. The long, heated look that she was giving him.

But both the heated stuff and the drool came to a quick halt when Anna got a better look at his face. "Heath?"

He blinked. "Anna?"

Good gravy. It was Heath Moore, all right. Well, a grown-up Heath anyway. The last time she'd seen him had been nine and a half years ago when he was barely eighteen, but he had filled out a lot since then.

Oh, the memories she had of him came flooding back.

He'd been naked then, too—for part of those memories anyway, since she'd lost her virginity to him. Though she certainly hadn't seen as much of him during that encounter in the hayloft as she'd just witnessed. He had filled out *everywhere*.

He sat up, dragging the sheet over his filled-out parts, and still blinking, he yawned and scrubbed his hand over his face. More memories came. Of his memorable mouth. The equally memorable way he'd kissed her.

She fanned herself like a menopausal woman with hot flashes.

"Why are you here?" she asked at the same moment that Heath asked, "Why are you here?"

Anna figured he was going to have a lot better explanation than she did. "I thought I might have left a book in here," she told him.

A total lie. She had been in search of a book that the housekeeper, Della, had said she'd left in her room on the nightstand. But when Anna had seen the guest room door slightly ajar, she'd opened it and had a look.

She made a show of glancing around for a book that had zero chance of being there since it was all the way at the end of the hall.

"This is your room now?" Heath asked.

"No. But I come in here sometimes. For the view." Anna motioned to the massive bay window. She wouldn't mention that every bedroom on the second floor had similar windows, similar views. As did her own room on the first floor.

Heath glanced in the direction of the bay window as if he might get up to sample that view, but his next glance was at his body. Considering he was naked under the sheet, he probably didn't want to get up until she'd left, and that was her cue to leave. First though, she wanted an answer to her question.

"Why are you here?" she repeated.

"Riley. He saw me at the base in San Antonio and said I needed some…R & R before I left on assignment. He was headed back here to the ranch to finish out his leave, and he asked me to come."

All of that made sense because Riley, too, was an Air Force officer and had indeed been at the base the day before. Yes, it made sense except for Heath's hesitation before R & R.

"You weren't here last night when I went to bed." She would have noticed Heath, that's for sure.

"We stopped for a bite to eat, then to visit some mutual friends, and we didn't get in until late. We didn't want to wake anyone up so Riley just sent me here to the guest room." Heath paused. "Riley's my boss."

Uh-oh. That wouldn't play well with Riley if he found out about her lustful thoughts over his subordinate. It wouldn't play well with Heath, either, since he probably didn't want to do or think anything—or have *her* do or think anything—that would cause his boss to hit him upside the head with a shovel.

A threat that Riley had first rattled off nine and a half years ago when he thought a romance was brewing between Heath and her.

If Riley had known what had gone on in the hayloft, he might not have actually carried through on the shovel threat, but Anna would have never heard the end of it.

And there was that whole underage-sex thing.

When Heath had first started working at the ranch, he'd been eighteen. But she'd been only seventeen. Riley and her other brothers had made a big deal about the attraction they'd sensed going on between Heath and her.

The term *jail bait* had been thrown around.

Since Heath had been making a big deal of his own about going into the military, it was an issue. Heath wanted to go into special ops, which would have required a lengthy background check for a top-secret clearance, and Riley had brought up her age for the sole purpose of scaring Heath into keeping his jeans zipped.

It had worked. Until the day Anna turned eighteen,

that is. After that, she'd made the trip to the hayloft with
Heath, and she had the memories of the orgasm to prove
it.

Heath smiled at her, but it felt as if he'd had to rummage it up just to be polite. Again, the nudity was probably driving that. But the nudity didn't stop him from
looking at her with those sizzling blue eyes. Also bedroomy like his hair. He slid his gaze from her head to
her toes, lingering in the middle. Lingering especially
on her breasts. Perhaps because she was wearing a T-
shirt and no bra.

"Riley didn't mention you'd be here at the ranch,"
Heath said.

"Oh? Well, usually I leave the day after Thanksgiving, but I decided to stay a little longer." Since it was already two days after Thanksgiving, she probably hadn't
needed to add that last part. "I'm in law school at University of Texas, but I finished my courses early this se-
mester. I'm also planning a transfer. I need a change of
scenery…or something."

And a life.

And perhaps sex, but she'd only gotten that idea when
she'd seen Heath naked.

"Yeah, a change of scenery," he repeated, as if he were
aware of what she meant by the *or something.*

"So, how long will you be here?" Anna tried to keep
her eyes directed just at his face, but her gaze kept drifting a bit to that incredibly toned chest. Either he'd gotten very good with contouring body paints or the man
had a six-pack.

"Until the cows come home," he said.

That's when she realized both her eyes and her mind

had seriously drifted off, and she didn't have a clue what he'd been talking about before that.

The corner of his mouth lifted. A dreamy smile, and he hadn't had to rummage up this one. It was the real deal.

"I'll be here about two weeks," he said. Probably repeated information. "How about you?"

"Two weeks. More or less. I was going to stay until the final exams were over and the campus was less busy. Then, the plan was to talk to my advisor about the transfer."

"For that change of scenery or something?" Heath made it sound like a question.

Anna pretended not to hear it. No need to get into all that. Instead, she glanced at his left hand, the one part of his body she'd failed to look at during her gawking. No ring.

"I'm not married," Heath volunteered. "Never have been." He looked at her left hand, too, where she was still wearing the opal ring her Granny Ethel had left her.

Anna shook her head. "No I-do's for me, either." Close, though, but best not to get into that after her change-of-scenery slip. "So, catch me up on what you've been doing."

"Maybe I can do that after I've put on some clothes? Or we can talk like this?" Another smile.

He was flirting with her, a ploy she knew all too well since she'd been on the receiving end of his flirting that summer. Well, she could flirt, too.

"I guess I can restrain myself for a quick catch-up," she joked. "A *quick catch-up*," she emphasized. "What are you doing these days? I mean, other than sleeping naked, that is. How's the job going?"

The smile faded, and she was sorry she'd taken the

conversation in that direction. Of course, it was something a normal nondrooling woman would have asked the man who had been her first.

Even though it was a dumb-as-dirt thing to do, she went closer. Much closer. And she sat down on the bed. Not right next to him, though, because she didn't want to move into the dumber-than-dirt category, but it was still too near him. Six miles would have been too near.

"Sorry," she added. "Didn't mean to hit a nerve. And I should have known better because Riley doesn't like to talk about his assignments, either. I think he believes it'll worry me, but whether he talks about it or not, I still worry."

"You shouldn't. Riley's been on plenty of deployments and hasn't gotten a scratch. Some guys are just bulletproof, and Riley's one of them."

Maybe. But Anna had a bad feeling about this deployment coming up. A bad feeling she definitely didn't want to discuss with Heath. Or Riley. If she didn't mention it aloud, maybe the feeling would go away. Maybe the danger would as well, and her brother would come back with his bulletproof label intact.

"You okay?" Heath asked.

That was a reminder to push aside her fears and get on with this catch-up conversation. "Riley always says if he tells me about his job, he'll have to hit me with a shovel afterwards. Riley really likes that shovel threat."

"I remember." Heath took a deep breath, causing the muscles in his chest and that six-pack to respond. "Well, shovels aside, I can tell you that I just finished up a deployment in a classified location where there was a lot of sand, followed by eight months in Germany where there was a lot of paperwork. That's where Riley became my boss. Small world, huh?"

Yes. Too small, maybe. "Riley and you are in the same career field?"

"For now." The short answer came out so fast. As did his hand. He brushed his fingers over the ends of her hair. Even though he didn't actually touch skin or anything, it was enough of a distraction. "Your hair is longer," he said.

"Yours is shorter." And yes, she achieved dumber-than-dirt status by touching his hair, as well. Since it was on the short side, she also touched some skin.

She felt everything go still, and even though Anna was pulling back her hand, it seemed to be in slow motion. The only thing that was in the revving-up mode was this flamethrower attraction that had always been between Heath and her.

"Yeah," he drawled. No other words were necessary. They were on the same proverbial page along with being on the same actual bed. The flamethrower had had a go at him, too.

"I, uh…" Anna stuttered around with a few more words and syllables before she managed to say something coherent. "This could be trouble."

"Already is." He drawled that, too. Hitched up another smile.

The past nine and a half years just vanished. Suddenly, Anna was eighteen again and was thinking about kissing him. Of course, she hadn't needed vanishing years for that to happen, but it was as if they were back in that hayloft. On all that warm, soft hay. Heath had taken things so slow. Long kisses. His hand skimming over various parts of her body.

Then, into her jeans.

That had been the best part, and it'd all started with a heated look like the one he was giving her now.

Even though they didn't move, the foreplay was in full swing. His gaze lingered on her mouth. She picked up the rhythm of his breathing—which was too fast. Ditto for her heartbeat. Everything was moving in sync.

"Anna, we're playing with fire," he whispered. It was a drawl, too.

She was near enough to him now that his breath hit against her mouth like a kiss. "Yes," she admitted, but she was in the "fire pretty" mindset right now, and she inched closer, her drifting gaze sliding from his mouth to his abs.

"Is it real?" she asked, but was in the wrong mindset to wait for an answer. She touched that six-pack.

Oh, yes. Definitely real.

It probably would have been a good time to snatch back her hand and be outraged that she'd done something so bold, but she kept it there a moment and saw and heard Heath's reaction. He cursed under his breath, and beneath the sheet his filled-out part reacted, as well.

He cursed some more, but it was all aimed at himself. "I really do need you to leave now so I can get dressed. Once I can walk, that is. Maybe you can shut the door behind you, too."

That caused the past nine and a half years to unvanish. Heath was putting a stop to this. As he should.

Anna was about to help with that stopping by getting to her feet and doing something that Heath clearly would have trouble doing right now—walking. But before she could budge an inch, she saw the movement in the doorway.

And saw the source of that movement.

Riley.

His eyes were so narrowed that it looked as if his eyelashes were stuck together.

"What the hell's going on here?" Riley growled. He opened his eyes enough to look at her. Then at Heath. Then at the other *thing* that was going on. "And what are you doing with my sister?"

No way was Heath going to be able to explain with the bulge of his filled-out part beneath the sheet. And neither could Anna.

Chapter Two

Well, hell in a big-assed handbasket. This visit was off to a good start.

Heath had known it wasn't a smart idea to come to the McCord Ranch, and he was getting a full reminder of why it'd been bad, what with Riley glaring at him.

"Get dressed," Riley ordered, and yeah, it was an order all right. "And we'll talk." Then he turned that ordering glare on his sister.

But Anna obviously wasn't as affected by it as Heath was, even though Riley was in uniform and looked thirty steps past the intimidation stage. Still, Anna matched Riley's glare with a scowl and waltzed out.

Thankfully, Riley did some waltzing as well and left, shutting the door behind him. Though it was more of a slam than a shut. Still, he was gone, and that gave Heath some time to take a very uncomfortable walk to the adjoining bathroom for a shower. Cold. Just the way he hated his showers. And if he stayed on the ranch, there'd be more of them in his near future.

It was time for a change of plans.

Not that he actually had plans other than passing time and moping. Yeah, moping was a definite possibility. At least it had been until Anna had shown up in the doorway. Difficult to mope in his current state.

Regardless, Anna was off-limits, of course.

He repeated that while the cold shower cooled down his body. Repeated it some more while he dressed. Kept repeating it when he went down the stairs to apologize to Riley and tell him that he'd remembered some place he needed to be. Riley would see right through the lie, but after what he had witnessed in the guest room, he'd be glad to get Heath off the ranch.

Heath made his way downstairs, meandering through the sprawling house. Since he was hoping for some coffee to go along with the butt-chewing he would get from Riley, he headed toward the kitchen.

He heard women's voices but not Anna's. He was pretty sure they belonged to Della and Stella, sisters and the McCords' longtime housekeeper and cook. Yep. And Heath got a glimpse of them and the coffeepot, too, before Riley stepped into the archway, blocking his path.

"I know," Heath volunteered. "You want to hit me on the head with a shovel."

"Hit who with a shovel?" Della asked, and when she spotted Heath, she flung the dish towel she was holding. Actually, she popped Riley on the butt with it and went to Heath to gather him into her arms for a hug. "It's good to see you, boy."

Heath hadn't even been sure the woman would remember him after all this time, but clearly she did. Or else she thought he was someone else.

"Nobody's gonna get hit with a shovel in this house," Della warned Riley, and then she added to Heath, "Have you seen Anna yet?"

"Earlier," Heath settled for saying.

"Well, I hope you'll be seeing a lot more of her while you're here. Never could understand why you two didn't just sneak up to the hayloft or somewhere."

Heath choked on his own breath. Not a very manly reaction, but neither was the way Riley screwed up his face. Della didn't seem to notice or she might have used the dish towel on him again.

"Have a seat at the table, and I'll fix you some breakfast," Della offered.

"Heath and I have to talk first," Riley insisted.

"Pshaw. A man's gotta have at least some coffee before he carries on a conversation. Where are your manners, Riley?"

"I think I left them upstairs."

Della laughed as if it were a joke and, God bless her, she poured Heath a cup of coffee. He had a couple of long sips, figuring he was going to need them.

"Thanks. I'll be right back," Heath said to Della, and he followed Riley out of the kitchen and into the sunroom.

No shovels in sight, but Riley had gone back to glaring again, and he got right in Heath's face. "Keep your hands off Anna, or I'll make your life a living hell."

Heath had no doubts about that. He didn't mind the living hell for himself so much, but he didn't want any more of Riley's anger aimed at Anna. "I'll get my things together and head out."

Riley's glare turned to a snarl. "And then Anna, Della and Stella will think I've run you off."

Heath had some more coffee, cocked his head to the side in an "if the shoe fits" kind of way. Because in a manner of speaking, Riley was indeed running him off. Except that Heath had already decided it was a good idea, too. Still, he didn't acknowledge that. He was getting some perverse pleasure out of watching Riley squirm a little.

"I'm guessing Anna, Della and Stella will make your life a living hell if they think you've run me off?" Heath asked. And he said it with a straight face.

Riley opened his mouth. Closed it. Then he did a wash, rinse, repeat of that a couple more times before he finally cursed. "Stay. For now. And we'll discuss it later. I've got to do some more paperwork at the base. Just keep your hands off Anna while I'm gone. Afterwards, too."

His hands were the least of Riley's worries, but Heath kept that to himself. Besides, Riley didn't give him a chance to say anything else. He lit out of there while growling out another "Stay" order.

Heath would stay. For the morning anyway. But it was best if he put some distance between Anna and all those parts of him that could get him in trouble.

He went back into the kitchen, got a hug and warm greeting from Stella this time, and the woman practically put him in one of the chairs at the table.

"How do you like your eggs?" Della asked.

"Any way you fix them." Heath added a wink because he figured it would make her smile. It did.

"Tell us what you've been doing with yourself for the past nine years or so," Della said as she got to work at the stove. "I seem to recall when you left here that summer you were headed to boot camp."

Heath nodded, took a bite of the toast that Stella set in front of him. "I enlisted in the Air Force, became a para-rescuer and took college classes online. When I finished my degree, I got my commission and became a combat rescue officer."

"Like Riley," Stella said.

"Yeah, but he outranks me."

"How is that? Didn't you go in the Air Force before Riley did?"

Heath nodded again. "Only a couple months earlier, though. We've been in the service about the same amount of time, but for most of that I was enlisted. I've only been an officer for three and a half years now. And Riley's my boss. Well, until the rest of my paperwork has cleared. That should be about the time Riley leaves for his assignment in two weeks."

Della stopped scrambling the eggs to look at him. "You won't be going with him?"

There it was. That twist to the gut. Heath tried to ease it with some more toast and coffee, but that was asking a lot of mere food products. And Della and Stella noticed all right. He'd gotten their full attention.

"No, I won't be going with Riley this time," Heath said.

He still had their attention, and judging from their stares, the women wanted more. Heath gave them the sanitized version. "The Air Force feels it's time for me to have a stateside assignment. It's standard procedure. A way of making sure I don't burn out."

His mouth was still moving and words were coming out, but Heath could no longer hear what he was saying. That's because Anna walked in. Or maybe it was just a Mack Truck that looked like Anna because he suddenly felt as if someone had knocked him senseless.

She'd changed out of her sweats and T-shirt. Had put on a bra, too. And was now wearing jeans and a red sweater. Heath tried not to notice the way the clothes hugged her body. Tried not to notice her curves. Her face.

Hell, he gave up and noticed.

Not that he could have done otherwise. Especially when Anna poured herself a cup of coffee, sat down next to him and glanced at his crotch.

"Back to normal?" she whispered. Then she gave him a smile that could have dissolved multiple layers of rust on old patio furniture. Dissolved a few of his brain cells, too. "So, did Riley try to give you your marching orders?"

Since Della and Stella got very, very quiet, Heath figured they were hanging on every word, so he chose his own words carefully and spoke loud enough for the women to hear. "Something came up—"

Anna glanced at his crotch again and laughed. Obviously, a reaction she hadn't planned because she clamped her teeth onto her bottom lip after adding "I'm sorry." Too late, though. Because Della and Stella weren't just hanging on every word but every ill-timed giggle, too.

"Well, I'm sure whatever came up—" Della paused "—you can work it out so you can stay here for at least a couple of days. That way, Anna and you have time to visit."

"Especially since Anna needs some cheering up," Stella added.

Anna certainly didn't laugh that time. She got a deer-about-to-be-smashed-by-a-car look. "I'm fine, really," Anna mumbled.

Which only confirmed to Heath that she did indeed need some cheering up. Maybe this had to do with the "change of scenery or something" she'd mentioned upstairs.

Well, hell.

There went his fast exit, and no, that wasn't the wrong

part of his body talking, either. If Anna was down, he wanted to help lift her up.

Stella dished up two plates of eggs for Anna and him, and she smiled at them when she set them on the table. "You two were as thick as thieves back in the day." She snapped her fingers as if recalling something. "Anna, Heath even gave you that heart necklace you used to wear all the time. It had your and his pictures in it."

Hard to forget that. Heath referred to it as the great engraved debacle. He'd spent all his money buying Anna that silver heart locket as a going-away gift. Something to remember him by after he left Spring Hill and the McCord Ranch. It was supposed to be engraved with the words *Be Mine*.

The engraver had screwed up and had put *Be My* instead.

Since Heath hadn't had the time to get it fixed, he'd given it to Anna anyway, but he hadn't figured she would actually wear it. Not with that confusing, incomplete *sentiment*.

"Where is that necklace?" Della asked.

"I'm not sure," Anna answered, and she got serious about eating her breakfast. Fast. Like someone who'd just entered a breakfast-eating contest with a reprieve from a death sentence waiting for the winner.

Della made a sound that could have meant anything, but it had a sneaky edge to it. "I think Heath needs some cheering up, too," Della went on. "And not because Riley was going on about that shovel. That boy needs to get a new threat, by the way," she added to her sister before looking at Anna again. "I get the feeling Heath could use somebody to talk to."

Heath suddenly got very serious about eating his

breakfast, as well. Either Della had ESP, or Heath sucked at covering up what was going on in his head.

Anna finished gulping down her breakfast just a bite ahead of him, gulped down some coffee, too, and she probably would have headed out if Stella hadn't taken her empty breakfast plate and given her a plate of cookies instead.

"I need you to take these cookies over to Claire Davidson at her grandmother's house."

"Claire's back in town?" Anna asked, sounding concerned.

Heath knew Claire. She'd been around a lot that summer he'd worked at the McCord Ranch, and if he wasn't mistaken Claire had a thing for Riley. And vice versa.

"Her grandmother's sickly again. Thought they could use some cheering up, too." Della shifted her attention to Heath. "And you can go with Anna. Then maybe she could show you around town."

"Spring Hill hasn't changed in nine and a half years," Anna quickly pointed out.

"Pshaw. That's not true. The bakery closed for one thing. And Logan bought that building and turned it into a fancy-schmancy office. It has a fancy-schmancy sign that says McCord Cattle Brokers. You can't miss it."

Logan—one of Anna's other brothers who ran the family business and probably also owned a shovel. Ditto for Logan's twin, Lucky. At least the two of them didn't stay at the ranch very often, so Heath might not even run into them. Well, he wouldn't as long as he avoided the fancy-schmancy office and any of the local rodeos since Lucky was a bull rider.

"I thought I'd go out and see if the ranch hands needed any help," Heath suggested.

That earned him a blank stare from the women. "You don't have to work for your keep while you're here," Stella said. "You're a guest."

"I know, but I like working with my hands. I miss it." He did. Not as much as he'd miss other things—like having the job he really wanted—but grading on a curve here, ranch work was missable.

"All right, then," Della finally conceded. "At least walk Anna to the truck. There might be some ice on the steps. We had a cold spell move in."

"Now, go," Stella said, shooing them out. "Della and I need to clean up, and we can't do that with y'all in here."

This wasn't about cleaning. This was about match-making. Still, Heath grabbed his coat so he could make sure Anna didn't slip on any ice. He only hoped Anna didn't ask why he needed cheering up, and he would re-turn the favor and not ask her the same thing.

"So, why do you need cheering up?" Anna asked the moment they were outside.

He groaned, not just at the question but also because it was at least fifty degrees with zero chance of ice.

"Is it personal or business?" she added.

"Is yours personal or business?" he countered.

She stayed quiet a moment and instead of heading to-ward one of the trucks parked on the side of the house, she sat down in the porch swing. "Both. You?"

"Both," he repeated. But then he stopped and thought about her answer. "Yours is personal, as in guy troubles?"

For some reason that made him feel as if he'd been hit by the Anna-truck again. Which was stupid. Because of course she had men in her life. Heath just wasn't sure he wanted to hear about them.

She nodded to verify that it was indeed guy trouble.

No, he didn't want to hear this, so he blurted out the first thing that popped into his head. He probably should have waited for the second or third thing, though.

"I had a girl break up with me once because I kept calling her your name," he said.

"*My* name?" She didn't seem to know how to react to that.

"Uh, no. I kept saying *your name* because I couldn't remember her name." And he added a wink that usually charmed women.

But, of course, it'd been Anna's name. The way stuff about her often popped into his head, her name had a way of just popping out of his mouth.

"Any other confessions you want to get off your chest and/or six-pack?" she asked. And she winked at him.

Man, that's what he'd always liked about Anna. She gave as good as she got. "Let me see. I don't wear boxers or briefs. I like mayo and pepper on my French fries. And my mother's in jail again."

All right, so that last one just sort of fell from his brain into his mouth.

Anna didn't question the *again* part. Maybe because she remembered the reason he'd ended up at the McCord Ranch all those years ago was that his mother had been in jail then, as well.

In jail only after she'd stolen and spent every penny of the money that Heath had scrimped and saved for college. She'd also burned down their rental house with all his clothes and stuff still in it.

Heath had snapped up Riley's offer of a job and a place to stay—since at the time Heath had had neither. His father hadn't been in his life since he was in kindergarten, and what with him being broke and homeless, he'd had few places to turn.

If it hadn't been for his jailbird mom, he would have never met Anna. So, in a way he owed her.

In a very roundabout way.

"Want to talk about why your mom's in jail?" Anna asked.

Well, since he'd opened this box, Heath emptied the contents for her. "Shoplifting Victoria's Secret panties. She'd stuffed about fifty pairs in her purse—guess they don't take up much room—and when the security guard tried to stop her, she kicked him where it hurts. Then she did the same to the manager of the store next door. Then to the off-duty cop who tried to stop her. My mom can be a real butt-kicker when it comes to high-end underwear."

Anna smiled, a quiet kind of smile. "I do that, too, sometimes."

"What?" And Heath hoped this wasn't about butt-kicking or stealing panties.

"Diffuse the pain with humor. I'm not very good at it, either. Pain sucks."

Yeah, it did, and he thought he knew exactly what she was talking about. "You lost your parents when you were a teenager."

"Yes, they were killed in a car accident before you and I met. I was fourteen, and I thought my world was over. That was still the worst of the *world's over* moments, but I've had others since."

"Is that why you need cheering up?" he asked.

She didn't answer. Anna stood. "I should deliver these cookies before the ice gets to them."

Heath put his hands in his pockets so he wouldn't touch her as she walked away. Not that he would have had a chance to do any touching. Because someone pulled up in a truck. Not a work truck, either. This was a silver one that Della would have labeled as fancy schmancy. It went well with the cowboy who stepped from it.

Logan McCord.

The top dog at the McCord Ranch and the CEO of Mc-Cord Cattle Brokers. He made a beeline for the porch, passing Anna along the way. She said something to him, something Heath couldn't hear, but it put a deep scowl on Logan's face.

"Smart-ass," he grumbled. "She threatened to hit me with Riley's shovel if I didn't make you feel welcome. So—welcome."

Warm and fuzzy it wasn't, but at least it wasn't a threat. Not yet anyway.

"Riley called," Logan continued. "He said I was to come over here and convince you to stay."

"Because of Anna, Della and Stella."

Logan certainly didn't deny that, and his gaze drifted to Anna as she drove away before his attention turned back to Heath. "You're only going to be here two weeks at most, and then you'll leave, right?"

Since that pretty much summed it up, Heath nodded.

"Well, the last time you did that, it took Anna a long time to get over you. *Months*," Logan emphasized. "We all had to watch her cry her eyes out."

Hell. Crying? Months? This was the first Heath was hearing about this, but then he hadn't been around to see those tears. He'd been off at basic training at Lackland Air Force Base. He'd written her, of course. In the beginning at least. She'd written back to him, too, but she damn sure hadn't mentioned tears.

Logan took a step closer, got in his face. So close that

Heath was able to determine that he used mint mouthwash and flossed regularly. "You won't hurt my kid sister like that again."

"The shovel threat?" Heath asked, aiming to make this sound as light as a confrontation with Logan could be. Heath wasn't sure friendly bones in a person's body actually existed, but if they did, Logan didn't have any.

"Worse. I'll tell Della and Stella what you've done and let them have a go at you. If you piss them off, the shovel will be the least of your worries."

Heath didn't doubt that. In fact, the whole McCord clan would come after him if he left Anna crying again. And that meant Anna was way off-limits.

He'd survived months in hostile territory. But Heath thought that might be a picnic compared to the next two weeks with Anna and the McCord brothers.

Chapter Three

Heath had been avoiding her for the past three days. Anna was certain of it. And she was fed up with it, partly because if Heath avoided her, it was like letting her knot-headed brothers win.

The other *partly* was that she couldn't get him off her mind, and she didn't know what riled her more—her brothers' winning or her own body whining and begging for something it shouldn't get.

Shouldn't.

Because another fling with Heath would only complicate her life and possibly get her heart stomped on again. That was the logical, big-girl panties argument, but the illogical, no-underwear girl wanted Heath in the hayloft again.

And the hayloft was exactly where she spotted him.

He was standing in the loft, tossing down bales of hay onto a flatbed truck that was parked just beneath. He was all cowboy today: jeans, a blue work shirt, Stetson, boots. Oh, and he was sweaty despite the chillier temps.

She wasn't sure why the sweat appealed to her, but then she didn't see a single thing about him that didn't fall into the appeal category.

Anna stood there ogling him, as she'd done in the bedroom, and she kept on doing it until his attention landed on her. Since she should at least make an attempt at not throwing herself at him, she went to the nearby corral and looked at the horses that'd been delivered earlier. It wasn't exactly the right day for horse ogling, though, because the wind had a bite to it.

An eternity later, which was possibly only a couple of minutes, the ranch hands drove off with the hay, and Heath made his way down the loft ladder. Then he made his way toward her.

"You've been avoiding me," she said. All right, she should have rehearsed this or something. For a soon-to-be lawyer, she was seriously lacking in verbal finesse when it came to Heath.

"Yeah," he admitted in that hot drawl of his. And he admitted the reason, too. "Your brothers are right. I'm not here for long, and they said you cried a lot the last time I left."

Her mouth dropped open, and the outrage didn't allow her to snap out a comeback. But her brothers were dead meat. Dead. Meat.

"They told you that?" She didn't wait for an answer. "I didn't cry. That much," Anna added.

Heath lifted his eyebrow, went to her side and put his forearms on the corral fence. "The fact that you cried at all tells me that I should keep avoiding you."

"Should?" she challenged.

He cursed, looked away from her. "You know I'm attracted to you. You saw proof of that in the bedroom."

She had, indeed. "And you know I'm attracted to you."

There, she'd thrown down the sexual gauntlet. But it caused him to curse again.

"I don't want to hurt you," he said.

"And I don't want to get hurt—"

A commotion in the corral nipped off the rest of what she was about to say. And it wasn't a very timely commotion.

Sex.

Specifically horse sex.

It went on a lot at the ranch. So often in fact that Anna rarely noticed, but because Heath was right next to her, she noticed it now. And he noticed that she noticed.

With all that noticing going on, it was amazing that she remembered how to turn around, but she finally managed it. She took hold of Heath's arm and got him moving away from the corral and toward the pasture.

Where she immediately saw cow-and-bull sex.

Dang it. Was everything going at it today?

Heath chuckled. "The Angus bull was getting restless, trying to break fence, so the hands brought in some company for him."

The ranch's version of Match.com. And the icy wind definitely didn't put a damper on things. Not for the bull anyway, but it did for Anna. She shivered and wished she'd opted for a warmer coat instead of the one that she thought looked better on her. It was hard to look your best with chattering teeth and a red nose.

"In here," Heath said. He put his hand on her back and maneuvered her into the barn.

"The scene of the crime," Anna mumbled. She'd fantasized about getting Heath back in here, but not like this. Not when she needed a tissue.

He glanced up at the hayloft, his attention lingering there a moment before coming back to her. The lingering lasted more than a moment though, and he took out a handkerchief and handed it to her.

"I should probably take you back to the house so you can warm up," he offered.

She considered it just so she could blow her nose. It was tempting, but Riley was inside. Della and Stella, too. So Anna touched the handkerchief to her nose and hoped that did the trick. In case it didn't, she went for what Riley would have called a tactical diversion.

"I'm surprised you're not off somewhere enjoying some *company* like that bull before you leave for your deployment," she said.

Anna figured that would get Heath to smile. It didn't. And she saw it again—the look on his face to remind her that he needed to be cheered up about something. Apparently, it had something to do with his assignment.

"Unless a miracle happens, I won't be deploying," he finally answered. The strewn hay on the floor was suddenly riveting because he stared at it. "The Air Force wants me to take an instructor job in Florida."

With the hay-staring and the gloomy look, Anna had braced herself for something a lot worse. "You make it sound as if you're being banished to Pluto."

"In a way, it is like that for me. I trained to be a combat rescue officer, like Riley. I didn't go through all of that to work behind a desk."

Anna wasn't sure how far she should push this so she just waited him out. Waited out the profanity he muttered under his breath. Waited out more hay-staring.

"I feel washed up," he added.

Ah, she got it then. "But the instructor job is temporary, right? You'll go back to being a combat rescue officer?"

"In three years."

She got that, too. It was an eternity for someone like Heath or Riley.

Anna touched his arm, rubbed gently. "The three years will fly by. Look how fast the past nine and a half years went."

The hay finally lost its allure for him, and he looked at her. "Yeah." Not so much of a sexy drawl this time. The hurt was still there. Time to pull out the big guns and do a little soul-baring.

"Remember when I told you I needed a change of scenery? Well, what I really need is to get away from my ex-boyfriend," Anna confessed. "We had a bad breakup."

Evidently, Heath didn't like this soul-baring so much because he frowned. "Are you telling me this is rebound flirting you've been doing with me?"

"No. The breakup happened two years ago, but he's getting married to one of my classmates. And they're having a baby. Twins, actually. The classmate is a former Miss Texas beauty pageant winner."

He nodded, made an "I got it" sound. "You're still in love with him."

"No!" And she couldn't say that fast or loud enough. "He's a lying, cheating weasel. My need for a change of scenery isn't because I still care for him but because I'm sick and tired of everybody walking on eggshells around me."

Her voice had gotten louder with each word, and she couldn't stop the confessions now that the floodgates were open.

"Poor pitiful Anna McCord got dumped for the beauty queen," she blathered on. "It reminds me of the stuff my brothers pull on me, and I'm tired of it. Tired of being treated like someone who needs to be handled with kid gloves."

She probably would have just kept on blathering, too, if Heath hadn't slid his hand around the back of her neck, hauled her to him and kissed her.

All in all, it was the perfect way to shut her up, and Anna didn't object one bit. In fact, she would have cheered, but her mouth was otherwise occupied, and besides, cheering would have put an end to this kiss.

She didn't want it to end.

Apparently, neither did Heath, because he put that clever mouth to good use and made the kiss French. And deep. And long.

All the makings of a good kiss even if Anna's lungs started to ache for air.

Heath broke the kiss just long enough for them to take in some much needed oxygen, and he went in for another assault. Anna was no longer shivering, could no longer feel her nose, but the rest of her was hyperaware of what was happening. The heat zoomed from her mouth to her toes, but it especially fired up in her orgasm-zone.

Soon, very soon, the kiss just wasn't enough, and they started to grapple for position. Trying to get closer and closer to each other. Heath was a lot better at grappling than she was because he dropped his hands to her butt and gave her a push against the front of his jeans.

Anna saw stars. Maybe the moon, too. And she darn near had an orgasm right then, right there while they were fully clothed.

Her heart was pounding now. Her breath, thin. She was melting. And there was a roaring sound in her head. That roaring sound was probably the reason she hadn't heard the other sounds until it was too late. Not horse or bull sex this time.

Footsteps.

"Interrupting anything?" someone asked.

Not Riley or Logan. Her brother Lucky.

And he was standing in the barn doorway with a shovel gripped in his hand.

ONCE AGAIN HEATH was facing a McCord brother when he was aroused. Hardly the right bargaining tool for dealing with Anna's older siblings who were hell-bent on protecting their sister.

Anna stepped in front of him as if she were his protector, but Heath remedied that. He stepped in front of her. But that only prompted her to attempt another stepping in front of him, and Heath put a stop to it. He dropped a kiss on her mouth, a chaste one this time hoping it would get her to cooperate.

"I need to talk to your brother alone," Heath told her.

"No way. He's here to browbeat you, and he's got a shovel."

Lucky shrugged. Propped the shovel against the wall. "Riley said I should bring it and do my part to remind Heath that he should keep his jeans zipped around you." He shrugged again when he glanced at the front of Heath's jeans. "The zipper's still up, so my work here is done."

Lucky turned to walk away.

"That's really all you've got to say?" Anna asked.

Her brother stopped, smiled in that lazy way that Lucky had about him. Heath knew Lucky loved his sister, but he'd never been as Attila the Hun as Riley and Logan. Heath suspected that's because Lucky got out all his restless energy by riding rodeo bulls. And having lots of sex.

"Should I ask you two to stay away from each other?" Lucky didn't wait for an answer though. "Wouldn't work. You two have the hots for each other, and there's only one way to cool that down." His gaze drifted to the hayloft before he turned again to leave.

Was Lucky really giving them his approval?

No.

This had to be some kind of trick.

Heath went after Lucky. Anna, too, and they caught up with him by the porch steps. However, before Heath could say anything else, the door opened, and Della stuck her head out.

"Anna, you got a call on the house phone. It's Claire."

Anna volleyed glances between Heath and her brother and then huffed. "Don't you dare say anything important before I get back."

She hurried inside. So did Lucky and Heath, but they stopped in the sunroom.

"Zippers and haylofts aside," Lucky said. "I don't want Anna hurt again. She sort of fell apart the last time you left."

"Yes. I heard about the crying from Logan." Heath paused. "Define *fell apart*."

"It wasn't just the crying." Lucky paused, too. "It was the pregnancy scare."

Heath felt as if all the air had just been sucked out of his lungs. Out of the entire planet. And if there was air on Pluto, it was also gone.

"Anna doesn't know that I know," Lucky went on. "No one does, and I'd like to keep it from my brothers. If Riley and Logan find out, they'd want to kick your ass. And mine since I didn't tell them. Then I'd have to kick theirs. If you don't mind, I'd rather not have to go through an ass-kicking free-for-all."

"Pregnancy?" Heath managed to ask. Considering there was still no air, he was doing good to get out that one word.

Lucky nodded. "A couple of weeks after you left, I went into Anna's bathroom to get some eye drops, and I saw the box for the pregnancy test in her trash can. She'd torn up the box, but I was able to piece it together to figure out what it was."

Heath managed another word. "Damn."

"Yeah. Two words for you—safe sex."

"I used a condom."

Lucky shrugged again. "Then, it must have worked because when I found the pee stick—it was in the way bottom of the trash can, by the way—it had a negative sign on it."

Heath heard the words. Felt the relief at that negative sign. Then managed another word.

"Hell."

Anna had gone through a scare like that, and she hadn't even told him.

"The only reason I dragged this up now was so that you'd understand why I'm protective of her," Lucky went on. "Now, go find her. Confront her about all of this. Then use a condom when you have makeup sex."

There'd be no makeup sex. Because Heath wasn't touching her again. Hell. She could have had his kid.

Heath went looking for Anna, and when he didn't find her in the kitchen or any of the living areas, he went to her bedroom. Of course she was there. The one room in the house where he shouldn't be alone with her. The door was open, and she was still on the phone, but she motioned for him to come in. He did, but only because he wanted answers and didn't want to wait for them.

But he had to wait anyway.

He listened to Anna talk niceties with Claire. Several "you're welcomes" later, she finally ended the call and looked at him. The smile that was forming froze on her mouth though when she saw his expression.

Heath shut the door just as he blurted out, "You had a pee stick in the bottom of your trash can."

Anna gave him a blank look.

"The pregnancy test from nine and a half years ago," he clarified. "Lucky found it and just told me about it. I'm wondering why I had to hear it from him."

She laughed. Hardly the reaction he'd expected. "It wasn't my pee on that stick. It belonged to Kristy Welker. I bought it for her so her folks wouldn't find out, and she did the test here."

Heath had vague memories of this Kristy. Anna and she had been friends, and Kristy had come over a couple of times that summer.

Anna's laughter quickly stopped. "What the heck was Lucky doing in my bathroom?"

She was using her sister voice now, and it wouldn't have surprised Heath if she'd gone running out of there to confront her brother about it. She might have done that if Heath hadn't done something so unmanly as having to catch on to the wall to steady himself.

"Whoa. Are you all right?" She slipped her arm around his waist, led him to the bed.

Heath didn't even try to say he didn't need to sit down. He did. "I thought… Well, I thought…"

"Trust me, if you had knocked me up, I would have told you about it."

Of course she would have. But it might take a year or two for his heart rate to settle down.

She gave his arm another rub like the one she had in the barn. "Relax. You were my first, but I wasn't totally clueless." She stopped, paused. "I wasn't your first though, and that's why you knew to bring a condom to the hayloft."

Even though Heath was still coming down from the shock-relief whammy, he heard her loud and clear. She'd given him something that a girl could only give once. Her virginity. That upped the encounter a significant notch, and maybe she was looking for some kind of assurance that she'd given it to the right guy.

"You were the first one that mattered," he said. "I risked being hit by a shovel to be with you. That should have told you something."

No smile. No more arm rub, either. "And yet you left."

He nodded, tried to ignore the sting of that reminder. "I was leaving for basic training, and you were barely eighteen."

Anna waved that off. "I know where this is going. We were too young for it to have been real love."

"No, we weren't too young."

Okay, he hadn't meant to say that, and it was another opened box with contents that Anna was clearly waiting to be spilled.

"What I felt for you was real," Heath said. And strong.

He hadn't cried as Anna had done, but leaving her had left a hole in his heart. Best not to mention that, especially since he would be leaving again soon.

"I knew I couldn't give you a good life," he added. "Not when I was still trying to figure out my own life."

She stayed quiet a couple of seconds. "Fair enough. And if you'd stayed, you would have resented me because you gave up your dream of being in the military. Your wanderlust and need for an adrenaline fix would have come into play. We would have fought, broken up, and all these years later we would have cursed the mere mention of each other's names."

Heath frowned. He didn't like that version of what could have been, but she was probably right. Probably. Now he was cursing her name for a different reason. Because it reminded him of how much he wanted her.

"I still have the need for that adrenaline fix," he admitted. "The need to be…something. Somewhere. It's easier if I stay on the move."

"I get it." She motioned around the room. "That's why it's hard for me to be at the ranch sometimes."

He was pretty sure they were talking about her parents now, about the hole in her heart that their deaths had no doubt left. "Are the memories of your folks harder to deal with while you're here?"

"Every now and then. But sometimes it's hard no matter where I am. Sometimes, I wake up, and I can't remember what they looked like. That sends me into a panic. So I run to grab one of the photo albums just to remember their faces."

"It's your way of keeping them in your life," Heath said around the lump in his throat.

"Yes. The past has a way of staying with you like that." Anna took a deep breath, then sighed. "And you can't run away from your past. I know, I've tried. It's like that little mole I have on my right butt cheek. It just goes with me everywhere." She looked at him. "I know what you're thinking."

Because he thought they could use some levity, Heath asked, "You have a little mole on your butt cheek?"

"All right, I didn't know what you were thinking after all. I thought you might be wondering if I was trying to outrun my past by transferring colleges."

That hadn't even crossed his mind, mainly because he wondered why he hadn't noticed that mole on her butt cheek. He was also wanting to see that mole. Clearly, he had a one-track mind here.

He shook his head. "I didn't think the transfer was about running, more like ulcer prevention. No need for you to have to face a daily dose of Mr. Wrong and his new family."

"Exactly." She smiled in a triumphant *I didn't think you'd get that* kind of way.

Heath got it all right. He got a lot of things when it came to Anna. A lot of things because of her, too. Like that tug below his belly that nudged him to kiss her again. That was his red-flag warning to get moving, and he would have done just that if he hadn't spotted the silver heart locket on her nightstand.

When she saw that he'd spotted it, she tried to put it in the drawer, but Heath took hold of her hand to stop her.

Yes, it was the locket he'd given her all right.

"After Della asked about it, I found it in my old jewelry box," she said. Then, she frowned. "All right, I wear it sometimes. Okay?"

She didn't sound especially happy about that, but it pleased Heath that she still had it. Pleased him even more than she occasionally wore it. What didn't please him was the reminder of the two words engraved on it.

"Be my." Anna ran her fingertips over it. "I wasn't sure what you were saying—be my heart, be my locket. Be my lay in the hay." She chuckled, poked him with her elbow.

"It was a fill-in-the-blank kind of thing," he joked, poking her back with his elbow.

"It sounds to me as if you didn't know what you wanted to say." No elbow poke that time.

"I was eighteen. I didn't know."

"And now?" she asked.

For two little words, it was a mighty big question. One that he didn't have to answer because there was a knock at the door, and the knocker didn't wait for an invitation to come in. The door opened.

Riley.

Well, at least Anna and he weren't in a butt-grabbing lip-lock as they'd been in the barn when Lucky had found them.

"I need to talk to you," Riley said, looking at Heath. Then his gaze swung to his sister. "And no, this isn't about you. It's business."

Damn it. That didn't sound good.

Anna must have thought so, too, because she gave Heath a sympathetic look as Riley and he headed out. They didn't go far, just into the foyer.

"I just found out that you're still trying to get out of your instructor assignment, that you put in a request to go on another deployment," Riley threw out there.

Heath cursed. He wasn't exactly keeping it from Riley. Okay, he was, but he didn't want to justify what he was trying to do.

"You've already had two back-to-back deployments as

an officer," Riley reminded him. "Before that, you had back-to-back-to-backs as a pararescuer."

"You're going on another one," Heath reminded him just as fast.

"I've had breaks in between. In the past ten years, the only time you've been stateside is for leave and training." He put his hand on Heath's shoulder. "You don't have anything to prove."

"No disrespect, *sir*, but I have everything to prove. To myself anyway."

Riley huffed. "You can prove it by being the best Air Force instructor you can be."

"That sounds like a recruitment pitch."

"It is." Riley took his hand from Heath's shoulder, and his index finger landed against Heath's chest. "And here's some more advice—sometimes life gives you crap, and you just have to make crappy lemonade out of it."

Heath frowned, thinking he might never again want another glass of lemonade. Or another lecture from Riley. Of course, there wouldn't be any more Riley lectures if Heath got stuck with that instructor job he didn't want. Then Riley would no longer be his boss.

Frowning, too, possibly over that bad lemonade analogy, Riley walked away. Heath would have, as well. He would have headed back to the pasture to do something, anything, to burn off some of this restless energy inside him.

Yeah, he needed an adrenaline fix *bad*.

He figured in that moment that his thought must have tempted fate, because his phone dinged with a text message. There was that old saying about when the gods wanted to punish you, they gave you what you wanted. Well, it wasn't from the gods.

It was from Anna.

And the text flashed like neon on his phone screen. A sort of warning from the gods out to punish him.

Meet me in the hayloft in one hour.

Chapter Four

Anna figured she wasn't just going to be able to sneak out of the house without anyone seeing her.

And she was right.

As she was cutting through the sunroom, Della spotted her. Anna smiled, tried to look as if she weren't up to something, but that was sort of hard to do considering she had a six-pack of beer in a plastic grocery bag. A six-pack Anna had just scrounged from the fridge.

Della glanced at the bag and its distinctive shape. Then gave Anna no more than a mere glance.

"What are you up to?" Della asked.

Anna shrugged. "I'm considering playing with some fire. Running with scissors. Taking candy from some guy I don't know."

Falling hard for an old flame she shouldn't fall hard for was something Anna could add to that list of no-no's.

"So, you're going to the barn again with Heath," Della said. It wasn't a question.

"No. Yes," she admitted when Della gave her that liar-liar-pants-on-fire look. Anna huffed. "Don't give me a hard time about this. I'm tired of everyone babying me."

"They do that because you're the baby."

"*Was* the baby," Anna corrected. "I'm a grown woman now, but none of them can seem to accept it."

"They love you," Della pointed out.

"And I love them, but I want the key to my own chastity belt."

Della smiled that sly little smile of hers which meant she could be up to something. But she only kissed Anna on the cheek. "Honey, you've had that key for a long time now. Might be time to see if it works the way you want it to work."

Anna opened her mouth to respond, but she had nothing to say. Not a word. Instead, she returned the cheek kiss, tucked the beer under her arm so the bottles wouldn't jiggle and clang, and headed out the back.

No brothers in sight. No ranch hands, either.

But she also didn't see Heath.

Since it was—Anna checked the time on her phone—three minutes to rendezvous, she'd hoped she would see him waiting for her. He better not have blown her off. Except Heath wouldn't do that. Well, he might have done it with a text, call or chat, but he wouldn't do an unannounced blowing-off.

And he hadn't.

The moment she stepped in the barn, she saw him. Not in the hayloft, but standing by the steps that led up to the loft.

"You came," she said.

"Of course I came. I'm a guy and I'm not stupid. All right, maybe I am stupid, but the guy part's still true, and I've got the junk to prove it."

She smiled, chuckled. All nerves, and she hated the nerves because they didn't go well with this blistering attraction. "Yes, I got a glimpse of your junk. You're definitely a guy."

He smiled, too. "Beer?" he asked, tipping his head to the bag.

"I thought you might be thirsty. It was either this, milk or a questionable green smoothie."

"You made the right choice. I've already had my quota of milk and questionable green smoothies for a while."

He reached out, took her by the fingertips. That was it. The only part of her he touched. It was like being hit by a really big dose of pure, undiluted lust.

"You may have made the right choice with the beer," he added a heartbeat later. "But asking me to meet you here might fall into the stupid category."

"Might?" she repeated. Well, it was better than an out-and-out "this ain't gonna happen."

"Is this going to happen?" Anna came out and asked.

With only that teeny grip on her fingertips, he inched her closer. So close that when she breathed, she drew in his scent. Mixed with the hay and the crisp November air, it gave her another dose of lust.

"It shouldn't happen," Heath said. "I've tried to talk myself out of it."

"And?" She was still breathing, through her mouth now. Still taking in that scent. Still feeling him play with her fingers. "I hope you're really lousy at talking yourself out of things."

He closed his eyes a moment. Groaned. And, as if he were fighting—and losing—a fierce battle, he brought her another inch closer. She figured if the lust doses kept coming that she was going to launch herself into his arms.

"I'm leaving soon," he reminded her. "And I'm trying to do the right thing here."

She wanted to point out that unless he was leaving within the hour, then this could indeed happen, but that would just make her sound needy. Which she was. So very, very needy.

He let go of her fingertips, and she figured this was it. Heath would send her on her way. But he took the beer from her, and as if he had all the time in the world, he set the bag next to a hay bale.

"So, what now?" she asked.

Heath didn't answer her. Not with words. He reached out, and just when she thought she was going to get more fingertip foreplay, he took hold of her, snapped her to him and kissed the living daylights out of her.

Anna forgot all about the stupid argument that he was leaving soon. She forgot how to breathe. But other feelings took over, too. Probably because Heath didn't just kiss.

He touched.

He slipped his hand between them and ran his fingers over her right breast. Nice, but he double-whammied it with a neck kiss, and Anna felt herself moving. At first she thought it was just her body melting, but nope, she and Heath were walking.

"What are we doing?" she asked.

"Complicating the hell out of things."

"Good. I like complications." At the moment she would have agreed to a lobotomy.

Heath kept kissing her, kept moving. Not up the steps of the hayloft but rather toward the tack room. Maybe because it had a door. Maybe because it didn't require the coordination of step climbing with an erection. Maybe because it was just closer.

It was the erection thing, she decided, and since she

could feel it against her stomach, Anna added some touching of her own. She worked her hand over his zipper and would have gotten that zipper down if Heath hadn't stopped her.

She heard herself make a whiny sound of protest, but then he put her against the back of the door that he'd just shut, and he lifted her. Until his hard junk was against her soft junk. Everything lined up just right to create a mind-blowing sensation.

"Let's play a game," he said. And yeah, he drawled.

Anna nodded. She would have agreed to a second lobotomy.

"On a scale of one to ten, rate the kisses, and then I'll know which parts to concentrate on."

She wasn't sure she could count to ten, much less rate kisses, but Heath jumped right into the game. He kissed her mouth.

"A ten," she said after he left her gasping for air and reaching for his zipper again.

He put his hand over hers to stop her, but Anna just used the pressure of his hand to add pressure to his erection.

"We'll play that particular game later," he promised.

Heath moved on to the next kiss. He placed one in the little area just below her ear, and he must have remembered that was a hot spot for her because it didn't seem like a lucky guess.

"Fifty," she blurted out. If Heath hadn't held her in place with his body, she would have dropped like a rock. There were no muscles in her legs, and her feet had perhaps disappeared.

"I'll definitely put that on my playlist," he said and

added a flick of his tongue in that very hot spot that needed no such licking to further arouse it.

She went after his zipper for a third time, and the only reason she failed, again, was because he pushed up her sweater, pushed down her bra and did that tongue-flicking thing over her nipples.

"A seventy," she managed to say.

"Scale of one to ten," he corrected.

"Ten plus sixty."

He chuckled, which made for some very interesting sensations since he still had his mouth on her nipple.

"And this one?" he asked. He went lower, kissed her stomach.

"Ten," she admitted, and she was about to pull him back to her to breast and neck.

Then he went down a few more inches.

Heath clearly had some experience in zipper lowering. *Fast* zipper lowering. He slid down, unzipping her and dragging her jeans just low enough so that he could plant the next kiss on her panties.

Anna threw back her head, hitting it against the door and perhaps giving herself a concussion. She didn't care if she did. That's because the only thing that mattered now was the pleasure. Such a puny word for the incredible things Heath was doing with his mouth.

"Your rating?" he asked, and mercy, he added some breath with that question.

"Six million," she managed to say.

He laughed.

"One more kiss," he said. "Then it'll be your turn."

Oh, she wanted a turn all right. Wanted it badly. Until he shimmied down her panties, put her knee on his shoulder and kissed her again. A special kiss.

Tongue flicks included.

After a couple of those flicks, Anna went into forget mode again. The thought of taking her turn went right out of her head. Everything vanished. Except for the feeling that she was about to shatter. And fall. And shatter some more.

Heath made sure he gave her the *more* she needed for shattering. One last well-placed kiss. An equally well-placed tongue flick. And all she could do was fist her hand in his hair and let him shatter her.

She had to take a moment to gather her breath. Another moment to keep gathering it. But even with the ripples of the climax tingling through her, she wanted to get started on her turn. And she was going to torture the hell out of Heath and his junk.

"Damn," Heath growled.

It took her a moment to realize that he was reacting to something he heard.

A knock at the tack room door.

"Heath?" Riley called out.

Hell.

"Uh, Heath, I need to talk to you," Riley added. "It's important."

Unless the world was about to end and Heath could stop it, then it wasn't that important, but Anna conceded that was the lust talking.

"How important?" Heath asked.

"Very."

Heath and she both cursed.

"Anna's in here with me," Heath volunteered.

It took Riley several snail-crawling seconds to respond to that. "Yes, I figured that out. Didn't think you'd go into the tack room alone and close the door. But this isn't about Anna. It's about your assignment."

Heath groaned, stood back up, helping her fix her jeans and panties. "You can wait in here if you want," he offered.

"Not a chance," Anna argued. "Riley knows what we've been doing. Or rather what we started doing, and the assignment thing could be a ruse to draw us out so he can ambush you with a shovel."

He brushed a kiss on her mouth. "You've got a very active imagination." Though she knew there might be a grain of truth in her theory.

Heath went out ahead of her, and Riley was indeed right there. He was sitting on a hay bale, drinking one of the beers. She braced herself for him to say something snarky like had she been trying to get Heath drunk or why did she have this thing for barn sex?

He didn't.

Riley did give her a look that only a big brother could have managed, but it had some, well, sympathy mixed in with the brotherly snark. A strange combination.

"I just came from the base," Riley said to Heath. "They want to see you about your deployment request."

"Deployment request?" Anna repeated. "I thought Heath was going to Florida."

Riley remained quiet, clearly waiting for Heath to explain.

"I asked to be diverted from the instructor job to another deployment," Heath said.

Riley's arrival had been a killjoy in the sexual-pleasure department, but hearing about Heath's request was a different kind of killjoy. Although obviously not for Heath since this was something he wanted.

Very much.

After all, he'd told her that the instructor job made him feel washed up, and maybe now he wouldn't have to feel that way because he could go back to one of those classified sandy locations. Where people shot at him and where he could be hurt or killed.

Mercy.

That felt as if she'd been slammed with a truckload of bricks. And there was no reason for it, because this was Heath's job. No logical reason anyway. But Anna wasn't feeling very logical at the moment.

"They want to see you out at the base right away," Riley added.

Heath nodded, looked at her as if he needed to say something, but Anna let him off the hook. She smiled, brushed a kiss on his cheek.

"Go," she insisted, trying to keep that smile in place. "We can talk when you get back."

Heath hesitated, gave another nod and then walked toward the house. Anna managed to keep her smile in place until he was out of sight. Riley opened a bottle of beer and handed it to her.

"Will he get to come back here to the ranch if the deployment is approved?" Anna asked, though she was afraid to hear the answer. "Or will they send him out right away?"

"Hard to say."

Or maybe not. The next thing Anna saw was Heath leaving the house, carrying his gear. He put it in his rental car and drove off. Obviously, he was prepared to go.

Anna took a long swig of that beer and wished it was something a whole lot stronger.

"Best to forget him," Riley said as they watched Heath drive away. "Heath isn't the settling-down type."

If only that weren't true.

"It's just a fling," Riley added. "That's what it was nine and a half years ago, and that's what it is now."

If only that were *true.*

Chapter Five

The McCord brothers were waiting for Heath when he got back from the base, and they didn't even try to make it look like a friendly, casual meeting. They were in the living room just off the foyer, and the moment Heath stepped inside, they stood.

No shovels. Not physical ones anyway.

"Where's Anna?" Heath asked. "You didn't lock her in her room, did you?"

The joke didn't go over so well, but Heath didn't care. He was tired, frustrated and wanted to talk to Anna, not the kid-sister police.

"Anna's Christmas shopping in San Antonio," Logan answered. "She'll be back any minute now."

Good. Well, sort of good. Heath definitely wanted to see her even if she probably hadn't liked his news. Hell, he hadn't liked it much, either.

"My request for deployment was denied," Heath explained. "The Air Force wants me to report to the base in Florida day after tomorrow so I'll have to cut my visit here short."

He expected them to jump for joy. Or at least smile. They didn't.

Riley immediately shook his head. "I didn't have anything to do with that."

Heath nearly snapped out "Right," but he knew in his gut that Riley was telling the truth. He wouldn't do anything like that even if it meant saving his sister from having sex with a guy Riley didn't think was right for her.

And Riley was spot-on.

Heath wasn't right for her. End of subject.

"I'll leave tomorrow," Heath added. "I just want a chance to say goodbye to Anna first."

None of the brothers objected, and Heath wouldn't have cared if they did. Yeah, it was the pissed-off mood again, but he had to get something off his chest.

"I know you think I'm a jerk, that I'm here only to try to seduce Anna, but I do care about her. Always have. If I hadn't cared, I would have never had sex in the hayloft with her nine and a half years ago."

There. He'd said it. But they weren't saying anything back to him. Maybe because Riley and Logan hadn't known about the sex. Lucky had, of course, because of the pee stick discovery, but even Lucky might have been stunned to silence to hear the de-virgining had taken place in the barn.

"Anna cares about you, too," Lucky finally said.

"She'll cry a lot again when you leave," Logan added.

"She'll be hurt," Riley piped in.

Maybe. Probably, Heath silently amended. Yeah, he was a jerk all right, but he was a jerk on orders, and that meant leaving whether he wanted to or not.

And he did want to leave, Heath assured himself.

He did.

Silently repeating that, Heath went to the guest room so he could finish packing.

HER BROTHERS WERE waiting for Anna when she got home. Hard to miss them since they were on the sofa in the living room.

She so didn't have the energy to deal with them now.

"You're all grounded," Anna said, going on the offensive. "Now, go to your rooms."

Of course, they didn't budge. Well, except to stand, and judging from the somber looks on their faces they had something serious to tell her. But she had something to say, too.

"I already know about Heath's deployment being denied. He texted me right after he got the news. He was at the base and couldn't talk, but he wanted to let me know that he's leaving tomorrow."

They stared at her as if expecting her to sprout an extra nose or something. Then Riley's hawkeyed gaze moved to the Victoria's Secret bag she was holding.

"Yes, I bought it for Heath," Anna admitted. "For me to wear for Heath," she amended when their stares turned blank. "It's red and slutty, and if you don't quit staring at me like that, I'll give you lots of details about what I want Heath to do to me while I'm wearing it."

Logan's eyes narrowed. Riley's jaw tightened. Lucky shrugged and went to her. He pulled her into his arms despite the fact she was as stiff as a statue from the mini hissy fit she'd just thrown.

"I've got two words for you," Lucky whispered to her. "Condom."

She pulled back, looked at him. "That's one word."

"If you wear what's in that bag, you'll need two condoms. Three if you skip what's in the bag all together and just show up in your birthday suit. Either way, condoms."

In that moment he was her favorite brother. Lucky had

always been her champion and not judgmental. Most of the time anyway. Plus, he was the only brother who talked safe sex with her. Or any kind of sex for that matter. He wasn't just her brother, he was her friend.

Anna kissed his cheek. "Thanks."

He shrugged in that lazy but cool way that only Lucky or a Greek god could manage. It was as if he drawled his shrugs. And his life.

Lucky returned the cheek kiss and apparently considered his brotherly/friendly duties done because he strolled toward the door and headed out. Logan went to her next.

"I love you," Logan said. "And no matter what happens, I'll be here for you. You can cry on my shoulder all you need. Or if you prefer, I can kick Heath's ass for you. Your choice."

She had to fight a smile, but she didn't have to fight it too hard because the nonsmiling emotions were just below the surface. "I don't want his ass kicked, but I might need the shoulder."

Logan tapped first one shoulder, then the other. "Any time. They're reserved just for you, and I swear *I told you so* will never cross my lips or my mind. You're a grown woman, and if you want to wear what's in that bag, then you have my blessing."

In that moment she loved Logan best. Logan had been her father more than her brother, mainly because he'd been the one to step up after their folks died. He'd been the one to bust her chops when she needed it and had been a whiz helping with her math homework.

Logan would walk through fire for her and not once complain. Well, maybe he would complain, but he'd still do it.

He kissed her forehead and headed off, not out the

door but to his old room. Since he lived in town and no longer spent many nights at the ranch, Logan must have wanted his shoulders to be nearby in the event of an impending crying spell.

Uh-oh.

It was Riley's turn.

"If Heath makes you cry again, I'm hitting him with the shovel," Riley growled. "And wear a robe with whatever's in that bag."

Anna sighed. The support of two out of three wasn't bad.

Riley sighed as well, and he pulled her into his arms. "FYI, Heath did some crying, too, after he left here that summer."

Anna wiggled out of his grip so she could see if he was serious or not. He was.

"I don't mean he actually shed tears," Riley went on, "but he cried in his own man kind of way."

"How do you know that?" she asked.

"Because I'm the one who drove him to his basic training." A muscle flickered in his jaw. A sign that he was remembering that day as unfondly as she was. Some of the anger returned. "Heath asked me to make sure you were okay. Can you believe it?"

"The bastard," Anna joked.

"He said it as if I needed to be reminded of it. I didn't. Not then, not now. If you need someone to make sure you're okay, I'll do it. As long as I don't have to hear any sex details. Or see what's in that bag. And I'll do that—minus the exceptions—because you're my sister."

Anna blinked back tears. In that moment, she loved Riley best. Yes, he was hardheaded, and they had a history of sibling squabbles. Plus, there was the time when he'd ruined all her dolls with camo paint and duct-tape combat boots, but still she loved every stubborn, camo-painting ounce of him.

Riley wasn't her father or her friend. He was her brother.

And sometimes, like now, that was exactly what a sister needed.

Chapter Six

Heath paced. Cursed. He figured this much debate hadn't gone into some battle plans, but a battle plan would have been easier than trying to figure out what to do about Anna.

Or better yet what to do *with* Anna.

If he went to her room, sex would happen. Then tomorrow he would leave—just as he'd done nine and a half years ago. That hadn't turned out so well, what with all the crying and her brothers wanting to shovel him.

If he didn't go to her room, sex wouldn't happen. But then he would have to leave things unsettled between them—again—as he'd apparently done before.

He was screwed either way, so Heath decided he might as well go for it. He threw open the door and nearly smacked right into some idiot wearing a hoodie and an army-green vinyl poncho.

Except this was no idiot. It was Anna, and in addition to the garb, she was also carrying a blue sock.

She practically pushed him back into his room and shut the door. "Shhh," she said. "Della and Stella's book club is meeting tonight."

He was still wrapping his mind around the fact that Anna was there, that she had come to him, and maybe that's why Heath couldn't quite wrap his mind around the book club or the poncho.

"There are six of them in the living room, and I had to sneak past them," Anna added when he gave her a blank look.

When Heath kept that blank look, Anna pulled off the poncho, and he saw the hoodie. No pants. No shoes.

Just a pair of really tiny devil-red panties.

He was sure his blank look disappeared because his mouth dropped open. This was the best kind of surprise.

"I didn't have a robe here at the ranch, and the plastic poncho felt sticky against my skin so I put on the hoodie," she explained. Then she unzipped it.

No top. No bra. Just the Be My heart locket dangling between her breasts. Heath thought maybe his tongue was doing some dangling, too.

"And the sock?" he asked.

She smiled and emptied the contents onto the bed. Condoms. At least a dozen of them.

"I took them from Lucky's bathroom," Anna explained. She was still whispering, but it had a giddiness to it. "The poncho and hoodie didn't have pockets so I put them in the sock. I only brought the normal-looking ones. Some had pictures on them and some were glow in the dark." Anna looked at him. "Why would a man need that?"

Heath didn't have a clue. He didn't need any illumination to find anything on Anna's body. His most vital organ agreed. In fact, it wanted to go on that particular search mission right now.

But there was a problem.

"You got my text saying I was leaving, right?" he asked.

She nodded. "Tomorrow. That's why I didn't want to wait until after the book club left. Sometimes they hang around until midnight if Della breaks out the tequila, and we don't have much time."

Not if they were planning on using all those condoms, they didn't, but Heath had to make sure that Anna was sure. She stripped off the hoodie, and he was sure she was sure.

At least he wanted her to be.

He wanted that even more when she slipped into his arms and kissed him. Heath was stupid and weak so it took him a moment to break the kiss.

"Anna, I don't want you hurt," he said.

She frowned. "I think that ship's sailed. I'll be hurt, but I'll get over it. And tonight you'll give me some really good memories to help me get over it, right?"

Yeah.

Whether they had sex or not, Anna would be hurt. Or at least she would be sad to see him go. Ditto for him being sad to leave her. But at least this way they'd have new memories, and they didn't need glow-in-the-dark condoms to do it.

Now that he had a clearly defined mission, Heath pulled her back to him to kiss her. One of those kisses that reached scorch level pretty darn fast. But Anna was aiming for fast, too, and not with just the kisses. She was already going after his zipper.

"We're going to play that scale-of-one-to-ten game," she insisted.

Maybe. But the way she was tugging at his zipper, it was possible she was also trying to finish this all way too fast. Tonight, he didn't want the kissing game, and he didn't want fast.

Heath stopped what she was doing by catching on to
her wrists and putting her against the wall. He liked walls
because it gave him some control…

Damn.

He had no control. Anna ground herself against him,
sliding her leg up the outside of his so that the millime-
ter of red lace was right against his crotch. Apparently,
the orgasm she'd had earlier in the barn hadn't done anything to take the edge off because she was going for another one very quickly.

Again, Heath tried to slow things down. With her
leg still cradling his, he turned her, intending to put her
against the dresser, but he tripped over the poncho and
fell onto the bed.

With Anna on top of him.

"Let's play a game," she said. Definitely not a virginal
tone or look. "I'll use just my tongue to find all your special spots. You don't have to give it a number rating. Just
a grunt for pleasure. A groan for find another special spot
that's more special."

"Men only have one special spot," he told her. Heath
took her hand and put it over his sex.

She laughed. Not a humor kind of laugh but the sound
of a woman who'd come to play. Or maybe give a little
payback for the things he'd done to her in the tack room.
Well, Heath wanted to play, too. After all, he had a nearly
naked Anna straddling him, and her breasts were making his mouth water.

He managed a quick sample of her left nipple before
she moved away. Anna didn't waste any time. With her
hand still on his special spot, she went in search of others. His earlobe.

He grunted, but Heath didn't know if that was because, at the same time, she started lowering his zipper.

"That wasn't a loud enough grunt," she said and went after his neck.

Heath grunted. Again, mainly because she lowered the zipper, and when she did that, her breasts got closer to his mouth again. She didn't grunt when he kissed her there, but she did make that silky sound of pleasure that Heath would never tire of hearing.

He would have kept on kissing her breasts, but apparently it was special-spot search time again because she scooted lower and ran her tongue over his own left nipple.

Oh, yeah. He grunted.

Grunted some more when she circled his navel with her tongue. All that tonguing and circling though didn't stop her from getting his zipper all the way down, and as he had done to her earlier, she shimmied his jeans lower.

"You really do go commando," she said.

"Yep—"

He might have added more. Something clever or at least coherent, but her hands were on him. The condom, too. Heath wasn't sure when she'd opened one of the packets. Nor did he care. The woman had clever hands after all—

Hell.

He grunted loud enough to trigger an earthquake when she dropped down onto him. That's when he figured out really, really fast that the panties were crotchless and that he was in her warm and tight special place all the way to the hilt.

"That's not your tongue," he said through the grunts.

"So, I cheated."

The woman was evil. And damn good. Heath usually

liked to be the alpha when it came to sex, but even more than that, he liked taking turns with Anna. Apparently, she was going to make the most of her turn, too. She had the whole *ride 'em, cowgirl* motion going on. So fast that Heath knew this would all end too soon.

Of course, sixteen hours was going to be too soon.

As if she'd read his mind, she slowed. Anna put her palm on his chest and, still moving against his erection, leaned down and kissed him.

"After this," she said, "I want you all the way naked."

Heath thought that was a stellar idea. He wanted those panties off her, too, even though they fell into the *why bother* category of women's undergarments.

The locket whacked him in the face, but even that didn't put a damper on the moment. Heath just pushed the locket aside, gathered her close and let his cowgirl screw his brains out.

Chapter Seven

Anna wished there were some kind of anticry shot she could take. Even one that worked for just an hour or so would do. She figured she'd do plenty of crying after Heath had left, but she didn't want any tears shed in front of him.

Or in front of her brothers.

She wanted Heath to remember her smiling. Or maybe naked, since that's how he'd seen her for a good portion of the night. It was certainly how she wanted to remember him.

With that reminder/pep talk still fresh in her mind, Anna left her bedroom and went in search of Heath so she could give him that smiling goodbye she'd practiced in the mirror. But he wasn't in his bedroom. Or the living room. Or the kitchen. In fact no one was, and she figured they'd all cleared out to give her a chance to have a private goodbye with Heath.

Or maybe they'd cleared out because Heath was already gone. She had several moments of panic when she sprinted to the back porch to make sure his rental car was still there.

It was.

And so was Heath.

He was at the fence pasture, looking at some cows that'd been delivered that morning. He made a picture standing there with his foot on the bottom rung of the fence, his cream-colored cowboy hat slung low on his face.

He must have heard her approaching because he turned, smiling. It looked about as genuine as the one she was trying to keep on her face. Until he reached out, pulled her to him and kissed her.

Then the smiles were real.

"How soon before you leave?" she asked.

"Soon."

That reminder made her smile waver. Anna wasn't sure how far to push this part of the conversation, but there was something she had to know. "Are you feeling any better about the instructor job?"

"I've accepted it. Sometimes, that's the best you can do with crappy lemonade. Sorry," Heath added when she frowned. "It was just something Riley said. An analogy of sorts."

Riley not only needed a new threat, he needed new analogies, as well.

Since their time together was about to end, Anna reached into her pocket and took out the "gift" she'd gotten him on her shopping trip the day before. She hadn't wanted it to be a big gift because that would have made this goodbye seem, well, big.

Which it was.

But she didn't want it to feel big to him.

She took his hand and dropped the smashed penny in it. "It reminded me of your dog tags, and it's supposed to be good luck."

He stared at it, gave a slight smile. "Thanks."

"I was going to give you the red panties," she added, "but I thought it would look strange if the TSA went through your luggage."

Now she got the reaction she wanted. A bigger smile. A bigger kiss, too.

"I have something for you," he said. He took out a silver heart locket. It was similar to the other one he'd given her nine and a half years ago. Very similar.

Right down to the Be My engraving.

Anna checked to make sure she had on the original one. She did. And she was shaking her head until Heath opened it, and she saw what was inside. Not pictures of him and her.

But of her parents. Her dad on one side of the heart. Her mother on the other.

"Della got the pictures for me," he explained. "You said sometimes you forget their faces, and this way you won't forget."

Oh, God.

She was going to cry.

No matter how hard she blinked, the tears came, and they just kept coming.

"I'm sorry." Heath pulled her back in his arms. "I didn't know it would upset you."

"It doesn't," she said, sobbing. "It's a good kind of upset." Still sobbing. "Thank you, Heath, thank you."

He held her while she sobbed, and it took Anna several long moments to stop.

"I got you something else," he added.

Anna couldn't imagine getting anything better than the second locket. It was even more precious to her than the first one. But Heath must have thought "the more the better" because he took out a wad of lockets from his coat pocket.

"I went to the jewelry store this morning and bought every locket they had."

She had no doubts about that—none. There was another silver one, one gold and another in the shape of a cat's head.

"They're, uh, beautiful." Though she couldn't imagine needing that many lockets. Or the ugly one with the cat's head.

"I had them engraved," he added, "and this time I watched to make sure they did it right. You can choose which one you want."

It took her a second to realize he'd finished his sentence. Not "which one you want *to wear*." Not "which one you want *to keep*." Not "which one you want *to remember me by*."

Heath turned over one of the silver ones, and she saw the engraving there. One word.

Lover.

He put the Be My locket next to it, and she got the message then. Be my lover.

She laughed. "Does this mean you want to see more of me?"

"Well, I've already seen more, but I'd like to see more of you more often."

That dried any remnants of her tears, and she blurted out an idea she'd been toying with for days. "I could look into transferring to a law school in Florida." And she held her breath.

No smile from him. "I don't want you to sacrifice going to a school that maybe doesn't have as good of a reputation as the one you're in now."

"No sacrifice. There are a couple of really good ones. And besides, I was transferring anyway. Might as well transfer so you can—" she held up the two lockets to finish that thought "—Be My Lover."

Anna tested his neck again with a kiss. And her tongue.

"Keep that up, and you'll be my lover again right now," he grumbled.

"If that's supposed to make me behave, then it won't work. Not with the hayloft so close. How much time do you have before you need to leave for your flight?"

"Not enough time for the hayloft."

She kissed him again, and he seemed to change his mind about that. He started leading her in that direction.

"Not enough time for the hayloft unless we hurry," Heath amended.

Good. The kisses were working.

Since she'd already put her heart on the line, Anna put the rest of herself out there, too. "I don't want a fling."

"Good. Flings are overrated." He kissed her again. "And temporary."

She released the breath she didn't even know she'd been holding. Heath didn't want temporary. Nor a fling. He wanted sex.

That was a solid start since she wanted that, too.

"I'm not done," he said. "Remember, you pick the locket you want." He held up the next one, the gold one, and it also had a single word engraved on it.

Woman.

As in Be My Woman.

Yes, they were so going to that hayloft, and then she was going to the university to start that transfer to Florida.

"Can I wear both the *Lover* and *Woman*?" she asked. Because she wanted both.

"You haven't seen the third one yet."

And she probably couldn't see it before the next kiss crossed her eyes. Along with singeing her eyelashes.

Still, he put the locket in her hand just as her butt landed against the ladder. Anna backed up one step at a time, which wasn't easy to do with Heath kissing her like that. And he kept on kissing her until they made it all the way to the top of the hayloft.

But Anna froze when she saw what was engraved on the tacky cat's head locket.

Love.

"Be My Love," she said, putting the words together.

Putting *everything* together.

"The *L* word?" she asked.

Heath nodded. "Sometimes it's the only word that works. What about you? Does the *L* word work for you?"

Anna had to catch her breath just so she could speak. "It works perfectly for me." She kissed him. "Does this mean we're going steady?"

"Oh, yeah," Heath confirmed. "That, and a whole lot more."

* * * * *

COMING NEXT MONTH FROM

◆H HARLEQUIN®

INTRIGUE

Available March 22, 2016

#1629 TROUBLE WITH A BADGE
Appaloosa Pass Ranch • by Delores Fossen
Lawman Levi Crockett would never turn his back on PI Alexa Dearborn
and the baby girl in her care. But as a serial killer stalks them, Levi must
fight a powerful enemy—the desire between them.

#1630 DECEPTIONS
The Battling McGuire Boys • by Cynthia Eden
Secrets from their pasts threaten Elizabeth Snow and Mac McGuire—as
much as the killer who seems to know their every move. Can they trust
each other again? Or will a shocking truth prove fatal?

#1631 NAVY SEAL CAPTIVE
SEAL of My Own • by Elle James
Being abducted wasn't part of Sawyer Houston's R & R mission. Jenna Broyles
claims she's rescuing the navy SEAL from unknown assailants. Only, it's
her life on the line when the jilted bride becomes a target.

#1632 HEAVY ARTILLERY HUSBAND
Colby Agency: Family Secrets • by Debra Webb & Regan Black
When someone tries to kill security expert Sophia Leone, she's rescued
by her husband, Frank—an army general she *thought* died a year ago.
Now Sophia must trust her life to the man she married...the man she
never stopped loving.

#1633 TEXAN'S BABY
Mason Ridge • by Barb Han
Bodyguard Dawson Hill is committed to protecting the woman who left
him two years ago. Melanie Dixon has returned to Mason Ridge...with his
son. Now a madman is threatening the family Dawson never dreamed he
could have.

#1634 FULL FORCE FATHERHOOD
Orion Security • by Tyler Anne Snell
Fatherhood was never in the cards for Mark Tranton, until widow Kelli Crane
and her daughter wrapped themselves around his heart. But digging into
their past riles someone who won't rest until Kelli pays the ultimate price...

**YOU CAN FIND MORE INFORMATION ON UPCOMING HARLEQUIN® TITLES,
FREE EXCERPTS AND MORE AT WWW.HARLEQUIN.COM.**

HICNM0316

REQUEST YOUR FREE BOOKS!
2 FREE NOVELS PLUS 2 FREE GIFTS!

H HARLEQUIN®

INTRIGUE

BREATHTAKING ROMANTIC SUSPENSE

HI15

SPECIAL EXCERPT FROM

⊕ HARLEQUIN®
™

I N T R I G U E

*When a Texas lawman discovers a woman from
his past and an innocent baby in danger, he has every
intention of keeping them safe...even though it could
cost him everything.*

Read on for a sneak preview of
TROUBLE WITH A BADGE,
the next book in USA TODAY *bestselling author*
Delores Fossen's gripping new miniseries,
APPALOOSA PASS RANCH.

Levi eased into the shadows away from the pulsing neon
bar lights, and he listened. Waiting. It was hard, though,
to pick through the sounds of the crackling lights, the
wind and his own heartbeat drumming in his ears.

But somewhere there was the sound of an engine
running.

Because the driver had the headlights off, it took Levi
a moment to realize the car wasn't approaching from
the street but rather from the back of the bar. No road
there, just a parklike area that the local teenagers used for
making out. It could also be the very route a killer would
likely take.

Before the car eased to a stop, Levi whipped out his
gun and took aim. He froze. And not because of the
weather.

The person stepped out from the car, the watery lights
just enough for him to see her face. Not the Moonlight